DUCK DIVE

MALLORY RAE

www.malloryrae.com

Cover art and design by Alicia Cartrite.
Page design by Reagan Wilcox.
Author Photo by Lindsey Cram.

Published September 2023

"Instill commonplace detail alongside a single extraordinary assumption."
Wells's Law

Great instructions for writing a book.
Perfect instructions for living a life.

DEDICATION
For Andrew, Staley, and Gunnar ~ my very best friends.
MR

PHASES

BEFORE YOU DIVE IN

I wrote this book to music. As I went, I started making a playlist of the songs that particularly inspired me or seemed to magically fit with the section I was working on at the time. And then I started to wonder...what if the songs that helped me get in the flow of writing could help you get in the flow of reading? So at the beginning of each chapter, you'll find I've noted a song that was particularly meaningful while I was writing that portion of the book. It's just a small offering, friend to friend. I hope it enriches your reading experience.

Create your own playlist, mixtape, or record collection using the full song list in Appendix A or you can find my playlist on Spotify by searching "Duck Dive."

Phase One

NEW

YEAR	DATE	TIME
1995	21-Jun	1:34 PM PDT

YEAR	DATE	TIME
2023	21-Jun	7:57 AM PDT

Listen: "Back To The End Of The World"
by Jim James, Teddy Abrams,
Louisville Orchestra

ONE

~~~~~~~~~~~

When your name is May, people tend to assume that you were born in the fifth month. But people tend to assume a lot of incorrect things.

EXHIBIT "A"

In 1582 the world skipped ten days. True story. It turns out the Julian Calendar (attributed to the reign of Julius Caesar and instituted in 45 BCE) had assumed that there were exactly 365.25 days in a year (it is actually 365.2422). Due to that flawed assumption the Julian Calendar Year was eleven minutes too long. That meant that by 1582 CE the calendar had drifted by ten days. The Spring Equinox that should have been happening on March 21, was happening on March 11. Uncorrected, the calendar would become meaningless, offering people an inaccurate representation of the lunar and solar cycles that served as guideposts for planting and harvesting, for feasting and fasting. The calendar would be saying one thing, and the sky would be saying another. This was a job for Pope Gregory XIII.

By Papal Decree, Thursday, October 4, 1582 was followed by Friday, October 15, 1582. Ten days, sucked into the void. The Gregorian Calendar reigned.

Most people assume that today will be followed by tomorrow, but sometimes the universe has other plans.

NEW

Listen: "Lady May"
by Tyler Childers

TWO

~~~~~~~~~~

JUNE 2018 CE

Friends aren't that hard to make. Not really. You bring an extra pack of Swiss Rolls at lunch. You join orchestra and student council. You remember things that people tell you about themselves. You smile, you laugh, you go to the beach when they invite you, even though you hate everything about the beach. You're friendly. You make friends. Not hard. But best friends. Now they're a whole different species. In May's experience, best friends weren't made, they were born. And if you were lucky, your best friend was someone who would come help you dig a hole in the backyard if you asked him to.

Abee pulled up the bottom of his shirt to wipe his forehead. The marine layer was just starting to burn off. The ground was sandy-ish which May deemed helpful for digging, but Abee kept reminding her that sand was still just small rocks.

"I think you need a new dream, Mays."

"Shut up, Andrew Bartholomew Berenson." May used his full name when she was feeling particularly feisty. She had battled the cobwebs of the shed to get two shovels, a big blue tarp, and some yellow plastic stakes out into the middle of the yard. Feisty was an understatement. The shovels were flat blades, not great for digging. The tarp was full of spider nests, terrifying. And the stakes were plastic, not exactly construction strength. But May was determined. They were going to build a pool, right here, right now. This was their summer plan.

"Please refer to me as *Andraus Bar Talmai Berenson* if you insist on using my full name." Abee could play this game too.

"Okay, *Manly–Son of Giant–who is Son of Bear Man*, please shut up." May would not be bested. She had been helping Abee get ready for his bar mitzvah, and while he was an obliging Hebrew student, May found it all utterly fascinating—in Abee's name he carried the story of three generations.

"We *can* do this." May was adamant.

9

"I hear you, and I retort with a—can we though? Can. We." Abee let it hang for dramatic effect. May was having none of it.

"Yes. Well, if you grew some muscles, it would be easier, but yes, we can." May didn't have time for this second guessing.

"I have plenty of muscles, thank you very much. Mom just bought me some new shirts yesterday cause I grew three inches this year."

"Hate to break it to you, but tall doesn't equal strong."

"Do you have someone else who can help you dig this hole?" Abee ducked as he said it, knowing full well May wasn't above throwing the next shovelful right at him.

May looked up, he was right, she should be nicer to him. "No. Just you and your long, skinny arms. Sorry. But it's already too hot and if dad won't put a pool in or buy one of those that you put on top of the ground, we are going to make our own."

"An above ground pool, here...I'm pretty sure there are laws against that. And have you ever heard of someone digging their own pool?" Abee preferred teasing her to picking up his shovel again.

"No, but there are probably a lot of things I've never heard about. Just keep digging, okay?"

"I heard some people saying that there is this thing called the ocean right down the hill there. Think of it as one of those infinity pools." Abee knew he shouldn't bring up the ocean, in her ten years she had never once actually gone swimming in the ocean. Well, maybe she had gone with her dad at some point when she was a baby. But May didn't go now.

"I didn't know you started doing stand-up...and no, I'd rather not." May delivered, *rather not* in the exaggerated English accent they were experimenting with that week, graciously attempting to deflect any tension that talk of the ocean would bring. It wasn't Abee's fault she was so weird.

The restaurant, May's family's restaurant, attracted tourists from all over the world. Well to say it more truthfully, the ocean and the views attracted the tourists, the restaurant just happened to be on the cliff that offered the views of said ocean. This week a big group of important looking English people had come rolling up in dark green Range Rovers. Everyone here had Range Rovers, but these were fancy even for Malibu. They had found the restaurant very charming. It was charming. It was actually a pretty great place to grow up, pool or no pool.

May's posture slackened. She let her shovel fall to the ground. She wiped her sweaty hands on her bare knees and grinned her crooked smile at him.

Abee rolled his eyes. "I know, Mays. I was just kidding. I'll go get the pointy shovel from my house —it is your birthday after all." Abee's voice trailed off as he walked across the yard.

He was her very best friend.

~~~~~~

It took Abee a while to find the good shovel. By the time he got back, May was gone. But Abee had watched enough *Odd Squad* and *Spy Kids* over the years to put a few clues together. May's no-good shovel was on the ground. A piece of the wooden handle, about the size of a carpenter's pencil, had splintered off. It was also on the ground a few inches away from the rest of the handle. A splattering of blood dotted the wood, the shovel, the whole general area. The honeycomb pattern from the bottom of May's shoes was pressed hard into the sandy ground, and her strides became longer as they reached the house. She had been impatient, pushed too hard on the shovel, broken the handle, and presumably cut her hand.

Abee found her on the couch. Her right hand was wrapped with a kitchen towel and propped up on her head. "You have to elevate to stop the bleeding," May said calmly. Abee nodded and plopped down on the couch next to her, like they'd been-here-done-this a million times before. Abee grinned. May had turned on *Spy Kids: All The Time In The World*. Sometimes it felt like their brains were connected. Timekeeper was monologuing about living life forward. Abee would dig a pool or he would watch this movie for the thousandth time; he was just glad they were together.

May was staring at him. The stare that meant she wanted something.

"Will you go get me a blanket?"

"The Juni and Carmen one?"

"Obviously."

"I'll be right back. It is your birthday after all."

She was his very best friend.

DUCK DIVE

Listen: "Ready or Not"
by Shakey Graves
and Sierra Ferrell

THREE

~~~~~~~~~

JUNE 2023 CE

There was Dad, in the kitchen, where he always was. Dressed in his white, double-breasted chef's jacket, with *Shep Thomas, Chef de Cuisine* embroidered in small cursive script across the right side. The restaurant might look quirky, but the kitchen, her dad's kitchen, was the real deal. Shep got his first Michelin Star a few years ago, and rumor was that this year it might be two. He was making a yellow dal for family meal tonight. Everyone loved when Shep cooked family.

"Pad-May, my queen. What's cooking?" This was his favorite pun. May had moved beyond being annoyed by this comment. She was even past just accepting it. May had now reached the stage where she realized she would actually be sad if he stopped saying it someday. The pot Shep was stirring smelled of coriander, cumin, and Kashmiri chili. May watched as he added a dash of salt.

"Yellow dal, Dad. That's what's cooking." The pun was meant to be instructive as well as funny. May had answered correctly and then quickly went on to offer the obligatory run down of her day. "And my day of sitting in a hard chair listening to people try to inspire me to memorize some facts was good. It was a perfectly good-ish day. And guess what, it is sunny and 72 degrees again, who wouldn't have a good day. The blondies are still blonde, surfing is still cool..." May would have continued, but there was a spoon hovering in front of her face. It smelled even better up close. It tasted even better than it smelled. Buttery, tangy, warm, what had she been talking about?

"I'm good, Dad. Really though, I am. And school's almost over. So, there's always that. And you have sauce on your shoes."

"*My* shoes, impossible." Shep's eyes gleamed. He loved this. He loved his kitchen. He loved her. "Can you take the Joshua Tree room tonight? Abee has a game, and the summer tourists are coming early this year, apparently. We were buried last night. I'll pay you extra. Unless you have finals to study for. Are finals still a thing?"

Shep was very chill as far as parents went, but sometimes he would remember to say parent-y things.

"Yeah Dad, finals are still a thing, I'm good though. My schedule is wide open believe it or not. And don't pay me extra, this will all be mine someday anyways. God knows Abee can't cook or think or...what can he do, why do we keep him around?" May grabbed a cloth to wipe the counter, absentmindedly, automatically.

"Abee's great at bringing in the blondies with their dad's credit cards."

"Well, you're not wrong about that."

~~~~~~

The restaurant was the best and the worst. There had to be more to life than feeding other people all day, every day. But May actually *did* love cooking, and she knew, even though she hated to admit it, that one day she would follow in her dad's footsteps and she would be thankful for every minute of it. Malibu had more than a few bright, white, crisp, kind of Asian, kind of Scandinavian, made for tv restaurants. Duck's was not that kind of place. And *Duck's* had been around long before *Duke's*. It was admittedly confusing for the tourists.

May's grandpa opened Duck's in the 70's. No one was exactly sure what year, let alone what day. It was kind of an accidental restaurant. Grandpa Gene chased his endless summer to the cliffs of Malibu, where in between sets he found a bungalow that was for sale. They were all bungalows back then. He used his newly come upon inheritance to purchase said bungalow and at night after the sun had gone down, everyone would come back to Duck's. Duck was Gene's nickname in the water, and it followed him on land. Duck dive or bail, the eternal conundrum of the surfer. Gene would always duck.

In the kitchen of his bungalow, Gene would magically throw some things that had come out of the ocean into a pot with some things that had come out of his garden and people would eat and laugh and smoke and drink until the wet air chilled them to the bone and they were forced to let the day be done. May suspected there was more than just nicotine and beer being passed around on those nights, it was Malibu in the 70's after all, but Grandpa Gene never talked about that.

Then one night, somebody put out an empty coffee can, Gene swore it wasn't him, and people stuck a few dollars in before they left. The can kept showing up on the counter, people kept showing up to eat, and so on some random day, in some year in the early 1970's, Duck's was born. The full name, when Gene finally got around to filing papers with the county, was Duck's Dive.

The origin story wasn't even the most interesting thing about the place though, at least in May's opinion. Because, as Grandpa Gene told it, one day a young woman who also loved to surf—but loved Gene's chowder more—started showing up, and one night as the others crawled out into the mist, Gloria stayed. And Gloria stayed the next day, and the next. And then one day Gloria and Gene stood out on the sand, surrounded by their friends, and promised to love each other always. Gene spread out a whole clambake right there on the beach. Gloria sang her favorite song by the Carpenters, and nobody went home that night. They never got around to filing any papers with the county. Gloria kept her name.

And then as the haze of the 70's started to clear, they realized they needed more room. Duck's was growing, and so was Gloria. More people were coming to the restaurant, a lot more people. Gene took out a loan to build a real kitchen and add another room for seating. Gloria sketched out a design for a room that was deep blue, with can lights tucked behind faux rocks shining up at three giant papier-mâché humpback whales hanging from a lofted ceiling—Gloria had half of a fine arts degree from Berkeley. Gene loved it. Everyone loved it. People loved California kitsch, and Duck's delivered on the kitsch. Duck's would grow five more times over the years. Gloria only grew that once. She gave birth to a baby girl they named Amy. Though Gene, who was half French from his father's side, would always call her *Aimée*.

Duck's was Gene and Gloria's life, but Amy was their world.

~~~~~~

May's favorite room in the restaurant was the Hollywood room. The Hollywood room had a giant circular table that sat twelve, or fifteen if the people really liked each other. There was a Lazy Susan in the middle of the table and in the middle of that sat a bust of James Dean. May thought the bust was better than the one at Griffith Observatory. Her Nonna had made this Jimmy.

Nonna Gloria died before May was born, but Grandpa Gene made sure that May knew every little detail about her. Gloria loved to cook, and sing, and read poetry, and drink coffee. In kindergarten May's teacher read the class a book about an Italian family, the kids in the book called their grandmother *nonna*. May wasn't sure if Gloria was Italian or not, but the pictures she had seen of her resembled the drawings in the book. No one ever told her she should or shouldn't, but that day May decided that Gloria would have wanted to be called nonna too.

As much as the restaurant was meant to memorialize the spirit of California, for Grandpa Gene it also memorialized the spirit of his lost loves. May knew he sat in the Hollywood room late at night with a martini and talked to Gloria. It always looked like he was talking to Jimmy.

One wall of the room was painted with a giant mural of the Hollywood sign and Grandpa Gene had tacked real wooden letters "H-O-L-L-Y-W-O-O-D" to the wall to make it three dimensional and then lined the letters with lights. The other walls were covered with autographed Polaroid's, headshots, and posters of all the celebrities who had come to Duck's over the years. Dolly in a pink satin suit, a young Tom Hanks, Paul and Joanne, a poster of Brittany from the "...baby one more time" era, Miley, Jack Nicholson, Barbara Streisand, a young Leo (Oh Leo). May liked to walk around the room and touch all the pictures of the red heads, Lucille Ball (south wall, center-center), Carol Burnett (right next to Lucy), Molly Ringwald (south wall, left-center), Conan (as you turned the corner to the east), then on to a picture of her Dad and Prince Harry (that was a recent addition), a clipping from the *Malibu Times* that featured her mom and grandparents (it was black and white but she knew her mom had red hair), and she'd always end with Robert Redford in his cowboy hat (Grandpa Gene always called him Bob). Hollywood loved a good red head. May knew every inch of this room. On summer evenings the ocean breeze would come across the deck and in through the west facing French doors. Grandpa Gene said he often caught whiffs of Chanel No. 5 on those nights. It was Gloria's signature scent. May never told him that at any given moment at least half of their guests were probably wearing Coco's most famous fragrance.

But tonight, May was covering the Joshua Tree room. As the restaurant was added onto over the years—each room a new homage to some part of California—an atrium popped up in the middle of the sprawling bungalow. Gloria gave the atrium a Saltillo tile floor, filled it with teddy-bear cholla in giant terracotta pots, hung air plants in macramé baskets, painted the walls a shade of desert rose, and strung twinkle lights across the open ceiling. She was ahead of her time. Joshua Tree was easily May's second favorite room.

~~~~~~

May found a clean-ish white button-up shirt and slipped on her black Vans. Dinner service started in thirty minutes. Luckily the restaurant was just across the yard. Winding her way through the kitchen she slid silently onto the bench next to Louis, their head server, just as her dad was describing the halibut that was on tonight's menu. May rushed through her yellow dal, as everyone else headed to their stations. May hated to rush, it was so good. Just as she was about to stand up, Abee popped his head around the corner. Abee's black hair was wet and somehow perfectly tousled. He had been surfing.

"I thought you had a game tonight, that's why I'm working for you." May was only slightly perturbed.

"I do. It's a make-up from when we couldn't get to Carp a few weeks back. I just smelled dinner and thought I'd grab some for the road. Keep it quiet, I don't want my mom to see me and ask me about my Pre-Cal test. It was no bueno. My Spanish test though...well also no bueno." Abee quickly ladled the yellow mush from the pot into a deli container. The cartoon shark on Abee's gym bag winked at May as it jostled around on his shoulder.

"Three more days and we're free. What are we doing this summer?" Abee looked back to catch her reaction. They both laughed.

"I'm leaving for Portofino on Saturday, did I not tell you?"

"Oh yes, yes, and I'll be doing a summer program at Oxford. See you in September. Really though, I'm not gonna let you hide in the kitchen for two months, Mays. This summer is going to be our best one yet." Abee was stuffing a spoon in his back pocket, one of the nice ones.

Abee had said *best*. May couldn't help but hear *last*. Next summer Abee would graduate and he'd be getting ready to head off to—somewhere. May shook her head as if to clear the Etch A Sketch inside. He was half-way out the door now.

Abee looked back at her. "Hey, birthday bonfire next week? I'll tell some people, you tell some people. I'll try to not catch anyone's hair on fire this time."

"Sounds like a plan. To be safe I won't invite..." May stopped and turned, she could hear Louis calling for her. She looked back. Abee was gone. "...anyone with hair."

He was still her very best friend.

NEW

Listen: "Mother, Mother"
by Rayland Baxter
and Dylan LeBlanc

FOUR

~~~~~~~~~

May generally had good self-esteem, she was happy enough with the way she looked, her red hair and freckles made her unique in a literal sea of blondes. She knew that she'd be able to go to culinary school, maybe even in Paris. May wasn't ever going to be homecoming queen, but she had plenty of friends. And what probably made her feel more confident than anything else was her birthday.

Well not the actual day, she didn't remember that obviously, but the date and the time. May was born on June 20, 2008 at 4:59 p.m. PDT, the precise moment of the summer solstice. Not a minute earlier, not a minute later, but the exact moment when the tilt of the earth put the northern hemisphere as close to the sun as it could be.

As far as omens went, this seemed like a pretty good one. The word solstice comes from the Latin words *sol* for "sun" and *sistere* for "to stand still." Solstice is the time when the sun appears to stand still for just a moment before the world keeps turning and another cycle of life begins.

~~~~~~~~~~~~~~~~~~~~~~~~~~~~~~~~~~~~~~~

On June 20, 2008 at 4:59 p.m. PDT Elise Berenson gave birth to her best friend's daughter. She was named May Vere Thomas, and her hair was as fiery as a Malibu sunset, just like her mother's had been. The sun stood still for more than a moment that day.

Listen: "Something You Get Through"
by Willie Nelson

FIVE

~~~~~~~~~~

JUNE 2023 CE

Tourists were always surprised by how cold a June day on the beach could be. June gloom was a real thing. But the force of the sun was too much for the gloom today. The sun couldn't help but shine. It was May's birthday.

Abee had his bar mitzvah when he was thirteen. Lily had her quince back in February. Caleb's parents let him ride his bike from San Francisco to San Diego last summer when he turned sixteen. May was fifteen and she was going to have a bonfire tonight. It wasn't nothing. It felt right for her. May was coming of age one stereotypical teen event at a time.

The sun was sneaking in through the cracks between the slats of her shutters. May looked at her clock. It was 7:45 a.m. Her body didn't know it was summer yet. Without getting up, May felt on the floor next to her bed for her hoodie. She tugged it over her head and convinced herself to get out from under the covers. She looked around her room as she blinked the sleep from her eyes. Above her desk was a poster that charted all of the winter and summer solstices from 1950 – 2050. May knew what it said, but she checked the line for 2023 again anyway.

2023 / 21-Jun / 7:57 a.m. PDT

Summer Solstice Times

BY YEAR

YEAR	DATE	TIME	YEAR	DATE	TIME
1995	21-Jun	1:34 PM PDT	2023	21-Jun	7:57 AM PDT
1996	20-Jun	7:23 PM PDT	2024	20-Jun	1:50 PM PDT
1997	21-Jun	1:19 AM PDT	2025	20-Jun	7:41 PM PDT
1998	21-Jun	7:02 AM PDT	2026	21-Jun	1:24 AM PDT
1999	21-Jun	12:49 PM PDT	2027	21-Jun	7:10 AM PDT
2000	20-Jun	6:48 PM PDT	2028	20-Jun	1:00 PM PDT
2001	21-Jun	12:38 AM PDT	2029	20-Jun	6:47 PM PDT
2002	21-Jun	6:24 AM PDT	2030	21-Jun	12:30 AM PDT
2003	21-Jun	12:10 PM PDT	2031	21-Jun	6:16 AM PDT
2004	20-Jun	5:57 PM PDT	2032	20-Jun	12:08 PM PDT
2005	20-Jun	11:46 PM PDT	2033	20-Jun	6:00 PM PDT
2006	21-Jun	5:26 AM PDT	2034	20-Jun	11:43 PM PDT
2007	21-Jun	11:06 AM PDT	2035	21-Jun	5:32 AM PDT
2008	20-Jun	4:59 PM PDT	2036	20-Jun	11:30 AM PDT

That was tomorrow morning at 7:57 a.m. on the west coast. The day after her birthday this year. The solstice liked to hop. It wasn't a fixed day and time. The calendar had to answer to it, not the other way around. So sometimes it was on June 20 and sometimes it was on June 21. And the solstice didn't happen in procession, moving from one time zone to the next, like New Year's did. It was a global moment. It happened everywhere all at once.

May walked down the hallway. The smell of bacon and coffee called her to the kitchen. Shep was sliding a crêpe out of a pan. Elise was cutting up strawberries. Elise saw May first.

"My May." Elise wiped her hand on the white towel she had hooked through her left hip belt-loop. Elise pulled May into a full body hug. Elise's long, dark hair smelled like grapefruit and oranges. Over her shoulder, May saw the "HAPPY BIRTHDAY" banner hanging above the breakfast nook.

"Good morning, birthday girl. You're up early. We're just getting things ready. Talmai and Abee will be over in a bit." Shep kissed the top of May's head as he scooted past her to grab the bowl of batter.

"Well, Tal will be here. He was just coming back from his run when I headed over, but Abee might be dead to the world for a while still. I swear, that child is a sleeping giant." A twinkle passed over Elise's eyes as she spoke. The ever observant May had seen that look in Elise's eyes many times throughout the years. The simple look of a mother thinking about her child.

"Here, start with some coffee." Elise poured her a cup from the French press. "You're fifteen now, coffee is allowed." Elise winked at her. May had been drinking Elise's coffee since she was ten. May grabbed the half-and-half from the refrigerator. Just enough left. She'd get another carton from the walk-ins later.

Music was coming from the deck. Tal had them singing about Bacardi on their birthdays for as long as May could remember. The music was in the living room now and getting louder.

"Tal, we are not in the club and it's not even eight o'clock in the morning!" Elise just barely tolerated Tal's taste in music. Talmai popped around the corner, larger than life, muffling his phone in his pocket just as Elise snapped him with the end of her towel. He lifted May up in a bear hug and gave her a good shake before putting her back down on the ground. Talmai was still just a bit taller than Abee. But Abee was catching up. They were both huge.

The strawberries, fresh whipped cream, lemon curd, Nutella, and bacon all got shuffled over to the breakfast table. Shep pulled the crêpes from the warming tray. They all tucked into the u-shaped banquette. The sun poured through the windows. When everyone you know and love works in a restaurant, birthday dinners and parties don't happen like they do for normal people. Birthday breakfast, that was what May had always had.

In between bites, May peeled the wrapping paper off of a vinyl, Willie Nelson's *Last Man Standing* from Talmai, a gift card to Nordstrom from dad, a Lulu tennis skirt and a giant squishy loaf of bread that was made out of a magic memory foam and smelled like cassis when you pushed your fingers into it from Elise. And then there was one small box left.

"This one is from..." Shep's voice hitched, and then he finished, "...your mom. I've been saving it for you. She told me once that she got it on her fifteenth birthday. So today seemed like the perfect time."

The box was wrapped in delicate blue paper. Not butcher paper as per Shep's usual. A satin white ribbon that was tied into a perfectly symmetrical bow sat atop the package. May slid the ribbon off and popped the tape that held one end of the paper down. May had lots of her mom's things—some jean jackets that were actually back in style now, her collection of original *Baby-Sitters Club* books, a bunch of yearbooks and photo albums and old letters, and a skateboard—but this felt different.

The box was a creamy velvet. It was a jewelry box, of course. May pulled back on the top of the box. Inside, resting on a perfect little pillow, was a delicate gold chain that anchored an equally delicate gold heart. Etched into the heart, May read the words, *Mon Amie*. May felt about ten emotions all at once. Her hands were tingly. Her ears were flushed. Her face was frozen. Talmai loudly cleared his throat. May appreciated the momentary distraction.

"Mon Amie, it's a play on her name, which is kind of your name. Grandpa Gene would always say her name in French. I thought it would be special..."

May knew what *mon amie* meant. She had just aced her French I final. Shep on the other hand, though highly trained in French cuisine, was woefully bad at the language. What it meant wasn't the problem. It *wasn't* her mom's name. And her mom's name *wasn't* her name. *Mon amie* was a cliché that French people didn't even actually use. It was a phrase that was decidedly in the realm of Americans writing French characters in movies and books. But none of that was the real issue.

May took a deep breath, "I love it, Dad." May looked around the table, "Thank you all, for everything." She meant it. Here she was sitting with the three people who loved her most in the whole world. Her mom's three best friends. She would never, could never say this out loud, but sometimes May worried that they didn't love her for her, not really. May worried that they just loved her because she reminded them of someone else.

They all cleaned up breakfast together. When May got back to her room, she shoved the jewelry box in her sock drawer. The necklace was still tucked in its perfect little pillow.

Listen: "The Breeze"
by **Dr. Dog**

SIX

~~~~~~~~~~

JUNE 2023 CE

"So what's up with yall? Are you like dating...or related..." As Bella asked the question her face twisted in a way that wasn't unfamiliar to May.

In Malibu there were two lower level schools and both those schools fed into an upper school campus that served all the kids that lived in a roughly 22-mile strip that stretched from Topanga to South Beach. So it was forgivable if early on there were some kids that you didn't know. But once you got to high school, you knew everyone, and everyone knew you. But there were some outliers, kids who went into LACHSA (the Los Angeles County High School of the Arts), or kids who got shipped out to Ojai (for boarding school), and you never saw them until summer rolled around. There were also the visitors as the locals pejoratively called them. Kids with a parent who had come into some money, rented an overpriced house on the cliffs, and then disappeared back to the valley when the money ran out. May suspected this wasn't a normal dynamic to grow up in, but it was theirs.

So the kids who knew them hadn't thought about who May and Abee were to each other in years, if ever. They were May and Abee. But once every few months, one of the outliers would fumble through a question similar to Bella's.

The answer was simple. That was a lie. They were best friends. But as May sat next to Bella, a LACHSA outlier, letting the sand fall through her fingers, squinting as she stared into the fire, she hesitated. Was it weird to say Abee was her best friend? Did he still consider her to be his best friend? Why was this bothering her, tonight of all nights?

"We've been friends, since like forever." May tried to sound nonchalant.

"Yeah, y'all seem really tight. I mean he's throwing you this party, right?" Bella said *y'all* a lot. Bella's family had come from Dallas, her dad did something with oil. May suspected they wouldn't be leaving for the valley anytime soon.

Was it weird that Abee, the 6'-2" captain of the volleyball team (who could be a pro-surfer if he wanted to be, but he didn't want to be), general heart-throb Abee, was throwing a party for a red-headed freshman (well, technically sophomore now), who played the stand-up bass, and exclusively read cookbooks? Yeah, it was probably kind of weird. But so what? Tonight was May's night. Bella was talking to Caleb before May could say anything else. Someone turned up the music. They were all up. They were all dancing. The stars were all shining.

~~~~~~

Tap. Tap. Tap. Tap. Tap. Tap.

Was it raining?

Where was she?

Why wouldn't that tapping sound stop?

"May. May. May. Mayyyyyyyyyyy. You're gonna miss it."

Miss the bus? She didn't take the bus anymore. Abee drove her now. Abee could drive. Wait, it was summer. They didn't have to drive to school. Summer. Summer. Her birthday. Her birthday was yesterday. Last night. Ohhh, last night. It was the morning now. The morning of the day after her—

"I'm up! I'm up! How much time do we have?!"

"Five minutes, come on!"

May was still in her clothes from the party. Her feet slid into her shoes before she even knew her legs were moving. May squirmed out through her window; it was faster than going through the house. They were running through the yard, out the gate, into the parking lot, and over to the path hidden between the bougainvilleas. May had to take two strides for every one of Abee's, but she was keeping up.

"This way!" Abee called over his shoulder.

May thought they were just heading to the cliffs, but Abee was going all the way down to the beach. May followed. The goal was to be as far west as possible at the exact moment of the solstice. It was their version of a pilgrimage to Stonehenge. They'd started this on May's eighth birthday, after Elise had given her a children's encyclopedia about the solar system. They hadn't missed a year since.

They were running on the sand now. Running in sand was the worst. May was not keeping up. Abee stopped about ten yards ahead of her. He bent down, putting his hands on his knees, trying to catch his breath. Then he fell sideways into the sand and rolled over to his back.

"Abee!" May ran—stumbled—toward him and sank down into the sand next to him. Had he hurt his knee again, twisted his ankle, was he okay? Abee was laughing. Breathing hard, but laughing.

"We've got------plenty------of time------Mays." He spoke between alternating gasps and laughs. She looked around. It *was* suspiciously dim outside. The sun was up, but barely. May punched him in the arm as hard as she could.

"I freaking haven't run that much since fifth-grade field day!" May let herself fall back in the sand next to Abee.

"Chill out, I actually have a surprise."

May shifted her eyes toward him to see if he was serious. Abee twisted to his side and propped his head up with his arm. May could see on his watch that it was only 6:39 a.m. His face was close to hers. He smelled like kerosene and salt.

"Have you been up this whole time?!" May was just realizing what the early call time and lingering scent from last night both pointed to.

"I'll sleep when I'm dead. Come here." Abee was on his feet and towering over her. He stuck his hand out to help her. Abee pulled her up with a hop, May clumsily fell into him as she caught her balance. It might have seemed almost romantic to someone watching, but May had seen him do this exact motion 1,000 times. It's how you help someone up after they take a dive in sand volleyball.

"This way, please." They made their way around a bend, and then another, carefully through some tidepools, up and then down some boulders that dotted the shoreline, until they found themselves shimmying into a hole about ten-feet wide. Rocks surrounded them on three sides, and an unobstructed view of the ocean spread out in front of them to the west.

"Wow." May saw some version of this every day of her life, but it still took her breath away.

"I know, right! I found it this morning while I wasn't sleeping. The tide is crazy far out, you can't usually get down here. It occurred to me that this would be the perfect place to dig our own personal pool for solstice-ing."

May felt like her whole body was smiling. He remembered. Abee remembered her silly dream. May grabbed two clamshells that were peaking up out of the sand, fell to her knees, and started digging. Sand was flying everywhere, May was like a dog who had lost her bone. Abee was right there next to her. His hands were big enough to be their own shovels. They couldn't stop laughing—with every scoop they dug out, the surrounding sand slid in to take its place. This would never work. The beach had a way of evening things out. May's arms were burning. She had sand in her mouth. For all their work, they had managed to make a dent, but not a pool.

"Hey, what time is it?" May asked through the grit.

"It's 7:55."

Less than two minutes to go. May lifted a clam shell high into the air, swinging her arm down with one last delighted show of meaningless force. The pool had never been the point anyway.

THUD.

It knocked into a hard object in the sand. The shell slipped out of her grasp, slicing her palm as it did.

"There's something here." May winced.

"What?" Abee was already looking toward the ocean.

"Quick, help me pull it out." May could see a glint of blue shining through the sand where her shell had come down. With two meaningful swoops Abee cleared the sand away faster than it could slide back down. They were staring at half of a surfboard. May put a hand on either side of the board and wrestled it out of the ground. She was holding half of a bright-blue surfboard. It was so beautifully blue. It was like the color of the crayon that a kid would choose to fill in the ocean.

Abee reached up with the sleeve of his sweatshirt and wiped some muddy-sand off the nose of the board. A fluorescent-pink heart emerged, it had been layered into the resin. It wasn't just that though, it said something—*Mon Amie*—right there, scrawled through the heart. May threw the board like it had shocked her. Abee's watch was making a loud beeping sound. They locked eyes—wide. It was 7:57. It was solstice.

~~~~~~

"What the…" Abee wasn't averse to swearing, he was really just at a loss for words. "Is that what I think it is?" Abee's mouth was moving, but nothing else.

"I don't see how it's not." As she said it, May broke the spell and slunk to the ground.

"Your hand is bleeding."

May looked down, blood was trickling from her palm, into her sleeve. The bright-blue board was now half-way between them and the rapidly rising shore line. A particularly determined wave broke free of the line and lapped up against its side.

"I should pick it up, right?" Abee genuinely wasn't sure how to proceed.

"I don't think we can just leave it here."

Abee moved toward the board in slow motion. Or maybe it was quickly. May couldn't tell. Abee picked it up just before another rogue wave snatched it away. He tucked it under his right arm. The water was somehow up to his ankles now.

"Hey, I think we need to move up the beach. The waves are being weird." Abee's eyes were concerned. "Hop on my back?"

May didn't protest. Abee leaned down, she draped her arms over his shoulders, she was getting blood on the front of his sweatshirt. They were up and moving. The deck knocked against her thigh as he walked. The board's splintered stringer scratched at her calf. The water was up to his knees now. His breathing wasn't labored as much as it was panicked. They made it past the high-water mark and Abee let them all down into a heap. They sat in stunned silence. They were staring out at the ocean, but not comprehending. Abee finally diverted his stare when he felt a sand crab flutter up against his fingers. As he looked down, he saw his sweatshirt and remembered her hand. He was still frozen but he could feel the flight instinct thawing.

"I think we need to get you home and get your hand looked at. Is that the same hand? The hand you sliced when we were kids?"

May timidly released her clenched fist. The scar that had bisected her palm for the past five years was nowhere to be seen. Bright-red blood, and pink flaps of skin, where no flaps should be, had erased the past. Did she want to cry? Did she need to scream? Why did she kind of feel like laughing? May let her hand curl back into a ball. She took a deep breath. She just had to say it.

"That's my mom's board. The one she was riding the day she—I mean the half they never—well you know." There, she had said it, kind of. It was a real thing that—somehow—was really happening, and she had said what was real. That was a start. Her therapist would be proud. Abee gently put his arm around her, not sure what else to say. May propped herself against his chest, not sure where else to go. The busted board waited by their feet.

"Have you ever seen the tide do this?" Abee asked, realizing that the ocean had fully come in. Their alcove had vanished under the waves. It normally took around six hours for the water to go from low to high tide. Abee looked down at his watch. It wouldn't turn on. It must be water locked? Or dead? He didn't remember stopping the alarm. It had been beeping, right? This whole strange series of events couldn't have taken that long. Two minutes, three? How long had they been sitting here? May was shaking her head, confused. Abee realized he was making the same movement.

"If it's a tsunami or something, we gotta get out of here. Why aren't the sirens going off?" He was unfrozen. He was up. His arm was around her waist now. She was up.

"What do we do with this?" Abee asked matter of factly. He was looking at the board.

"I don't really want to just show up in the kitchen with it..." May's brain was moving slowly.

"Right. Okay. Umm, there's a cave around the corner. Let's stash it there until we figure out what to do. But we've got to move—fast." They were running again. But May didn't feel it this time. She was somewhere else entirely.

~~~~~~

It was a Wednesday morning, that meant no brunch service, and Shep and Elise would be out on their weekly rounds to see local vendors. Talmai was undoubtedly stuck on the 10, he had an important meeting in Culver City with their bank. They shouldn't have to answer any parental questions for at least another hour.

Abee helped May squeeze back through her bedroom window. She caught a glimpse of herself in the reflection of the glass. God, they looked like they'd just murdered someone or someones. There was blood everywhere.

Abee stayed outside. "Hey, hang tight, I'll go get the big first-aid kit. Just sit there I guess." May slid down onto the floor, everything was spinning, she closed her eyes.

Abee ran across the yard toward the restaurant. He was on the landing, and then the stairs, three at a time up to the back deck, and then he was at the back door. Abee was playing it all out in his mind—the kit was just inside the back door, to the right, in the broom closet. Get the kit, clean up her hand, stop the bleeding, figure out if the whole west coast was about to get swept away. Did they need to get to higher ground? What did that even mean? First, her hand. As Abee reached for the door it occurred to him that it might be locked. Shit. He didn't have his keys.

He grabbed the handle anyway, expecting it to give him a restrictive clunk as he put pressure on it. But the handle swung down with no resistance. Abee took a step inside and immediately turned into the broom closet. He didn't need the light, he knew right where it was. He had used it two days ago after he burned his arm getting some loaves out of the ovens. He opened the cabinet door and swooped his hand across the shelf. His hand came out empty. He shook his head, confused. He knew he had put it back right there. This was taking too long. Abee turned around toward the entry, fumbling for the light switch. A fluorescent tube buzzed to life overhead. The hell? Did someone rearrange this whole closet yesterday?

"Tal, is that you?" A voice called from the hallway.

The voice didn't sound familiar. It must be the girl who helped his dad with HR stuff. She was new. She had probably come to pick up some paperwork. Abee didn't say anything in response.

"Okay, fine. Be that way. I'm outtie. I'll be down there if you want to come."

Abee felt like his brain was glitching. What was going on? Whose voice was that? His eyes landed on a red box. It wasn't the first-aid kit that he had used on Monday, but it was red with a white-cross thing on it. It would do. He picked it up. He turned around just in time to see a flash of red hair walk past the closet and out the door he had just come in. May?

"It's gonna be gnarly, you probably couldn't handle it anyway," the redhead called out right before he heard the door swing shut behind her.

Abee's brain was at max capacity. Had he been dropped into another universe? He still had to get back to May. That couldn't have been her. Could it have? He reached to turn out the light. He stopped short.

Hanging there between the switch and the wire shelves was a tacky wall calendar, courtesy of the Hughes Aircraft Employees Federal Credit Union. This month featured a fairly low-res picture of Point Dume. He could take a better picture with his phone. And then he saw it. Abee wasn't sure if he was in another universe, but based on the current context clues he was pretty sure he was in 1995.

~~~~~~

JUNE 1995 CE

May opened her eyes. What was taking Abee so long? She was flat on the ground. Had she dozed off? Passed out? Shoot. She was probably getting blood on the carpet. May had begged her dad for this rug last year. Shep said it cost so much, it might as well have been a car. May gingerly brought her hand up to rest on her stomach instead of the floor. But now her awareness was focused on the feeling of the rug under her. Her rug was soft, but it wasn't a shag. Those were cool and all but she had gone for a woven graphic piece. Why did this rug feel like shag?

May brought her awareness up to her head. She opened her eyes and looked around. She was in her room. But this was also not her room. The dresser was the same, but the wallpaper was different. The light fixture was the same, but what she could see of the bed was different. And where was her poster? Had her dad redone her room? Was this all a giant decorating show prank? Were Nate and Jeremiah about to jump out from behind a screen? She must be dreaming. She closed her eyes again, hoping for a reset.

"Shit. Shit. Shit. Shit. Shit. Shit. May. Shit. Shit. Shit. Shit Shit." May could hear Abee coming across the yard. He had found his words again. Abee came tumbling through the window head-first as he continued to swear. The contents of the first-aid kit spilled out in front of him.

"May! We back-to-the-futured. I mean, I think we are in the back part, not the future, but yeah, we time traveled, or blipped, or hopped timelines. I don't know." He was talking faster than May had ever heard him talk.

Abee was searching through the strewn contents of the first-aid kit. He should rinse her hand. But if this was really happening, they couldn't just wander around the house like they belonged there.

"Wait, what would Marty do? Wait, Marty almost got sexed by his mom. Don't do what Marty would do." Abee sounded like a pinball machine. He was moving like one too. May hadn't said a word, or moved.

In lieu of a good rinse, Abee went with three antiseptic wipes. Then he wadded up a stack of gauze pads and shoved them into the gash. He wrapped it all into place with an unnecessarily long ace bandage. Abee patted the bandage as if to say, all done. Then he remembered. "You have to elevate to stop the bleeding!" He grabbed a pillow to prop her arm on. He smiled—proud of his work. May really was thankful, so she resisted rolling her eyes at his somewhat inappropriate giddiness. There was still an insane amount of blood all over both of them. He crammed all the supplies back in the first-aid kit and pushed it under the bed.

May adjusted her arm on the pillow. Where'd this pillow case come from? And had Abee really just been talking about time travel? Had she lost that much blood? Had she hit her head? If she had a concussion she shouldn't let herself doze off again. May willed herself to open her eyes. Abee was eagerly staring at her; his hair and the whole buzz of energy around him did remind her of Doc. She grinned almost involuntarily. "So, what year did the DeLorean bring us to this time?"

"I can't tell if you are trying to be sarcastic with me or what. So I'm just going to pretend like you're genuinely asking. Cause Mays, hold on to your butts, it's 1995."

May stayed completely still on the floor. Was Abee having a nervous breakdown? Or was this just another one of his pester May 'til she screams routines? This hardly seemed like the time. Her eyes were closed again. She continued to keep them closed as she started to speak.

"Okay Doc, if this is 1995, then this isn't my room. So, here's what we are going to do. You are going to stand up and open the top drawer of the dresser, and tell me what you see inside."

Abee had too much adrenaline running through him to do anything except hop into action. He pulled the drawer open. This knob had always been loose. It still was.

"I see a bunch of socks and a cream colored jewelry box."

"That's exactly what should be in there, in my drawer, in 2023," May said, unsurprised. May pushed up from the floor with one arm, glad she had quickly put a stop to whatever weird game Abee had going. She managed to slowly stand. From here she could see the drawer crammed full of unmatched, indistinguishable socks, just like always, and sure enough there was the velvety jewelry box shoved right down in the middle of them all. She walked to the dresser and reached in to pick up the box.

"There is going to be a gold necklace in here with a gold heart that says *Mon Amie*, cause this is all some sadistic prank that has gotten out of hand. Literally." May held up her bandaged arm dramatically. May opened the box. It was empty. Now that May was standing up, she could take in the entirety of the scene playing out around her. This was not her room. Yes, technically it was the room where she had slept for the past fifteen years, but this room did not belong to her. She was feeling woozy again.

May didn't have to say anything, Abee could tell by the look on her face that she believed him now. "Alright May, don't freak out. I've been preparing for this moment my whole life. I always knew this would happen," he added under his breath. "I have watched every movie and every tv show ever made about time travel. We've got nothing to worry about."

Why was he acting like this was a good thing?

"Abee, I was right there on the couch next to you for every movie and show. I just didn't realize we needed to be taking notes." May's voice went a little shaky at the end. With her left hand, May instinctively reached down and grabbed his right hand, hoping he would mete out some of his manic energy. He gave her hand a quick squeeze and then proceeded with his pinball dance around the room.

"Okay, first things first, we need to figure out the rules that are governing our current situation. The rules of time travel are not a given; they are always changing depending on the needs of the storyline."

Why was he talking about plot development?

"Wait, back up, actual first thing. We have to get out of these clothes. We are definitely giving athletic-murderers-from-the-future." Given their monochromatic, blood-soaked, slim-fit athleisure wear, it was a very apt assessment. Abee bounced over to the closet and opened the door; he flipped on the light, revealing a mound of pink – orange – blue – black – red plaid – yellow plaid – light washed – camo – mini – ringer – baggy – flannel – cotton – denim clothes from a vintage sourcer's wildest dreams.

Abee grabbed a few things off the pile and tossed them at May. She was now holding a yellow spaghetti-strap top and her favorite vintage Levi's cropped denim jacket. From the moment she opened the jewelry box she had known this was coming. How could she not have? May was obviously standing in her mother's bedroom, holding her mother's jacket. May had to put the clothes down on the bed and then she had to put herself down on the bed. There was no way this could really be happening. But May's life was full of things that couldn't happen and yet did. So despite the appeal to common sense that her brain was trying to formulate at the moment, May awkwardly pulled her arm in through the sleeve of her bloody shirt and then tugged the whole thing up and over her head with her good arm. And then May put on her mother's clothes.

Abee was still busy digging through the pile. He was low on wardrobe options but found a black and red striped oversized sweater that almost worked. On him it was undersized, but at least it was giving more of a jacked Curt Cobain vibe than murderer. May had managed to put on the yellow shirt and jacket. They looked at each other from across the room. This was ridiculous.

"So I'm assuming you've put two and two together...that this is your mom's room?" Abee was tying a flannel around his waist to add another layer to his new look. He smiled at himself in the mirror.

Why did it seem like he was having fun?

"Yeah, I guess I figured that out, Doc. I'm going to skip the obvious questions of *how* and *why* for now, because it's still very likely that we have lost our minds." May's voice was getting shaky again. She took in the room one more time. And once again it confirmed the absolute predicament they were in. They had not lost their minds, as much as she would have preferred that explanation.

"What do we do, Abee?" May had never been more earnest.

He had never looked happier to be answering a question. "Well, we need to get out of here for one. I think we are already pushing our limits. There's just one small detail that I haven't had a chance to tell you yet. I think I saw your mom—hold on—I'll answer questions when I'm done, but I'm pretty sure it was her, and I'm pretty sure she was heading down to surf. My watch doesn't work here, obviously..." Abee was proud of himself for figuring that detail out. "But that was probably like twenty minutes ago now, so she might be gone for a while if the waves are good, or she might pop in at any moment because she forgot a hair tie or something. Wait, the waves!" Abee was just realizing why the waves had been so weird. "There's no tsunami coming; the tides were just at different places! When we hopped, we hopped to a time where the tide was in." He was glowing, and out of breath.

May had a million questions, but she couldn't verbalize any of them, so she just shook her head. It was one of those shake-nod motions that seemed to be claiming yes and no at the same time.

"Mays, we are going to calmly make our way out the window, across the yard, to the street, down the block, and then turn off on the equestrian trail that goes to the waterfall." May could see another epiphany coming. "What if they didn't have the equestrian trails back then?! I mean now. When did they add those? Anyway, we'll figure it out when we get there." Abee grabbed her good hand, and they were sliding out the window.

~~~~~~

They obviously couldn't leave their old clothes in May's mom's room, so at the last minute Abee had swiped a red Jansport from the closet and shoved their stuff into it. The left strap was busted, which forced him to just sling it over his right shoulder. It was the pièce de résistance for his new 90's kid persona, the grunge surf rat.

Normally, in the present, the path to the waterfall would have been packed with day-hikers, trailrunners, and the occasional horse and rider, but for now at least, they were alone. If anyone had been there to see them, they would have thought these two teenagers looked like any other kids wandering around that day. More specifically, they would have thought they looked an awful lot like two locals who were about the same age.

As they walked, Abee looked up at the sky. He guessed it was around 9:00 a.m. He was no astronomer; May had done most of his Earth Science homework for him, but here you couldn't help but be in sync with the sun. It was the main character in every story, even when it was hiding.

Abee still had lots of things to say, but he could sense that May wanted—no needed—him to stop talking for a little while. So they walked along in silence, both of them unconsciously comforted by the familiar smell of the sagebrush and the rhythm of the California oaks throwing their dappled light down on the path from above. These trees had been around for hundreds of years; they weren't concerned if it was 1995 or 2023. It was just another day of sun to them.

With anyone else, May might have felt the need to fill the silence of such a preposterous moment with talk, but not with Abee. What do you even say when you have somehow magically traveled to the past and now apparently exist in the same time and place as your dead mother who you've never even met before. May had never met her mother. This hole in her life wasn't newly discovered, but here in this moment, May felt the weight of it in a way she rarely let herself think about. She had never known her mom, and now according to Abee, her mom, or some version of her mom, was probably right down on the other side of these cliffs. May's brain kept tempting her to dive into the swirl of questions waiting to erupt, but she did her best to just focus on the hard, solid ground in front of her.

Just off the path, Abee spotted a crook in a giant oak that he recognized. As kids they climbed these branches all the time. He didn't need to explain to May what he was doing. He pulled himself onto the massive bough and then leaned down to help her up. It was a perfect bench for two. Abee's long legs dangled in the air, just like they always did from this branch.

May was staring off toward the ocean. Abee was staring at May. She didn't seem to notice, or didn't care. Her long red hair, her flushed cheeks, her misty eyes, her favorite jacket, simple things he had seen countless times before, and here they were again...for the first time? It all made perfect sense, and it all made no sense whatsoever.

Abee knew that May didn't like to talk about her mom. He had noticed for years now that any time Amy's name came up, which was more often than you might think, May would get this strained look on her face like she was trying to spot something on the horizon that kept coming in and out of view. If May was forced to talk about Amy, she would say *mom* like she was saying it for the first time, every time. Like it was a word she was borrowing from some exotic language. For May, *mom* was an idea, not a reality.

Finally sensing his gaze, May cautiously lifted one leg and scooted around so that she was straddling the branch and looking straight at Abee now. When had he become such a—man? Abee was as long as ever, but he had shed his lankiness somewhere along the way. She had obviously noticed how he was changing over these past few years, but she had been afraid to look too closely. May couldn't help but look now. She needed to be certain that he was there with her, right next to her, every inch of him. With the chaos happening inside and all around her, she needed the certainty of him. And there he was. Abee held her gaze for just a moment before looking down at his feet.

A growl from her stomach interrupted the silence. Abee remembered he had seen a green-wrapped granola bar in the bottom of the backpack. Without even opening the package he could tell the 2-bar pouch was more like a 100-bits pouch. Good to know some things had always been the same. He handed her the pouch of crumbs and then fished out a wrinkled-up piece of paper and a chewed-on plastic pen from the bottom of the bag.

"Mays, I know this is a lot. It's too much. But we have some things we need to figure out."

May started to grin in spite of herself. They were here together. Whenever *here* was. They had always taken care of each other. She lifted her chin to the sky and blew the tension away from her body with a deep exhale.

"Alright, this is heavy Doc, but let's figure out when the hell we are and what we are going to do about it." Her voice was steady.

~~~~~~

THINGS WE THINK WE KNOW

1. We started today in 2023.
2. Something happened on the beach...solstice?...surfboard?????????
3. Now we are in 1995, but the same day? JUNE 21.
4. We can see other people and they can see us. Maybe - need to test this more.
5. Amy is here.

THINGS WE KNOW WE DON'T KNOW

1. WHYYYYYYYY?
2. HOWWWWWWWWWWWWWWWWW?
3. Are we going to butterfly-effect ourselves out of existence?
4. Can we get back to the future? Dear Marty, help us.
5. Are we gone from 2023 or have we started another timeline and are now living in two worlds at the same time? May says this is impossible.

NEW

Listen: "Lady by the Sea"
by Stephen Sanchez

SEVEN

~~~~~~~~~~

JUNE 1995 CE

It was a great session. The water was glassy with a strong swell; she got some long rides; the sun was warm on her back. But as Amy dropped her board on the porch and slid through her window, she felt a little irritated, or maybe disappointed. Tal had never come down.

Amy knew she should work on being less sarcastic with him. She should have just told him she wanted him to come with her when she saw him in the kitchen. Tal was her boyfriend after all. She could—and should—just be honest with him. This was new for both of them, but if it was going to work, and last, she knew she needed to be more mature about things, no games. Tal was her best friend, he always had been, and now he was more than that too. It felt complicated, but it felt good. Amy unconsciously reached up to touch the heart that hung from her neck. She couldn't make out each individual engraved letter with just the feel of her finger, but she knew what the ridges collectively added up to—he loved her.

Amy had to work the lunch rush, but first she'd take a quick shower and then go find him and apologize. Tal would laugh and say he didn't even know what she was talking about, and he would be right. All of the angst and conflict was confined to her own brain. Maybe she was just trying to find an excuse to go looking for him.

Before heading to the bathroom, Amy grabbed some clothes from the jumbled heap in her closet. She made a mental note to get better about putting her stuff away. But there was always tomorrow. She wriggled her still sandy toes in the deep shag of her rug as she walked across the room. She should make her case for a new rug again. Amy knew her mom was sentimental about this shag-tastic thing from the 70's, but it seriously must have had half of the Malibu beach in it by this point. Her right foot slid against something wet in the rug. But as she stopped and the feeling of whatever it was sank in, she realized it was actually more sticky than wet. Amy maneuvered herself into a sort of modified one-legged chair position to examine what was now on the bottom of her foot.

Sick. It was blood. Was she bleeding? Amy abandoned her one-legged chair stance and let herself sink to the ground. Maybe she had cut the bottom of her foot swimming up through the rocks. Amy pushed her fingers across her arch and the ball of her foot and between her toes. She didn't find any gashes. It wasn't coming from her foot. She timidly ran her fingers through the thick pile of the ombre orange rug. There it was. It was a small spot, but it was definitely a spot of blood. This was weird, and gross, but mostly weird.

Amy jumped as a tap tap at the window broke her concerned stare. The tap was just a courtesy though because Tal was coming in before she even had a chance to say anything. He pounced down on the rug next to her and scooped her into a rolling hug, rocking her back and forth and squeezing her ribs with his big hands. Tal knew that she pretended to hate being tickled. Amy screamed with laughter and joy. She wrestled out of his arms and flopped down flat on the rug as she tried to catch her breath. But there was no use in trying, because every breath she had ever had was gone as his face stared down at her and then his mouth was on her mouth. His tongue bumped up against her teeth. She let him melt into her; he tasted like honey. She didn't even care that she could feel the blood rubbing into the back of her head. And the last thing she wanted to think about was why there was a first-aid kit under her bed.

~~~~~~

"We've had a lot of really stupid ideas over the years," Abee whispered across the table, "but this is the tops, Mays." Now it was his turn to be shocked for a while.

"You're not wrong," May whispered back, "but I really think this is what we have to do." May hoped that by saying it, she would feel the truth of it. She fidgeted with the napkin on her lap.

It was in fact still June 21. The chalkboard out front with the *Menu Du Jour* had confirmed that bit of information. And everything else around them—as they started looking—solidified the added detail of 1995. There were the stickers on the license plates, "CA 95" in the upper right hand corner. There were the actual physical newspapers in the big box things on the street—and the boxes took coins! There were the fringy haircuts and the chunky highlights on the women at the table next to them. And there was the cigarette smoke—it was everywhere, people were even smoking inside the restaurant.

They had stopped by the gas station on the corner before heading to Duck's. Gas was only $1.29, another unbelievable detail from 1995. Tal had given Abee a hundred dollars last night to use for May's party. Had that really just been last night? Abee still had twenty bucks left. It wasn't much, but considering they almost never had actual cash on them it was a bit of good luck that they were happy to take. They didn't know anything about the history of currency, but Abee's twenty-dollar bill had some fancy watermarks and holographic strips on it that they guessed wouldn't have been used in the 90's. So, rather than show up at Duck's with money from the future, they decided to take their chances with the long-haired kid at the gas station. The gas station kid would have taken Monopoly money. Two minutes and $0.52 later they were back on the sidewalk with a pack of Bubble Yum and $19.48 in change. Hopefully it was enough to buy lunch.

May's reasoning for going to Duck's went like this…if time travel was something that could really happen, then anything could happen. And if anything could happen, then they very well could have shown up in London in 1613 to catch a matinee of *Henry VIII*, or they could have popped up at the end of the Cretaceous to see what really did in the dinosaurs. Abee felt the need to point out what a weirdo she was; these were the examples she thought of when she imagined unimpeded time travel? May ignored him.

But they hadn't shown up anywhere else. They had hopped to their hometown, at a time when their parents, or at least half of them, were there too. This wasn't a coincidence. May was certain of it. The universe had thrown them back here for a reason, and if she had to guess, she'd guess that reason had something to do with their own families. So why not just go to where their families were?

Abee's objection went like this…they were both the spitting image of their parents. Wouldn't someone start asking questions? What would they say? Were they long lost cousins who just showed up for lunch? Were they random exchange students who didn't speak English? And to top it all off, they had on Amy's clothes. May said they'd just know what to do when they got there. It made as much sense as anything, so Abee conceded. They were going to Duck's.

Lunch service started at 11:00 a.m. A young girl had ushered them to a table for two in the Humpback room. May had relaxed slightly as she walked in. It was exactly the same—three humpbacks keeping watch from above. So, here they were, sitting under the shadow of the whales, tensely whisper-talking, waiting to see what the universe would bring them next. They didn't have to wait long.

"Welcome to Duck's! I don't mean to be too nosy, but do we know each other? I just say that because, this will sound strange, but you look exactly like my daughter and her boyfriend. The resemblance is, well it's uncanny. " Gloria's eyes twinkled. May didn't know what she had expected. But she did not expect this. Gloria was radiant. Grandpa Gene's stories, the pictures, the spirit of her that lingered in every inch of this place, none of it had prepared May for the magic of her physical presence. May was smiling, but she wasn't talking. Abee spoke up.

"That is so crazy!" Abee did his best impression of a surprised person. "And no, I don't think we've ever met. This is our first time here." That was true in a sense. "We're just ummm kind of on a crazy trip—we're here visiting—I guess."

"Travelers. I like it. Well, you picked a great time to come. It's summer solstice today. In the land of sun and surf, this is kind of like our Christmas. In fact—" Gloria looked down at her watch, "we have about two and half hours until the exact moment. I'm sure you have plans, but you should try and be out on the beach here in a bit, well at 1:34 to be exact. It's pretty magical."

Gloria was telling Abee something about the weather and the surf conditions, but May's head was buzzing. In 2023 the solstice had been at 7:57 a.m., but here in 1995 it was going to happen at 1:34 p.m. The solstice hadn't happened here yet. It wasn't just her head now; all around her the universe was buzzing.

Abee was ordering a BLT. He and Gloria turned to look at May. She managed to say, "Chopped salad, and water please." She hadn't looked at the menu yet, but surely salads in the 90's weren't very expensive. Gloria nodded and turned to talk to the table next to them.

"Your grandma is hot," Abee whispered. The words sounded wrong even as they were coming out. "Do you think she suspects anything?"

"She is gorgeous, isn't she!" May felt drunk. "And do I think she suspects that her granddaughter, who she doesn't even know exists, has traveled back in time and is about to eat a salad at her restaurant? No, I don't think she suspects that. But Abee, did you hear what she said? Solstice is at 1:34. It hasn't happened!"

"Okay...I think I know what you're getting at, but say more." Abee's forehead was furrowed.

"Something happened this morning at solstice. It's possible we are stuck here in 1995 forever, but that's never really how it works in the movies. There is something we have to do and then there is always some way back. What if the solstice is our way back to the future? It makes a lot of sense." They both laughed at the absurdity of that statement.

And then, a flash of red hair caught May's attention. There she was, at the wait station. Amy's back was to them. May held her breath, afraid that if she moved, she might wake up from the dream. This was what she had wanted. This was why they had come. Her mom was alive. Her mom was here.

~~~~~~

They paid Gloria. They had enough to leave her two dollars for a tip. At least it was something. May waited on the bench out front, while Abee went to pee. Should she have gone up to her mom? What would she even say to her? She hadn't seen her straight on yet, but even from the back May could tell she was staring at a version of herself. The way Amy's hair waved into a curl just at the ends. Her freckled arms that could have disappeared into Point Dume's buff sand that was always spotted with chestnut cowries. Her slightly clipped torso and elongated legs. They were the same. And May was not ready to talk to her, not yet.

It had been a very enlightening lunch though. They had seen people and no one had immediately disappeared into thin air. They knew exactly when and where they were now. And they had a working theory on how to un-time-travel themselves. May wasn't ready to talk about the other working theory she had.

What was taking Abee so long? He must have had to do more than pee. Classic. May had seen thousands of people sit on this bench, but this was her first time. Most of the lunch-goers were inside now and the street was quiet. May heard the front door creak open behind her. Finally, he was done. But it was Gloria, not Abee.

"Hey, Hon. I'm glad I caught you. You left this at the table." Gloria held out the denim jacket.

"Oh gosh, thank you." May's fingers brushed against Gloria's as she handed it off. May's face flushed, realizing Gloria must recognize the jacket. But if she did, she didn't betray any familiarity; her eyes were more focused on May's bandaged arm. Then, instead of turning to go back inside, Gloria sat down on the bench next to her, like that had always been her intention.

"Feel free to write me off as some crazy old lady, but I wanted to give you something else too."

"You're hardly old, and I doubt you're crazy," May offered sweetly.

"I knew I liked you," Gloria smiled back with a wink.

Her presence was intoxicating. May felt right at home.

As if by magic, Gloria opened her hand to reveal a tightly folded piece of paper. "It's just a little token for your journey," she offered. Gloria set it on the bench between them, and then stood up as quickly as she had sat down.

"It was really nice to meet you—" Gloria stopped, realizing she didn't know the girl's name.

May and Abee had planned for this moment. If asked, they were going to say their names were Mel and Josh, but as May sat there looking up into Gloria's eyes, she couldn't do it.

"I'm May and it was really good to meet you too, G—."

"Lo—Gloria. I'm Gloria," Gloria interrupted. Her eyes were twinkling more than ever. "Oh right, right." Gloria looked down at her own name tag realizing she didn't need to introduce herself. "Come back and see us again sometime, May. You're always welcome here." Then Gloria turned and went inside.

May picked up the paper and held it for a breath before unfolding it. She recognized Gloria's handwriting. She didn't know she could recognize it, but she did. She had seen it scrawled on the backs of enough pictures and on the countless notes Grandpa Gene always had lying around. Her eyes raced to take in the words.

I dream of you
or maybe it's when I wake
that I hold your hand,
but either way
here we are.

I run toward you
or maybe it's the ground
that floats under my feet,
but either way
here we are.

I turn to you
or maybe it's that world
that turns around me,
but either way
here we are.

I reach for you
or maybe it's you
that reaches out for me,
but either way
here we are.

Dreaming.
Running.
Turning.
Reaching.
Here may we always be.

When Abee came out a few minutes later, May was still sitting on the bench, quietly crying.

~~~~~~

"Barukh atah Adonay, ---------------- Adonay, Barukh ----------------, Barukh atah ------------------ atah Adonay, ---------------- Adonay." In the few seconds of silence that came between each crash of the waves, May could just barely make out what Abee was saying. He was partly chanting, and partly mumbling. He was on his knees at the edge of the surf, praying and pleading, swishing and wringing. First her clothes and then his. Cold saltwater worked wonders on blood stains, apparently.

Barukh atah Adonay. All the good Jewish prayers started like this. *We bend to the Eternal One.* May knew it was a loose translation—the more classic interpretation being, *Blessed are You, LORD,* but it was how Elise had first explained it to her. Elise was the mystic of the family. Not knowing where else to go at the moment, May and Abee had come back to the water. Abee was closer now, draping their clothes over some rocks to dry. May could hear that he had moved past the first line of his prayer.

But the meaning of the rest of the words was beyond her. His work done, Abee came and dropped down next to May. The sun was high in the sky. It wasn't hot, but the sun was strong. Abee shimmied out of his too-tight striped sweater.

"Why do you think she gave me that poem?" They were well beyond the need for build up or explanation. They were in a say-whatever-you're-thinking-as-soon-as-you-think-it situation. "I don't get it..."

"Maybe she just always has a stack of poems ready to give out to people. It wouldn't be the weirdest thing to happen today." Abee grinned wryly. "I don't know Mays. I don't know. You're the one who said there was no way she could suspect anything."

"Well, I'm starting to think I was wrong. Yesterday, we had no idea that time travel was real."

"Speak for yourself," Abee said under his breath.

"Okay, fair, you've always been a believer," May smirked, "but whatever we thought was or wasn't possible, here we are now. The world is crazier and bigger than we—than I—thought it could be. So maybe my grandma knows something about all of this. Maybe. She talked to us about the solstice, she told me to come back anytime, and then she capped it off with a cryptic poem."

"I'm not sure if it's really that cryptic, to be honest."

May stared into his bright sea-glassy eyes, simultaneously afraid of what he was going to say next and aware that it had to be said.

"May, it's for you. And not just the random you who showed up for lunch today; the you who is her family. It's for you, as her granddaughter."

Abee was right. May knew he was right. But how? Gloria died before May was born. Gloria died before even the idea of May was born. Gloria died. Why was this the most constant theme in her life? People die. Her people die. Her people always died. The script supervisor over her life's story was nailing it, the continuity was impeccable, the story had never deviated. Her very existence was enmeshed with someone else's death in a way that felt cruel. It was cruel. May was alive because her mother had died. She hadn't asked for that. She didn't want that to be the story of her life, and yet the story seemed bent on repeating itself ad infinitum. Ad nauseum.

This wasn't something that was going to be resolved in one unbelievable day. This was chapter one. Or maybe even just the preface. May let her head sink in between her knees. Her kneecaps rubbed up against her temples. The pressure felt nice. She spoke, her voice muffled in her legs. "I think we just became the main characters in a story we aren't writing."

"Looks like we better up that main character energy then." May lifted her head. Abee's eyes promised her this would be fun.

~~~~~~

They weren't exactly sure what time it was, but they knew they didn't want to miss it. Would they magically be wrenched from the past at the moment of the solstice, without any effort on their part, or was it something they had to agree to in some metaphysical way? And what did the surfboard have to do with the mechanics of it all? Had it just been a coincidence or did they need to be touching the board again? Did they need to be standing in the exact same spot? Hopefully not, because they couldn't get all the way down there right now.

Backs turned, they put their own clothes on. The clothes were stiff with salt. The busted surfboard was right where they had left it. They put Amy's clothes in the backpack and tucked the bag in the cave where the board had been. May unwrapped her arm and buried the bandages in the sand near the bag. Maybe Amy would find her bag someday and wonder how it got there, or maybe she never would. Maybe it would still be there if they came back. But if the jacket was lost to the cave, how would May ever have it in the future? Could one jacket change everything? Or even one thing? But, ironically, they didn't have time at the moment to discuss theories of relativity. And leaving it seemed safer than taking it to the future. Right?

Not wanting to miss their chance, if that's what this was, they took the board and waded into the water. The spray of the waves burned as it splashed up into May's hand. She hated to do it, but she had to. She unclenched her fist and let the poem float out into the water. She couldn't take it with her. Or maybe she could. But she didn't. She had it with her now anyway. Even though she had to let it go, she held onto every word.

May could swim, she wasn't that crazy, but she had never been fully in the ocean. They went up to their waists. Whatever the rules of this were, they figured waist deep, as close to their original spot as possible would have to do. Then they stood there, each of them holding one side of the board, looking out to the horizon, trying not to flinch as the waves crashed around them. How long did they need to wait? Was it ten minutes until the solstice? Thirty? Would they know right away if it worked? How long were they just going to stand there? What if it didn't work? Better to stand there too long, than not long enough. And so they stood, and they waited. A shiver ran down May's back. The sun had gone behind a cloud. Had those clouds been there before? The water, almost imperceptibly, rose up to her ribs.

"Hey guys!! Guys! Is that you?!!"

They both knew the voice immediately. They kept their grasp on the board but slowly turned their heads to see which version of Tal was calling to them from the shore. Tal's strong jaw, his stubbly face, his hair that was more of a charcoal than a jet black, his expensive looking techy running shorts; it all proved what they had hoped for—they were back to the future. Abee's watch dinged to life with five and half hours worth of missed notifications and messages. May released her grasp on the board. Abee took it and tried to push it under the water, but it was half of a surfboard; it couldn't just disappear—again. And there was no way Tal hadn't already seen it.

Abee looked at May and shrugged. They couldn't just stand there forever. They sploshed through the water, making their way up to Tal. His expression was both amused and confused as he watched them come toward him.

"I thought that was you out there, but I couldn't tell until I got up close. It was like you were in a mirage or something. You guys alright? We hadn't seen you since last night. I wasn't worried, but you know your mom...she could see that you were down here on your location, but your board was at the house and we weren't sure if May was with you, and so I just came to check. I wasn't worried, but..."

Tal was speaking in a mostly normal tone and cadence, but his eyes betrayed him. His mouth was saying one thing, but his brain was obviously somewhere else. Tal's eyes were transfixed on the board. He had made a lot of surfboards over the years, but this had been his first.

"Dad," Abee kindly interrupted him, "we found this down in that alcove." Abee nodded his head in the direction of the rocks. "The tide was really far out, and well it was there, buried in the sand." He instinctively held it out toward his father, relieved when Tal's giant hand gripped one side, releasing Abee from the weight of it.

"I—I know we never found it that day, but I never, never imagined it was still—here." Tal's voice was low and heavy.

~~~~~~

They all tucked in around the banquette. Elise with smudges of flour on her cheeks, Shep smelling of hickory and oak tinged with melted pork fat. Lunch service was done. They could spare a few minutes before diving back into dinner. May was chilled in her still damp clothes, but she was avoiding going in her room. Her dad reached across the table and lightly squeezed her hand in his. She winced but squeezed back. Her wound was exposed, no covering.

Now that they were all sitting here, Tal wasn't exactly sure what needed to be said. He had given Shep and Elise the thirty second run down when he went to get them at the restaurant. *May and Abee are okay. Yes, they were right where the location said they were. But there's something else. Somehow...God how?....they found the other half of Amy's board that was never recovered. Yes, yes, I saw it. Yes, yes, I am absolutely sure it's hers.*

Tal's momentary absence at that point had given May and Abee a chance to quickly agree. Whatever conversation was about to take place, let the adults take the lead. Answer their questions about the board; don't bring up time travel. Not yet. Maybe not ever.

Shep was the first to speak. "I feel like Amy is here with us again, in a way I haven't felt in a while." He shifted his gaze to speak directly to May and Abee. "But I'm so sorry, sorry you had to be the ones to find it." Shep spoke more to himself now, "What are the chances of that?" His compassion-filled eyes had gone out of focus.

Elise picked up where Shep drifted off. "Did you realize right away what you had found? I can't even imagine what must have been going on in your heads." Elise was speaking to both of them, but she was looking at May. "Are you okay? Is your hand okay?" Elise's own hand rested over her heart as she spoke. May was shaking, partly because of the chill, partly because of everything else. She managed an affirmative nod to Elise's question. The motion was more emphatic than she intended, inadvertently letting everyone at the table know how *not okay* she was. May chewed on the inside of her lip and looked down at her lap.

"I think we really just want to make sure you both are okay and talk about anything you might want to talk about." Tal was still trying to find his way in this strange moment. "Do you have any questions..." It sounded more rhetorical than he intended. Obviously they had questions. The questions were a given; the answers were not.

"Well I know Amy was out surfing, but I've never really understood exactly how things went bad that day." Abee looked at May, hoping this was alright to ask about.

"I don't want to know all the gory details, but what happened?" Abee knew he was treading on sacred ground.

"That's a really good question, son." Tal's eyes filled with sadness and then tears.

"We failed her that day, that's what happened..." Shep met Tal's gaze and neither of them looked away as the tears freely streamed down their cheeks. Elise's eyes were closed. Her chest heaved up and down in quick silent gasps. It had been sixteen years, but anyone looking in the window that day would have surely thought this grief was brand new.

It's not that May didn't understand their pain, but for the very first time in her life she felt like she had power over it. She had just been in the same room as her mom—and not a ghost of her mom—the real flesh and blood person. She wanted to shout, *Mom is alive! And I think I can help her. I think I can help all of you.*

But instead, May just blurted out, "I want to keep the board!"

Obviously no one objected. Shep said that Amy would have wanted it that way. No one ever really answered Abee's question.

After a round of kisses to the forehead for May and hugs for Abee, the adults went back to their orderly, urgent worlds. The board lay on the kitchen island like it was there in state for viewing. May didn't want the board in any sentimental way; it actually seemed pretty morbid, but she knew that they needed it. Or they might need it. She still wasn't sure if the board was part of the magic or just a coincidence. Either way, it was best that she be the keeper of it for now.

Abee's head was down flat on the table. He hadn't slept in a long time. Was it days? Or years? It all felt the same at this point.

"Can you do one more thing with me?" May knew she couldn't avoid her room forever. Abee didn't lift his head, but May could see that he cracked one eye.

"Just one more thing?" he asked through a yawn.

"Well, just one more today. Then, you can sleep. Will you go check my room with me? I'm kind of worried about going in there again." May knew she sounded like a child.

"Worried your mom is hiding under the bed or what?" Abee picked up his whole head and opened both eyes now. "Let's go."

May timidly pushed the door open. It really was her room again. She stood at the threshold observing. It was her bed, her rug, her clothes—well sort of. Abee slid past her into the room. He dutifully opened the closet. He got down on his knees and looked under the bed. He was making a production of it all. Not to make fun of her, but to make her feel safe. He pulled back the covers, waving his hand over the empty bed like a magician. Then he literally fell into the bed. He couldn't make it next door. He couldn't make it another step. His breathing was immediately heavy. May took a deep breath herself. She stepped into her room.

She had to check one thing. She flipped through the crammed together hangers in her closet. She felt panicky inside. She wasn't sure which option was better. Should it be there, should it not be there? Where had she put it?

And there it was. Barely hanging on, the left shoulder lodged into one of the notches of the hanger, the other dangling toward the ground. She gathered it in her hands, like a nun beholding the Shroud of Turin. She turned it over. It was here. She ran her fingers up and down the button holes, then along the stitching on the sleeves. She froze. There on the cuff, it was muted, faded, a stain. An old blood stain. You wouldn't notice it if you didn't know to look for it. Had she ever noticed it before? May shoved the jacket back into the closet. It was there and that was all her brain could handle for now.

May sank down to her rug, tucking a pile of laundry under her head as a pillow. She needed to rest her eyes for just one second...

~~~~~~

SEPTEMBER 2023 CE

"We are such scientists. Should we be streaming this? We could get a Genius Grant, a Nobel, a Pulitzer! I don't know the difference to be honest, but I'm just saying. We don't have to keep this to ourselves." Abee talked to keep himself warm, like the way other people rubbed their hands together. It was almost midnight, late September, and the beach was dark and cold. Despite the darkness, Abee could still see May roll her eyes.

They definitely weren't scientists, but they were at the very least experimentalists. The earth spins along its orbit in relatively precise and predictable ways, which means that every year there are four distinct solar events: the summer solstice, the fall equinox, the winter solstice, and the spring equinox. Solstice happens when the earth is at its max tilt in relation to the sun (the northern hemisphere toward the sun in June and the southern hemisphere toward the sun in December), and equinox happens when the earth is neither tilted away from nor toward the sun. The solstices are the extremes;

the equinoxes are the means. They might have four chances a year to hop. They wouldn't know until they tried.

"Based on our last jump, I don't think we have to be in the exact spot where we found the board. But maybe our feet should be in the water?" May was trying to be practical about all of this, not emotional. But her mom was always on her mind which had a way of making things emotional despite her practicalities.

"I'm down with that. We would need wetsuits otherwise." Abee really was down for all of this. His excitement and joy with it had not waned over the past three months. He loved to talk about it. He loved to plan and ideate. May still had more of an apprehensive relationship with it all. But here they were, board in hand.

In preparation for tonight they had thrifted an outfit for May that consisted of a vintage Ralph Lauren sweatshirt, bright green, with a pair of high-waisted light-washed Guess jeans. And for Abee, an Alice in Chains 1995 tour t-shirt with a pair of distressed black Levis. And to finish off their looks, they were each sporting an analog plastic Swatch watch circa 1993. They didn't carry any other technology with them, May was pretty passionate about avoiding as much anachronism as possible. Abee thought their physical existence in a different time was more problematic than say an iPhone, but he didn't protest.

Over the past few months May had also been discreetly watching the cash coming through Duck's on the nights she worked. So far she had managed to find five twenty-dollar bills in the older style of currency. They weren't from the 90's; most paper currency only lasted seven or eight years—she discovered with a little research—but they weren't obnoxiously crisp and shimmery either. She had obviously replaced them with other bills of her own when she closed out. They were ready.

They walked down into the water, soaking the cuffs of their jeans. May had a tan canvas tote slung over her shoulder; it held their cash and two pairs of timeless black Chucks. If their hypothesis was confirmed, they were prepared for the outcome this time. They held the board between them. They looked at each other and smiled. This actually was fun. May counted to one-hundred. Then she counted to one-hundred again. She didn't want to jinx it by looking at her watch too soon. But then she couldn't wait any longer. She checked. The time had passed; if it had happened, then it had happened, but they wouldn't know just standing there in the dark. They'd have to get back to some landmarks.

They made their way across the sand. From the beach they could see the cliffs dotted with warm lights and the reflective glow of sparkling blue rectangles, but it was too dark to make out specific homes and judge if they were the mansions of the 90's or the fortified celebrity estates of modern Malibu. They kept walking. They would know one way or the other when they made it around the next corner.

The death stairs, as they were not so affectionately called, had precariously conveyed people from the cliffs to the beach for almost fifty years. They were a real Malibu experience. Missing steps, sharp edges, unsteady railings, holes in the landings, that kind of experience. But a few years ago the death stairs had been dismantled and a solid, sturdy, no death version of the stairs had taken their place. They would know when they saw the stairs. Death or no death.

As they walked, not yet knowing where they had landed, May realized that she felt—what was this feeling? She felt untethered. She felt like herself. Here in the darkness, for a few precious moments, she felt extraordinarily alive. She didn't know when she was, and she didn't care. Her parents might be here; they might not. She might belong here; she might not. It might all make sense someday, and it might not. But she was alive right now, right here. May slowed her pace. The ocean was full of silky ink. The deep sky was full of infinity. Saturn and Jupiter hung in the darkness; they could have been the lights from another window on the cliff, or they could have been the lights from a window to another world. It was hard to tell. If NASA ever put out a call for volunteer space pioneers, May would be first on the list.

"Hey, hold up." The words were out of May's mouth before she knew she was saying them.

Abee, realizing she had stopped a few steps behind, turned toward her in the darkness.

"I probably haven't said this enough, or at all, but thank you for being here. Thank you for everything. Thank you for giving up your Friday night to maybe time travel with me." May wasn't stupid, she knew there were at least a dozen girls who were feeling very dejected right now because Abee wasn't at tonight's party. There were probably even more guys feeling similarly. Abee was the life of everything. He was fun and funny, and cool and kind, and somehow he was hers, for at least a little while longer. May could feel herself blushing. Why was she blushing? It was just Abee.

May got sentimental sometimes; Abee liked that she still told him everything she was thinking. "What are you talking about? This is the best party in town, ya nerd. Race you to the stairs!"

Why was he always running? May's legs were flying after him. Abee let her win;

she knew he did. The stairs were perfect. They would probably hold up for at least 100 years this time. No death, at least for tonight.

They grabbed two slices of Elise's famous pineapple layer cake from the cold case and sat down across from Jimmy. The HOLLYWOOD sign glowed on the wall, like the original HOLLYWOODLAND sign had from its hill. Grandpa Gene's sign was a nod to both versions of the icon.

May loved the made for movies history of Los Angeles. Everything was more dramatic than it needed to be. Had the Hollywood royalty of the first half of the 20th Century known they were building a set? Building what would become the backdrop for the world's storytelling fantasies? There were the everyday apartment complexes you could still find on random street corners that glittered with fantastical mid-century flourishes; there were the pineapple palms lining the boulevards of Beverly Hills; there were the hands and the stars, and the roads where you could see straight to the beach even though it was still twenty miles away; there was the Roosevelt and the Chateau, and the seemingly impossible bowl of green earth where the best musicians in the world would come and spill out a soundtrack for the hills; there was the cemetery with the audacity to sell forever, and then of course there was the sign that presided over all of it, as if giving its blessing from Olympus. Did the place make the people or the people make the place? It was like the question of nature or nurture on a metropolitan scale. May was daydreaming. It was what this room did best. The cake was bright and rich in her mouth; it tasted like a burst of sunshine in the middle of a dark night.

"So it didn't work. No big deal." Abee's long legs were propped up on the round table. He rocked back in his chair. He shoveled another bite of cake into his mouth. "We can try again in December, and if it's a no go at winter solstice, then we just wait for next June." Abee ate and talked simultaneously. With his legs stretched out, his chair bumped against the wall. May noticed that the top rail of his chair lodged under a framed picture of a bow-tied Paul Anka from the 80's.

"Okay sure, but let's talk about something that's really important. Paul Anka's best song...five seconds...go!" Abee didn't need five seconds, he barely needed one. He answered in song. May couldn't help herself; she was belting it out too. She was up on her chair, stuck in a loop repeating the lyrics. Abee was up on his feet singing with her. They only knew one Paul Anka song, and only because it had been in the rotation of Duck's background music for as long as they could remember; they both knew every word. They were laugh-singing their hearts out. They weren't drunk, but they would have had a hard time convincing anyone of that. They were just the one o'clock in the morning, high on sugar, singing with your best friend after the ridiculous letdown of not traveling back in time, kind of drunk.

Abee's shoulders were about even with May's waist. Swept up in the moment, he swept her up, folding her in half like a sack of whatever people carry over their shoulders. She fake protested by punching at him. He danced her around the room; she was laughing too much to keep singing. Out of breath, Abee carefully lowered her down over his back so that she ended up in a handstand. May did a tuck and roll to the ground. Abee folded down on his knees next to her. Unconsciously, he brushed the hair out of her face. May smiled her crooked smile up at him. His hand lingered on her forehead. Hidden under the drape of her hair were two freckles like twin stars, forever emblazoned upon her temple. Castor and Pollux. If the door hadn't blown open at that very moment, he might have kissed the stars.

DUCK DIVE

Listen: "I Just Wasn't Made For These Times"
by Jim James

EIGHT

~~~~~~~~~~

JUNE 1995 CE

No child should have to lose a parent. But for a teenage girl to lose her mother, that is without a doubt one of the cruelest hands a person can be dealt. Lola was on the receiving end of one of those cruel hands. She hadn't asked to be dealt in. Apparently the game was obligatory.

As Lola sat there on the couch, she knew she should be hungry, but she wasn't. She hadn't seen her father since, when was that? Monday night? Yeah, he had come home with some burgers and fries on Monday and then left as quickly as he came, *thankfully.* What was today? It must be Wednesday now. No one had eaten the burgers. They were still there in the paper bag on the coffee table. Lola's father was only ever thirsty, never hungry. Maybe he was passed out in his room. She'd go check later to see if the car was in the garage. Or not. It didn't matter if he had come back. In fact she hoped he hadn't. The only person Lola wanted to see—couldn't come back. Would never come back. Her mom was never coming back.

Lola pulled her knees up into her sweatshirt. The shark winked up at her as her knees jostled him around. It looked like he was swimming across her shirt. The Malibu Sharks. Right. School. Lola looked at her watch. The school would call here in a few minutes, calling for her father, asking where Lola was, would she be coming in today? She'd let the machine get it. Lola had missed so much school in the spring; they understood why of course, but now she really had to do summer school if she wanted to stay on track and start her sophomore year with the rest of her class. They had made as many allowances for her as they could. They had given her all the time that they could. That's what the message would say. It hardly seemed to matter.

Like clockwork, the phone rang—five times—cue answering machine.

"Goodmorning Mr. Rossi, this is Mrs. Emil calling from MHS. It is Wednesday, June 21, and I am assuming you are aware that summer school started last week, and well, we have yet to see Lola. I hate to be the bearer of..."

Lola slouched back and pulled the couch cushion down on top of her head, muffling the sound of the machine, muffling her own breath. The world got slower, quieter; it was nice. She needed to take a deep breath, but instead she pushed the cushion into her face even harder, for as long as she could, until her arms betrayed her, and she threw it to the side.

Now that the sun was up, she could at least let herself fall asleep. Time was all backwards; she'd be awake all night and sleep all day—if she was lucky. If she could just lie here, motionless, long enough, just staring at the coffee ring on the table next to her, she would eventually...

Lola's mother had loved coffee. She sat here, right here, every day, leaning against the arm of the couch, coffee next to her on the table. She would drink her coffee and read her books. Read her books and gaze out the window. Gaze out the window and then go back to reading. Just like that, every day, for as long as Lola could remember. They weren't on the beach, but they could see the ocean from this window. Lola could still smell the smokey, nutty, earthy scent of her coffee wafting around the room. Lola could still see her mother smiling.

Then, the doctors said coffee was bad for her, too acidic, too hard on her stomach, possibly carcinogenic even. Lola knew her mom missed the coffee even more than she missed her hair. Lola would make the hot ginger lemon water instead and bring it to her, right here. She had always been right here. She would take a trembling sip and do her best to smile, but a few hours later Lola would pour the mug's tepid contents down the sink. She could see the lemon slice swirling around the drain, and then she was in the sink too, surrounded by rushing water, floating, slipping, shrunken, disappearing. It felt nice.

A door slammed. Slowly, her eyes opened. Good, he was gone. But now the coffee, and the lemons, and the water—they were all gone too. A car rumbled to life, clunked into reverse, and then squealed away. The room around Lola was bright now. Too bright. She must have been asleep for a few hours. How could her head hurt and feel numb at the same time? One of the few days she had shown up for school back in the spring, the counselor had pulled her out of class *just to chat* she promised: "Make sure you eat regular meals, Lola. Make sure you talk to someone about your feelings, Lola. Make sure you get some sunshine every day, Lola."

Lola gave the lady an affirmative nod after each instruction, like she understood. And she did. She understood that the person who made her regular meals was dead. She understood that the person she talked to about her feelings was dead. She understood that the person who was her sun, moon, and stars, was dead.

Lola pressed herself up and off the couch. She rolled up the waistband of her sweatpants one more time. This trick wouldn't work much longer; it wasn't really working now. She looked like she had a life preserver on, but it was just an illusion. Lola wasn't that lucky. She thought her clothes hid her, but if anyone had taken the time to look, they would have seen that she was drowning in them.

Lola walked out the front door, not bothering to close it behind her. She didn't have a plan, but the downward slope of the street led her toward the cliffs. The essing road lulled her on. She found herself by the stairs. The death stairs. Her bare feet accepted the slicing of the rough edges as necessary suffering. She haphazardly made her way across the sand, through some tidepools, taking no notice of the prickly stars under her feet. The sun was high overhead; the reflection burned into her eyes.

Get some sunshine. Get some sunshine, Lola. That's what the lady had said. Get some sunshine. Her mind was stuck in a loop. Get some sunshine. Get some sunshine. The sun was a warm ripply ball, bouncing up and down on the water. She could get it. It was just right there. Get your sunshine, Lola. You're my sunshine, Lola. You're my sunshine, Lola. That's how her mom had always said it. You're my sunshine, my only sunshine, Lola. Go get your sunshine back, Lola.

The water lapped at her toes, inviting her in. Her legs obliged, grateful to be wanted. She pushed on toward the sun. Her clothes swelled, pulling her in. Pulling her down. She tried to make her arms slice through the water, but the water cut first. The water wanted her more than she wanted air. Lola's arms didn't betray her this time. None of it was on purpose, but it wasn't an accident either. As her arms floated up over her head, she saw her watch still ticking away, not ready to give up. 1:34. 1:34, that's a nice time, she thought. One plus three equals four and four plus four equals eight, eight looks like infinity. Infinity, boundless, endless, always room for one more. And then graciously, mercifully, the thoughts stopped.

Phase Two

WAXING CRESCENT

YEAR	DATE	TIME
1996	20-Jun	7:23 PM PDT
1997	21-Jun	1:19 AM PDT

YEAR	DATE	TIME
2024	20-Jun	1:50 PM PDT
2025	20-Jun	7:41 PM PDT

Listen: "One"
by Sleeping At Last

ONE

~~~~~~~~~~

People assume that things are or they aren't. Black or white, dead or alive, yes or no. But that's not how things really work, that's not how life goes—on. Life happens in the grays and the maybes and the unobserved particles. These are the places where the fullness of life, in all of its infinite possibilities, exists. At least for a while.

EXHIBIT "B"

One day the star at the center of earth's solar system will explode. This is what stars do. Just because Earth dwellers call their star the sun, it is not exempt from the fate that comes for all stars. But the story will not be complete doom and gloom, at least not right away. The earth exists eight-ish light minutes away from the sun. So when the sun explodes there will be a period of eight minutes wherein the solar system will have fallen apart and yet we will not experience any change. Eight blessed minutes where the world has ended, but life on earth will go on as it always has. It is and it isn't. It's all beautiful and it's all falling apart, all at once. Of course it is.

The cup is broken even as we gently sip from it. Of course it is. Our star has exploded even as we walk our children to school. Of course it has. We will all vanish in the twinkling of an eye even as we fight to keep our eyes wide open. Of course we will.

May was learning that things—people—could be very alive and also very dead all at once. How could it be any other way?

WAXING CRESCENT

Listen: "Here Comes the Sun"
by The Beatles

TWO

~~~~~~~~~~

JUNE 2024 CE

"Andrew Bartholomew Berenson." The crowd erupted. There was no holding your applause when it came to Abee. For years, the Halls of Malibu High—well actually the beautifully manicured breezeways of Malibu High—had been home to some of the world's most winsome characters, but Abee's star was uniquely bright even in an already ridiculously lit sky.

Elise and Tal glowed too as they watched their boy take the stage. Shep and May were no different. Abee was a joy. He was joy. And he was about to leave them all. While in some ways Los Angeles and New York seemed like two sides of the same coin, bound by a quick five hour and twenty minute flight, in other ways they seemed like two different planets, cut-off and untraversable.

USC and Stanford were great west coast options of course, but they weren't NYU. And maybe more pointedly, they weren't in New York City. Someday Abee would be a fantastic Record Label Exec, or maybe he'd be a movie star, or maybe he would live out his days surfing in Costa Rica; all were plausible options, but whatever came after, being at NYU in the heart of the best city in the world was where he wanted to start. Plus, the city was where his parents had met and fallen in love, and he had inherited a bit of their nostalgia for the place. Going to New York kind of felt like going home, to a home you forgot you had.

And so now the count was on, 73 days til Abee left—her.

~~~~~~

The winter solstice jump hadn't worked. May knew it wasn't going to. Abee had been on his senior trip during the spring equinox, so they hadn't even tried that time, but it wouldn't have mattered. The magic was in the summer. And now with two practice runs under their belts, they felt extra prepared for this try. If there was any magic left, if the universe was still interested in relocating them for a few hours, they were ready, again.

May would find herself laughing randomly. They were insane. They had to be. This was a year long fever dream, a folie à deux, a madness by two, a shared psychosis, right? Was she so afraid of losing Abee that she was inventing ways to keep him close? Was he that afraid of losing her, too?

Of course May loved him, and of course she hated him. Of course she was attracted to him, and of course he was like a brother. But she never hated him for long, and they shared no genetic connection or legal relation—May had done lots of research to make sure of that.

64 more days.

~~~~~~

It was May's sixteenth birthday, and this year it was also the solstice. It was a big day with lots to do. But the universe had it all planned out perfectly for them. First, birthday breakfast like always; then, wardrobe change, quick lunch, and then, down to the beach for a 1:50 p.m. solstice call time. They had it all charted out and assuming time was traveling in parallel and equal increments, which they knew was a big assumption, they guessed they would hop to 1996 this time. In 1996 the solstice would happen at 7:23 p.m. So they would have five hours and thirty-three minutes to do whatever it was they were meant to do in the past.

And that was still the rub. Why had this magical time hop happened— it was still hard for May to actually say the words time and travel—and what were they supposed to do with this magic if it happened again? May was happy making spreadsheets, charting dates and times, and shopping for vintage props; it all had a game-like aspect to it, but why was the game happening? Abee had tried to bring it up a few times and May could never quite express what she was thinking. But it was almost all she thought about. *I think I am supposed to stop my mom from dying.* Obviously Abee knew that's what she was thinking, but he didn't force her to say it.

May was awake early. She checked and rechecked her outfits, her bag, the money. It was still only 7:15 a.m. Why couldn't she sleep in like a normal teenager? She got dressed, made her bed, and even put on some blush and tinted lip gloss. It was 7:30, she couldn't sit around in her room any more, she was getting too nervous. Surely dad was working on breakfast by now, but she wasn't picking up any of the telltale scents of a normal birthday morning.

"Hello? Helloooo? Dad. You here, dad?"

There was no answer, and the kitchen was empty. The lights were off, the kettle wasn't going, there was no birthday banner over the window. Had he forgotten? Had Elise forgotten? There was no way Elise had forgotten.

Not sure what to do, or what to think, she opened the fridge. And there on the carafe of orange juice was a sticky note:

Happy birthday!
-Dad
P.S. We didn't forget
P.P.S. Come outside

Of course they hadn't forgotten. She felt guilty for even thinking it. Orange juice in hand, she made her way out to the deck. No one was there, no one was on the lawn, and then she heard them, in the parking lot. Some laughter and a low rumble.

May opened the gate and there they were, Dad, Elise, Tal, Abee, and a sunshine yellow Volkswagen Type 2 Bus. Shep told her later it was a '73 and it was technically Saturn Yellow. The felt happy-birthday banner was strung across the front of the bus, each end hooked onto a small silver side mirror. Tal reached in the front window, hit a button, and the whole thing turned into a giant yellow speaker amplifying the Beatles' birthday message across the parking lot.

May had never seen her dad smile so big. She didn't realize that her own smile outdid his by far. This was the car of her dreams, beyond her dreams. May was hugging her dad; Tal was opening the door for May; Elise was recording it all; Abee was in the passenger's seat. Without any need for explanation the three adults piled in the back, May looked over all the dials and switches; Abee kept slapping her on the back like she was a new father, and then they were going in circles around the parking lot, Beatles still blaring. May turned a little too tight and the unbuckled parents all folded on top of eachother.

May knew how incredibly lucky she was. Not everyone got to have this many people to love. Maybe it was okay that someone else had loved them first. They were her people now, at least for a while.

~~~~~~

"So, just a what if...what if it hasn't happened? What if last year was some weird fluke? What if it really was just a one and done type thing? What if—"

"I get the premise of your question," May interrupted Abee with a smirk. "And I think I'm okay with that." May wasn't. She needed to meet her mom; she wanted to actually know Amy, not someone else's version of her.

They stashed the board in the cave. The red Jansport wasn't there; that was an inconclusive detail, but it was worth noting. It was a gloomy day. It had been and it still was, whatever that meant. As they walked along the beach they could see a group of surfers, but surfers looked like surfers, and presumably they always would. Abee said he wasn't opposed to just going up to someone and asking what year it was; it surely wouldn't be the weirdest thing to happen on a Malibu beach that day, but May liked the suspense of it all. She liked waiting for some irrefutable sign. She liked the thrill of wondering what the stairs would be. Last year in their panic they had gone up a private rocky side path and hadn't had to reckon with the stairs, but now the stairs were their surest and quickest way of assessing the situation. What would the stairs show them? Surely, the answer this time would be death.

But they didn't have to wait for the stairs. As they rounded the next corner, there in the middle of a somewhat secluded section of beach, half covered by a bright orange-striped sarape, were two people who were either a prince and a mermaid, or Tal and Amy, and the prince and the mermaid were kissing.

Go on and kiss the girl, and all that.

Abee was swearing again.

~~~~~~

JUNE 1996 CE

They had prepared for a lot of things. They had not prepared for this. Abee looked like he was holding back tears and laughter, all at the same time. "Did—did you know this was a thing? I mean that's my dad and your mom, right?"

"It sure looks that way, and no, no, this is all news to me. I knew they grew up together and were really close obviously, but that's—" May nodded her head up the beach, "that's like really close." May caught a giggle in her throat. The fact that she didn't actually know her mom and could somewhat dissociate from the scene in front of her made this situation more bearable for her. Abee was not so lucky. "I know burying your head in the sand, literally, feels preferable right now, but I think our plan just got fast tracked. Abee, it worked! We're here again, and I think we have to go make some friends."

Abee let out a roar that was half ewww and half ughhh. "Okay, this is so weird, but let's swimsuit up."

Along with their other accessories, the canvas tote bag was also packed with suits and towels this time. It was summer in Malibu; it would be weird not to have swimsuits and towels. May had a simple bubblegum-pink high-leg bikini. Abee had a pair of Body Glove trunks with palm trees on them. They were vintage cringe, but Abee actually loved them. May had talked him out of a straight up *Bay Watch* pair; they weren't trying to have the whole beach notice them.

May's plan for today had been to find her mom and then talk to her. She hadn't been sure how she'd do it or what she'd say, but it's what needed to happen. And amazingly, here she was, step one, done. Now May just had to say something. Suited up, towels in hand, they made their way along the beach. They tried to look casual. They looked like they were trying to look casual.

"Mel and Josh, from Pismo, and we're just hitchhiking up and down the coast, couch surfing and surf surfing. If they start asking too many questions, just act like you're high and stare off at the ocean." Abee nodded in agreement. Amy and Tal had come up for air and were out playing in the waves at the moment, which provided the perfect opportunity for May and Abee to set out their towels near the orange blanket without being too awkward about it all. They settled in. Abee was on his back looking up at the sky. May's eyes were on the ocean.

"Shoot, they're coming back. Be cool," May hissed.

"Actually, I'm going to pretend to be asleep, good luck." And with that Abee closed his eyes—tight. Too tight. May started to protest and then she started to laugh; he was a terrible faker, but it was too late. Tal and Amy were back. If they thought it was weird that all of sudden their doppelgängers were lounging next to them on the beach, Tal and Amy didn't show it. Amy might have done a slight double take when she first saw the newcomers but she quickly gave them a smile and a wave. May felt like she might throw up. Her mom had acknowledged her existence, even though Amy still technically didn't know May existed.

May matched her mom's smile and wave, and then quickly laid back next to Abee. "Hey Doc, I can't do this on my own, you gotta wake up," May whispered in his ear and then to really make her point she pinched the back of his arm.

"Yowwwwch!" May had pinched too hard. They were both sitting up. Amy and Tal were both looking. No turning back now. Before May knew what was happening, they were all introducing themselves—Talmai and Amy, Josh and Mel. Abee almost laughed as he said Josh. Then one thing led to another and they were standing in a circle peppering a volleyball back and forth. Some vague details about hitchhiking were exchanged for some vague details about a restaurant up the cliffs.

Tal was the same as always. But looking at this unlikely father and son standing just a few feet away from each other, May realized that Abee was now the oldest in the group, he was eighteen to their sixteens (if her math was right), and Abee was taller than his dad for once.

And then, there was Amy. Her mom. May unconsciously started keeping a mental list of the things she wanted to remember about Amy. She had light green eyes, lighter than in pictures. Her nails were painted a bright red, and they were just starting to chip. She smelled like coconut, but not overwhelmingly so. She had strong arms dotted with dark freckles, she obviously spent more time outside than May did. And she was funny, so funny. Everything about Amy was delightful, and to May's growing surprise, Amy was unabashedly in love—with Tal—the way only sixteen-year-olds can be. And Tal was right there with her. The lingering hands and glances, the smiles, the familiarity. May had to actively remind herself not to stare, but they were adorable together. The bizarre nature of it all was engrossing enough to keep her from wondering why Tal had never told them this part of the story.

May was by far the weak link in the volleyball circle—because, well she just was, but she was also very distracted—and so after she sent the ball flying into the waves a dozen times, Tal asked Josh if he was into body surfing. They hadn't brought their boards down this afternoon, Tal explained, but body surfing was still really fun. Tal grinned a little too much as he said *body surfing*. It was clear Tal and Amy had different plans for their afternoon, but they were pivoting and warmly welcoming these visitors nonetheless.

The boys were off to the waves. May was alone with her mom. "Are you into surfing? Body or otherwise?" Amy gave a knowing nod and eye roll toward Tal. They were talking.

"No, not really; well, it's complicated. A—Josh is really into it, regular surfing I mean, we're not like that, not that there's anything wrong with that, or not that I wouldn't—" Why was she being so awkward? May was freaking out inside, "So yeah anyways I watch him surf, but I don't love being in the ocean." May should have thought this through more. It was their first one-on-one conversation and it had already gone straight to the one thing—wait two things—she didn't want to talk about. If there was a universal rule to time travel, it had to be—don't tell someone how they die.

~~~~~~

"You should come up for dinner. Our treat." Tal looked at Abee. Abee looked at May. May looked at her watch. They still had two hours.

"Yeah, that would be great actually. Thank you." Things were potentially about to get more complicated if Gloria was going to be around, since Gloria knew her as May, and not to mention the whole poem thing, but it was a risk May was ready to take if it meant more time with Amy.

As they gathered their things and made their way up the beach, May mouthed to Abee, *Let them lead. Play dumb.* Abee nodded in agreement even though he had no idea what May was trying to say.

"Watch your step, these stairs are the worst." Tal held Amy's hand as they made their way up the stairs. May felt a ping of something come to life in her chest as she followed behind them. Longing? Jealousy? Probably a bit of both. She couldn't take her eyes off their tangle of fingers. It looked like it felt nice.

"What'd you say the restaurant is called?" Abee yelled up from a few stairs down. May turned and shot him a *don't play that dumb* look.

"Duck's, well technically Duck's Dive," Amy answered from a few stairs up ahead. "My dad's surfing buddies call him Duck, and the restaurant started out as a real dive, and in surfing duck diving is like a technique, but sorry you must know that."

"I think we stopped there last summer. We sat in a room with giant whales and a lady named Gloria was our server."

What was Abee doing; he was talking way too much.

"No way, that's my mom, and those whales are her pride and joy. You know what?! She actually did tell me about meeting some kids who looked like us," Amy nodded toward Tal. "I figured she was just exaggerating, but it's pretty trippy." Amy looked back at May for affirmation. "I wonder if we are related somehow; how crazy would that be?"

"That would be soooo crazy." Abee really was a terrible faker.

~~~~~~

May and Amy tucked in around the banquette. Tal took Abee over to the kitchen to pick up some food. The restaurant was too busy to eat in one of the dining rooms. As awkward as it was, Abee probably did have the better approach. May needed to talk more. If she was going to figure out how to help her mom, she needed to get to know her mom. So why not start with the most normal thing for two teenage girls to talk about...

"So how long have y'all been together?" May wanted to know; she really did, but also she knew it might get weird. Why hadn't she ever known that Tal and her mom had been, well been in love? Did Shep know? Granted, this was a long time before Amy would have ever met Shep, but it all felt like it was happening at once in May's brain. She had just been sitting right here with her dad and Tal.

"We've been official for a little over a year now I guess. We've known each other our whole lives, and then there was just a day when something clicked and I wanted to kiss him more than I wanted to punch him." Amy paused. "Not that you're asking, but it's worth the risk in my opinion. At first it was strange; I thought I had to be this new version of myself, the girlfriend version, but that was just me overthinking things. Now we've found our rhythm I think, we are still goofy best friends and also I get to enjoy how hot he is. I might have our kids' names picked out. Don't tell." Amy's voice got higher with every word she spoke.

May couldn't help but mirror her smile. "You both seem really happy, like it's meant to be." May hadn't meant to say something so honest, but it did seem that way. What was going to happen over the years that would pull Amy and Tal apart but still keep them so close together? As May sat there looking at her mom, who was hopelessly but not foolishly in love, May couldn't help but feel protective over her. Amy's life was not going to go the way she thought it would. That was a strange thing to know about a person. It was a strange thing to know about your mom.

Before May could say more, Tal and Abee were back carrying trays piled high with fish tacos and giant slices of pineapple cake. The recipe had been Gloria's before it was Elise's. The four of them sat in the kitchen eating Gene's tacos and Gloria's cake, talking about *ER,* and *The Simpsons,* and *Friends.* May had watched *Friends* all the way through at least three times. In a flash of momentary panic, May realized that she knew how *Friends* ended, but in 1996 they were only two seasons in. Luckily the roller coaster that is Ross and Rachel was a through line, no matter the season.

May checked her watch. She tapped Abee's leg under the table. It was time. They couldn't risk a turn-into-a-pumpkin situation when the magic wore off. They thanked their new friends profusely. Amy suggested that they should keep in touch. Did they have email? Did they even have a computer? Amy and Tal had just gotten Hotmail accounts. It was like letters, but they showed up on the computer. Abee would have loved nothing more than to think through the possibilities of digital communication across space-time, but they didn't have Hotmail accounts, only moms still had Hotmail accounts (that tracked), and to drop Gmail or iCloud on them would be akin to Marty with the *Almanac*. Abee froze. Tal and Amy read it as confusion over their new technology. May offered an awkward shrug, afraid that to say anything would be to say too much.

Before they walked out the back door, Amy grabbed May in a quick hug. "It's worth the risk," she whispered in her ear. They were barely out of the yard before Abee was howling. He couldn't stop laughing. It was all too much. Their parents were in love. Their parents wanted to email them. Abee was laugh-crying. May was cry-laughing. There was a subtle difference.

Tal and Amy watched out the window as their two new friends walked back toward the beach.

"They're really weird." Tal smiled.

"Totally weird." Amy caught a giggle in her throat.

"It's almost like they're from a different planet."

"Or a different time."

"Yeah, it's like they've traveled to the future, and they don't know what anything is. They don't have pagers or anything."

Amy shook her head, confused, amused.

"Wherever they're from, I hope they come back."

Listen: "Oh I Wept"
by Free

THREE

~~~~~~~~~~

AUGUST 2024 CE

Abee was leaving in the morning. One more night. Most of his things had been shipped in boxes a few days ago, but his room was still chaotic with the odds and ends he planned to stuff into his two duffle bags. Shep, Elise, and Tal had taken an unheard of night off. They had all gone into LA. Abee wanted to eat downtown and make a stop at The Last Bookstore to check the rare vinyls one last time. They would have said yes to whatever he wanted to do. Now they were back home, but the night was far from over. May was on Abee's floor doing her best to fold his clothes and talk him through how many pairs of sandals he would realistically need in New York.

For the past month, Elise had been trying to get Abee to tell her what he still needed, and the answer had always been nothing. But here they were, fourteen hours to go, and it turned out Abee needed some stuff after all. He and May would have to stop by the drug store before they went to Caleb's. Sleeping was not on the list of tonight's activities.

May and Abee strolled the aisles like two retirees who had come for batteries that they didn't really need. Once they showed up at Caleb's, the night would turn into a blur. It was here, with toothpaste on one side and adult diapers on the other where they would get to spend their last few moments as just May and Abee.

"You know what a shot clock is, right?"

May rolled her eyes. "Yeah, I've heard of a shot clock."

"So it's a timer within an already timed game. Before they started using a shot clock, players figured out that if they could get an early lead, for the rest of the game they just had to play keep away from the other team until the time ran out. No one would ever take a shot because they didn't want to lose possession. It was a boring way to play, and it was even more boring to watch. There was no skill involved. There was no excitement."

May was listening, she really was, but she was also wondering who Abee would find in New York to listen to his ramblings. Would he become friends with his roommate over late night pizza? Would he pal up with some kid next to him in class as they laughed about the professor's bad ties? Would he have a meet-cute with some girl in the laundry room because she needed to borrow a dryer sheet that he inevitably wouldn't have? May didn't like the thought of that last scenario.

Abee paused to see if May was still listening.

"You're talking about golf, right?" May batted her eyes at him mockingly.

"So anyways," Abee continued on, unphased by her sass, "these guys did the math and figured that on average each team, if they weren't trying to hoard the ball, would take 60 shots a game, so 120 total, and so they divided the total amount of seconds in a game by 120 and came up with 24 seconds as the average time there should be between each shot to keep the game moving. And then the league adopted the 24 second shot clock. But what's really interesting is that some teams impose even shorter windows on themselves, like 17 or 18 seconds, and they end up scoring and winning even more."

"Hold up. Are you telling me that you miss 100% of the shots you don't take?" May hadn't intended on being so sarcastic with him, but he was just making it so easy.

Abee stopped; they were in the middle of the greeting card aisle now. "Mays, I'm trying to say something serious here."

May gently put the singing cat card back in the rack. She turned to look at him. He was serious. What was Abee about to say? Was he about to take—a shot? Here next to the tissue paper and gaudy bows?

"What I'm trying to say is, I'm afraid I've been holding on to the ball for too long."

May scrunched her nose and wrinkled her forehead. Where was this headed?

"You're my best friend, and I don't want that to change. But it is going to change. It has to. And maybe right now we're just at a self-imposed time mark, we're at 18 seconds, but some day the real shot clock is going to go off, and then some day the whole game will be over, and–"

Why did he have tears in his eyes? God, why was he still talking about basketball? What was he actually trying to say?

"And–"

May couldn't take it. Abee was about to say too much again. He always said too much. She wasn't ready to lose possession. They were on the same team; they could hoard the ball all they wanted.

May shifted her weight to her toes and leaned forward. Her hands were on his shoulders. Her hands were on his face. She stretched up on the balls of her feet. He was so freaking tall. This was taking too long. She was losing the moment. Shit. This was about to be really awkward if he didn't...

Abee dropped his chin, his arms wrapped around her waist. Both of her feet lifted slightly off the ground. Her mouth was on his. Oh uh. Her mom had been right.

~~~~~~

Elise said it reminded her of the baby blues. You knew everything was good and as it should be, but you still wound up in the bathroom crying. They texted all the time and he did a good job of sending them videos of his dorm room and the things he found when he was out on his morning runs around the city, but he was still gone. They had to find new rhythms. May started going over and watching one of the late night talk shows with Elise at the end of each day. Tal would make them popcorn and hot tea. Tal was running more than ever. Elise was starting to work on a cookbook—an eclectic, California take on kosher cooking, which she had been dreaming about doing for years. Business at Duck's was surpassing their projections; Tal was managing upgrades around the property; Shep was solidifying the new dishes for the winter menu. May was busy with school, more so the social side than the academic side, and she was working with her dad in the kitchen a lot. Life was full, but it wasn't the same.

They only spent a few hours at Caleb's that night before Abee left. Then, they found some day-old donuts at the gas station. Then, they sat in the back of the Volkswagen and listened to music for a while. They must have fallen asleep at some point, but then the sunrise woke them up. They walked up and down the beach one more time. May sat on Abee's bed as he finished packing his bags. Abee sat down next to her. He pulled May into his chest. She tucked in under his chin. He kissed the top of her head. He ran his fingers over the scar on her palm. They didn't make any promises. No one took or missed any shots. They were who they always had been, May and Abee, except now the colors were just a bit richer, deeper. But no buzzers had sounded, not yet.

Then, May waved from the driveway as the car drove off toward LAX and Abee left her.

WAXING CRESCENT

Listen: "All Your'n"
by Tyler Childers

FOUR

~~~~~~~~~~

DECEMBER 2024 CE

Abee would be home in two days, his first trip back west since he'd left. He wouldn't get to stay quite as long as they had hoped, though. His suitemate was a film student who had obviously cast him as the lead in her short film. They would be shooting it at a hopefully snowy cabin upstate, during the second half of the break. Abee said things like *upstate* now.

May was trying not to get too excited, but she couldn't wait to see Abee. They had done a good job of being normal these past few months, but that probably wasn't as much of an accomplishment as she thought it was, given that they had 2,823.1 miles and a three-hour time difference between them. But now they were about to be as close as they wanted to be. So how close did they want to be? How close did he want to be?

May had given Abee plenty of presents over the years. She had mastered the art of the Chanukah gift. Something meaningful and not ostentatious. Hand knit beanies, old books, the occasional video game—she could tell Elise thought those were too much. One year she had gotten her dad to order them custom *Spy Kids* blankets; Abee's had a thumb on it; hers had Juni and Carmen on it. But this year felt special. She needed to give Abee something that really meant something. Right? She didn't have the idea fully fleshed out, but she was thinking she'd have hoodies made that said "HPATPOA" and she'd put her head on Emma's body and Abee's head on Daniel's body. She was imagining a still from the scene in the hospital wing when they have the time-turner around both of their necks. May would argue till her dying breath that *Harry Potter and the Prisoner of Azkaban* was the best time travel movie ever made. They never changed the past, but changes in the future depended on them reliving their past with open eyes and a bit of wisdom from their headmaster. Abee of course thought "BTTF" *Back to the Future*, held the distinction of best time travel movie, but he was obviously wrong. In *Back to the Future*, literally changing the past was the only way to change the future. Which version were they living out? Were those the only two options?

May and Abee had enough inside jokes that their parents didn't even bother to ask at this point. They had long ago abandoned any hope of discerning the secret language May and Abee spoke. No one would bat an eye at a weird sweatshirt. But first, May needed to find some pictures of her and Abee from when they were around thirteen. Bella, LACHSA Bella, had started designing clothes, May could use her screen printing machine to make the hoodies once she hacked together the graphic. Maybe she had this present idea more figured out than she realized.

May had a (too big) wicker basket on the top shelf of her closet which was a catch-all for mementos: birthday cards, stickers, orchestra programs, Polaroids, and pictures Elise used to print off for her—before everything just existed on a cloud. May awkwardly pulled the basket down, flinching as the wicker scraped against the wooden shelf.

The quickest way to go about this was to just dump the whole basket out on her rug. By tipping the basket upside down the earliest memories were now on top and more recent items were toward the bottom. As May started to push aside the papers and pictures, she half realized and half remembered that these memories were not just hers. The bottom of the basket, which was now top of the pile, held inherited memories. This basket had been her mom's first, of course it had.

There were newspaper clippings, pictures, ribbons, yearbooks, and ticket stubs from the 80's and 90's. It had been years since May had gone through these remnants of her mom's life, but they all looked vaguely familiar. For an instant May thought she had found what she was after, but as she looked closer she realized the picture was of Amy and Tal, not herself and Abee.

May eventually found the pictures she needed, set those to the side, and then scooped everything else back together and dropped the stuff into the basket one handful at a time. She decided to keep her mom's high school yearbooks out; there were only three of them though—not four—she shrugged, acknowledging this detail to an imaginary witness. May would look through them later as part of her deep-dive into all things 90's. At the very least there would be some good outfit inspo, and there might even be some helpful clues about her mom's teenage years.

May looked at the basket. Everything was seriously jumbled up now. The layers had been disturbed, the past had been contaminated with the present, and there was no going back to how it had been before.

~~~~~~

May and Abee walked along the beach in their matching sweatshirts. Abee told her all about Meredith's movie and how smart it was. Meredith was Abee's auteur roommate. It wasn't going to be just student-film-good; it was going to be good-good, Abee promised. May was half listening, half trying to convince herself she wasn't jealous. But as Abee kept and kept talking, May's right hand gradually found its way into a clenched fist. She pushed her nails into the line of her scar. She felt nothing. Nothing felt familiar.

"Hey, you with me?"

May blinked herself back to attention. "Sorry, I think I'm just tired," May lied. "The restaurant has been crazy." That was true at least.

"Well, do you have it in you for one more present?" Abee stopped and was standing in front of her now. May quickly scanned his hands, the shape of the front pouch of his hoodie, the beach around them. It was just the two of them, and he didn't seem to have a present with him.

"Uh, sure," May said, half smiling, half bracing herself to be punked. She barely had the words out before Abee was pulling his sweatshirt up and over his head. His skin was milkier looking than May had ever seen it before.

"In New York I don't walk around with my shirt off as much," Abee smirked, clocking her surprise. "But this isn't about me; this is about you. Mays, it's time for you to take a proper swim. I mean, no pressure. But you're a time traveler now." They both laughed. "If you can do that, this is no big deal. You're not your mom, Mays. It's okay to live your life. So, if you want, my gift to you is a swim in the ocean. I'll be right there with you, the whole time."

And with that Abee splashed into the water, stepping over the dying waves one effortless stride at a time. He was half-way in. He turned back and called out, "C'mon, the water is nice."

And even after all these years, apparently that invitation was all May needed. Her hoodie was off. Her feet were in the water. Her eyes were locked on him. Her skin prickled. Adrenaline flooded her system. His hand was reaching toward her. She lunged forward, clumsily. Her fingers found his. Abee pulled her through the water toward him. They were up to their necks, treading water. They bobbed up and down with a few passing waves. His eyes never left her. The next set was coming in, and as a growing wave rumbled behind them, May dropped Abee's hand and let herself sink. She held her breath, tightly at first, and then as the wave gently rocked her from above, she let her chest relax. The weight was gone. And then her arms were moving, pulling her back up. Her fingers broke through the surface, and like she'd been doing it her whole life, her arms started pulling her forward. Back, up, over, down, pull. Back, up, over, down, pull. Breathe. Back, up, over, down, pull. Back, up, over, down, pull. Breathe. And just like that May was out past the breakers. May was swimming in the ocean. She stopped and turned to look toward the shore. She had never seen her home, her life from this angle. She'd only ever looked out, never back. This must be what it felt like to look at earth from space. It all looked so small.

And just as she realized that she couldn't spot Abee from this angle, he popped up underneath her. He burst through the water literally whooping and hollering, lifting her with him. Abee's skin was warm and soft against hers. She gladly draped her arms over his shoulders. Her legs locked around his waist. Her temple pressed up against his.

Abee was right. May could let go of the fear that she had clung to. She wasn't her mom. And yet somehow here floating in this liminal space, she felt more like her mom than ever. Her salty tears ran down his cheeks and took their place in the sea.

WAXING CRESCENT

Listen: "The Long and Winding Road"
by The Beatles

FIVE

~~~~~~~~~~

JUNE 2025 CE

May wasn't exactly dreading this conversation, but she had chickened out at least five times already. In the background, she could hear that one of the Jimmys was already doing his monologue. Elise's sous was out sick today, so she was late getting home. May felt completely at ease with Tal; he was like a second father, he was a friend, he was a confidant, and sometimes it felt like he understood her in a way that no one else did. But it was rare that it was just the two of them together. Tal scooted a mug of green-ginger across the marble counter toward her. May breathed in the warm steam. Then she bent down to pull the creamy jewelry box from her bag, and scooted it across the marble toward him.

"Talmai, I, well I should have done this two years ago when I got it, but I think you should have this back." May had planned to say more, but his expression told her no more explanation was necessary. Tal gently pulled back the top of the box even though he knew exactly what was inside.

"My dad, bless him, he can slay all five of the French mother sauces at once, but he can't speak a lick of the language. Grandpa Gene called my mom his *Aimée*. But this necklace is for *Mon Amie*. I knew the minute I saw it that it wasn't from Grandpa. But, well, I just figured out that it was from—you." May paused, trying to gauge Tal's reaction. "I knew you and my mom were more than just friends growing up. But I didn't realize you were more than more than friends."

May let it out like a deep exhale. She looked down into the bits of leaves that had escaped the strainer. It felt too intimate to watch Tal as he freed the necklace from the box, threaded the chain through his fingers, and let the heart come to rest on his palm, so May pretended like she wasn't.

"Well May, here's the long and short of it...your grandparents, and your mom, they saved me."

~~~~~~

Tal grew up three houses down from Amy. Two houses from where he lived now. They were the feral sun-baked children of the 80's. The ocean was their playground, their school, their house of prayer, and their boards were their playmates, teachers, and priests.

Exaggerated landscapes tend to grow exaggerated people; exaggerated people tend to live exaggerated lives, and nowhere was more exaggerated than Malibu in the 80's. By the time they were twelve, Amy and Tal had lost their first friend to Malibu's excesses. Over the years Malibu would lose many of its children to the cliffs, or the chemicals that played as candy, or the carelessness of the adults who had abandoned themselves to their own siren's song. And with each strange absence Amy and Tal would link arms a little bit tighter, a child's promise to never leave the other to explore the landscape alone.

Tal was one of those rare people who had let the hard edges of life make him softer. While the unsurprising story of Malibu's lost boys eventually took its place in the zeitgeist, the people who lived it, like Tal, knew that was just the fallout of another, less movie-worthy tale. The lost mothers were the preterite of the story.

Malibu attracted a type of person whose last hope was finding heaven on earth. And those same people would eventually, ultimately, tragically find that wherever you go, there you are, and no Edenic city on a hill can save you from that. Salt can heal, but it takes time, and first it burns, and Malibu is notorious for its incessant burning. Lots of women never made it through the burn, and so yes, of course, there were also many lost sons and daughters. Of course there were.

Tal had his own lost mother. He was born as a pair on December 22, 1979, the eighth day of Chanukah. He was Baby B born via cesarean section at 3:09 a.m., and he took the record for the largest (length and weight) twin to be delivered at Good Samaritan. A record he kept for almost two decades. His mother's labor started right after they lit the fifth candle. They drove to the hospital before they had a chance to light the sixth candle. Baby B was so large and caused his mother and the doctors and his smaller brother, Baby A, so much trouble that no one even realized when the seventh night came and went.

The doctors called them Monochorionic Diamniotic Twins; they shared one placenta but they existed in their own amniotic sacs.

Baby B had taken more than his share of the placenta's necessary blessings.

Baby A was small.

Baby B was not where he needed to be.

Baby A's sac ruptured.

Baby B could not—would not move.

Baby A was running out of time.

So, the doctors rushed to move on Baby A's behalf. The mother was cut open and Baby A was wrenched from her womb at 2:55 a.m. Baby A never took his first breath. Baby B was delivered *en caul*, fourteen minutes later, warm and floating and perfectly unaware of the chaos surrounding him. Oblivious to the grief his own mother would come to believe he caused. One stillbirth, one veiled birth, one lost mother.

Isaac Berenson moved his lone infant child and his broken-hearted wife to a small cottage on a cliff, where sunlight poured in every window, and the thrum of the ocean rang in your ears and it was all medicine to soothe your soul, or so he hoped. Isaac asked too much of his hope. He asked too much of the sun and the water.

Over the next eight years, Isaac and Talmai lost Miriam again and again, in ways big and small. Some days she tried; some days she couldn't. And then one day the sun flooded in the cottage windows and found only two souls to soothe. Miriam was gone, and yet somehow there was a bit of the miracle left. The love was not gone. Talmai turned to his father, and his father turned toward him, and they remembered her kindly, and spoke of her fondly, and they did not let the light burn out.

Three houses down, Gloria watched the bear of a boy grow and did her best to stand in the gap with him. No child should have to lose a parent.

~~~~~~

"I hope you've got something stronger than tea going tonight," Elise called out from the mudroom. May could hear her clogs hit the ground with a thunk. Elise shuffled around the corner, still working her houseshoes onto her feet and sliding her arms into a camel-colored cashmere cardigan like she was a gorgeous Mr. Rogers.

"I've mostly been slinging stories tonight," Tal said with a smile as he helped straighten her sweater on her shoulders.

"I'm so sorry, my dear," Elise gave May her signature wink and walked around to squeeze her shoulders.

"I actually wanted to hear them this time, so it's on me." May was glad to be with the two of them.

Elise eyed the box and necklace that were now back on the counter, but she didn't ask.

"I was just going to tell her about Amy and me as teenagers, but of course I had to start at the very beginning."

"Of course you did." Elise playfully slapped Tal's butt as she walked past him toward the refrigerator. "Well, don't let me stop you. Keep going and I'll fill in any details you miss. Have we never talked about this? I mean all together?"

"Some of it, but not all of it I suppose. I mean the kids were young, and it was so long ago."

"Well Mays, I mean I wasn't there for the beginning. I showed up later, or actually they showed up in my life. Can you imagine, I was just living my cold New York life and then one day this god and goddess who I swear still smelled like the ocean just sat down at my table in the dining hall. They were tan and strong and were audacious enough to be happy. I was so annoyed and I was instantly in love...with both of them."

As Elise talked, her fingers found their way between Tal's, and as she finished talking she brought the back of his hand up to her mouth and kissed it like she had a million times before, because of course, she had. Tal shifted their tangle of hands toward him and brought the back of her hand to rest against his cheek as he went on with his story.

"May, your Nonna became my mom, or at least that's how I felt. I was still messed up, but Gloria helped make sure I didn't get too messed up. She started bringing us dinner every night, whatever they cooked for family at Duck's, and she'd always give us a giant slice of her pineapple cake. Gloria said it was so bright it could fight off any darkness. My dad grew wider and I grew taller the year that Gloria started feeding us. Dad tried to give her money every night for the first week until she looked him straight in the eyes and said, *Isaac, the only thing you owe me is your word that you'll do the same for us when we need it. And, no more gin - you owe him that.* I remember, Gloria nodded curtly toward the brown paper sack on the counter and then nodded in my direction. Dad nodded back, put his cash away, and kept both promises until the day he died. When Gloria thought I was staying inside with my mom's old records too much, she and Gene gave me my first surfboard. When I punched another kid who lived down the street because he made a *yo mamma* joke,

Gloria sat on the porch with me and asked me what I missed and loved about my mom. She knew I needed good food, and sunshine, and someone to talk to, and she made sure that I got all three."

~~~~~~

Isaac always suspected that his son needed a playmate, a soulmate, another half to to make up for the loss, to make him wholly himself, and so Isaac wasn't surprised when Talmai and the red-headed girl down the street paired up. Then, after Miriam left, and the two families found themselves even more intertwined, the matter was all but settled in Isaac's mind. His boy and their girl, the writing was on the wall. Gene and Gloria weren't Jewish, but times were changing, and they were good, decent people. The kind of people anyone would be proud to call family. And so when his fifteen-year-old son told him he was going to be taking the red-headed girl out on a proper date that night, Isaac smiled, gave Tal some money to buy her a nice meal and some flowers, and offered to drive them.

~~~~~~

"So I had the money to take your mom wherever she wanted to go for our first date, but she just wanted to go to Rae's for burgers. They were still open for dinner back then. Your mom shopped and ate local before that was a thing. Amy always said if she was going to pay someone to make her food it should be another family. We were just fifteen, so my dad drove us to Santa Monica and said he'd meet us at the pier in three hours. I always imagined he went back home, but now as a dad myself I'm sure he stayed nearby. Your mom and I might as well have been on a different planet for all we cared about who else was or wasn't around, though. Falling in love with your best friend, and having your best friend love you back at that age, it's pure magic." Tal paused. He was the one watching May this time, and based on her expression, Tal could tell that May knew exactly what he meant.

"That night is mostly a happy blur of the teal and burgundy palette that Rae's has going on and the smell of burgers cooking on the flat top, but I do remember a few specific things. I was nervous and wasn't sure what to talk about, like all of sudden we needed to talk about something different than the stuff we talked about all day every day. I think I downed four sodas and a whole jar of pickles before our food even came. I started the day feeling like I might puke from nerves, and then there were a few times there at Rae's that I was pretty sure it was really happening. We walked down to the pier after we ate. They were building, or rebuilding, the ferris wheel, so we rode the carousel instead. We each got a horse that moved up and down, and when I could feel that the ride was starting to slow down, I panicked and tossed this box at her." He acted it out by awkwardly chunking the jewelry box at May.

"In my mind, halfway through the ride, I was going to lean over and effortlessly put the necklace on her, and then she was going to lean in and kiss me, but I was too nervous until it was almost too late. And I really thought I was about to throw up. So, I just threw it at her, and she lost her balance trying to catch it and she hit her head on the horse next to her. Luckily, Dad was early, and the whole way back she just leaned on my shoulder. When we got home, Dad insisted I stay with her to make sure she didn't fall asleep for at least a few hours. I had to keep her talking to keep her awake. We sat on the couch like we had a million times before; we played *Zelda* like we had a million times before, but at some point she did lean over and kiss me. And after that, she never took this necklace off. Well, until she did, but that's a different story."

Tal was the one reaching for Elise's hand this time. A late late show was starting up in the next room. Tal promised to tell May more another time and promised he was happy to talk about it. But May knew that might not exactly be true.

WAXING CRESCENT

Listen: "Everywhere, Everything"
by Noah Kahan

SIX

~~~~~~~~~~~

JUNE 2025 CE

They waited for Abee to come home so they could all watch the film together. Meredith didn't have feedback from her professor yet, Abee prefaced, but everyone in the class had loved it. People wanted to know if Abee was interested in being in more projects. *Yes*, absolutely he was.

May had plenty of friends who, even in high school, thought they were the next Paul Thomas Anderson or Scorsese. And spoiler alert, they weren't. May was happy for Abee, but she was also prepared to notice every single amateur and hacky thing that this Meredith did. Abee pushed play from his phone. May sat motionless for thirteen minutes and twenty-two seconds.

The credits started rolling; May's eyes were fixed on the screen, waiting for the scroll to reveal what she already knew must be true. Though muffled by the pounding in her head, May could hear her dad and Elise and Tal saying nice things and asking appropriate follow-up questions. May needed some air. She headed toward the bathroom down the hall, but she kept going, out the back doors, to the deck, and down to the pool. A few years ago Tal and Elise had finally put a pool in their yard.

The air was warm, and the pool was bright and clear in the darkness. Why hadn't Abee told her? Was this all a joke to him? *Andrew B. Berenson* had shown up twice in the credits, once in the cast list and once as a producer. Abee had done more than just act this story out. He had helped create it.

For thirteen minutes and twenty-two seconds, May had sat transfixed as the unthinkable unfolded in front of her. For thirteen minutes and twenty-two seconds this Meredith—and apparently this Abee—had used one cabin, one slice of generational trauma, and one time-traveling Adonis to splay her pain for the world to see—or at least the Tisch Undergrad "Narrative Workshop." It was pretentious. It was trying—trying hard. And yet, somehow, it was good. It was actually good. Which made May hate it even more.

81

May could hear the door slide open and slide shut behind her. She was ready to be mad if it was Abee. She was also ready to be mad if it wasn't Abee. He sat down on the edge of the pool next to her. She was mad.

"Why'd you leave? Are you okay?"

Abee's eyes were full of stupid, genuine concern.

"You didn't think to mention that you were making a movie about time travel?" Her mouth hung agape, as if there were no more words or breath to be had.

"Mays..." Abee looked surprised. "I did. Or I tried."

Was that true? May couldn't remember.

"You don't own the idea of time travel ya' know." Abee said it with a laugh in his eyes, but May was in no mood for laughing.

"But I do have the rights to my own story!" May was yell-talking in a way he'd never heard her speak before.

"Mays, that's not you, that's not your story. It's me, it's mine. It's everybody, it's for anybody." Abee looked confused, like he didn't understand why he was having to tell her this. She looked back at him equally confused. And sitting there under the full moon of a warm June night, May realized that Abee wasn't just the best-friend slash love-interest who had a strong supporting role in her story. He had his own story going on. Shit. Maybe everyone had their own story.

Later in life it becomes a truth you can take for granted; you might even start to assume you've always known it to be true. But if you think real hard, and transport yourself back to that first time you found your dad with his head in his hands, or your sister, just sitting in her car, staring, no music, no movement, you might just remember that once upon a time it was a revelation.

Staring down into the pool, Abee finally broke the silence. "And believe it or not, Meredith actually had the broad strokes figured out before I ever got involved. I read the first draft; she asked for some notes; I gave her some. We started collaborating more, and she asked if I'd work on it as a producer. She laid the framework, and I filled in the details."

May bit her lip. She hated to say it. She hated herself for needing to ask it. "Does Meredith know about us?" Was she asking in regard to their yearly jumps across time or in regards to the gray edges of their relationship? May wasn't actually sure herself.

"No, no she doesn't know," Abee offered softly. Neither of them knew which question he was answering.

May was embarrassed. And confused. But mostly embarrassed. She had been operating under the assumption that all this hopping across space-time was because her story was so, well, so story worthy, and ultimately in need of a better outcome. And Abee just happened to be there too. Did Emma need Daniel, or was it just more fun to turn back time with a friend? Maybe the analogy didn't hold up, May realized, annoyed. That actually was all about one person. Or maybe it was really about the tortured godfather, and the kids were just pawns. But why'd the headmaster have them go to all that effort to save someone who ended up just falling into the veil two books later anyway? May had her concerns about the headmaster's methods.

That night after the film, Abee eventually went back inside. But first he stood up, stomping in place to shake some of the water off his legs. Then, he squatted back down to May's level, balancing on the balls of his feet, and kissed the side of her forehead, right up against her hairline. Abee smelled like eucalyptus and sea salt. May was pretty sure he hadn't been surfing yet; it was just baked in somehow.

"I'm gonna head back in. I don't want to bail on Mom and Dad my first night back. Is it okay if we talk more tomorrow?"

May nodded yes. And that was eight or nine days ago now. May never knew how to count days; did you include the day you were on and the day you were counting back or forward to? What she did know was how to count the 142 messages she had left unread, the six face-to-face conversations she had dodged, and the one tap on the window she had pretended to sleep through. This was not like her, and she knew it. This was not like them, and she hated it. But May needed some space and time, funnily enough.

The film went like this: open up on a cabin in the middle of a snowy forest. It's not a quaint amount of snow, it's an apocalyptic amount of snow. Meredith had gotten very lucky. Zoom in through an open front door, ominous, no door would intentionally be left open in this weather. A one room cabin with the simple boast of being able to keep you alive when winter shows up. Not a fancy second home, magazine cabin, but a dark wood, red wool, kettle hanging over the fire, pelts and hides on the floors and walls, could be 1920 or 2020 type cabin.

No one is home. But someone was, not long ago, because the fire is going, the kettle is whistling, cups and books and other signs of life are strewn about. This scanning of the room goes on just five seconds shy of too long. Just long enough for you to realize you should be taking in the details. The bed, mussed up just a bit too violently for normal sleep. Lots of old family photos, but of all men, no women. An insane amount of knives and guns; there's one tucked behind a pillow, one atop a coffee can, a blade poking out between some pages apparently serving as a bookmark. It is all like a Seek-and-Find gone mental.

And then behind the camera you hear a crashing and rolling, and you think the ceiling has fallen down, but as the camera whips around like it's a human head, you see Abee, who has apparated here from some unknown location and is the actual source of the crashing and rolling noise. You watch him writhe on the ground for, again, just five seconds shy of too long. He is wearing some timeless, as in you can't place what time they are from, off-white long underwear. He is a true spectacle. Meredith was apparently the star of her "Gender and Madness Advanced Seminar." Abee whispered something else about how you could see her exploring all facets of the female gaze. May whispered back, not so quietly, that she didn't need him to explain feminist theory to her. Tal shushed them both.

The camera focuses on Abee's feet. He isn't given a name in the film; he just shows up as *Person* in the credits. As Abee is the only person on screen for the entirety of the thirteen minutes and twenty-two seconds it is obvious who that credit belongs to. Then the camera travels up the length of his body, slowly enough to feel a bit cringy, too quickly to let the female gaze really sink in. The tremors in his body lessen as the camera moves from toe to head, and as it settles on his face, his expression is calm in comparison to the chaos marking his entry. His tone is deep and clear, but reserved enough that you want to lean forward toward the screen to make sure you're not missing anything.

"The past is just there on the other side of the curtain."

The curtains on the window behind him are drawn, but they flutter with some unseen breeze. He's not speaking of them literally, but it's an effective visual.

"Like the next valley over, you just can't always see it for the mountain in the way. But there are objects and forces that reach out, you just have to reach back, if you want. And sometimes even if you don't want."

And with that the camera pulls back and you see Abee fish a knife out from under the rug next to him. He sits up and moves his giant body into a cross-legged position.

"Some people wonder about the circumstances of their lives. What if they had been born at a different time, to a different set of humans, in a different spot? I've never found that possibility very interesting to think of; no point dwelling on the impossible. I could only exist at this time, in this place, to these people. I do not exist removed from the 23 chromosomes that came with the egg and the 23 chromosomes that came with the sperm. As the humans that grew the egg and sperm could not exist except for the 46 chromosomes they inherited, and so on, and way back, and on it goes. I carry them on with me, and they carry me back with them."

And with that Abee chaotically raises the knife up in the air, as if possessed, and then plunges it down into the floorboard in front of him. It's just a floorboard, but the knife and the hand move as if it is more. And the moment the knife pierces the oak, the hand that holds it, along with the rest of his body, vanishes from screen. The blade's vibrations fill the empty space. Hold for three seconds on the knife, and then head whip back around to the bed. He has tumbled back in, this time with a smattering of blood on his off-white pants and smeared across one cheek. It is unclear if the blood is his own or someone else's, but the knife is still humming in the floor.

"I am not their sins. But I am not apart from their sins. I am not them, but I am not here without them. I do not owe them anything, but I owe them everything. I would leave the house they built for me, but to go where?"

A gust of snow blows across the room reminding the viewer that the door is still wide open, and that outside these walls a storm is raging.

"My great-grandfather killed his own brother right there." He nods past the camera to the spot he just was. "Oldest story in the book. It was easier for him that way. I've tried to undo it. Surely the world is better without another dead brother, but the moment I lift my hand in protest, I am undone. Because I do not exist if their sins are wiped clean."

He pulls a tattered prayer book out from the bed sheets. "I pray their prayers for them and with them. But if it didn't work for them, I'm not sure why I keep on. I go to them; I demand they be better. They laugh, knowing I'm proof they cannot. I've watched the priest entrust my grandfather to his Creator, right here in this bed. Returning to the One who formed him from the dust. Dust, upon dust, upon dust, upon dust. I can't ever stop the dust from piling up." And this time lifting the book into the air, he again vanishes from the screen, the book tumbles back into the sheets, right back to the hiding spot he pulled it from just a moment ago.

Abee tumbles in and out of the cabin a few more times, revealing more about the past sins and puzzle pieces of this family, until he finally crawls out onto the front porch, blizzard swirling around him. He is bare chested, bruised and bloody, giant legs pulled up under him, so you can't quite tell if he's kneeling over or keeling over.

"They will not let me rest, but they will not let me help them. Where do I go? I've heard there is a place on the other side of that mountain. A place that isn't haunted yet."

And with that Abee heads out into the blizzard, as if it is the most sensible thing in the world to go to that place he first talked about on the other side, where, whether he knows it or not, he will start the cycle all over again. The place beyond the veil of snow. Abee disappears into the snow; the camera holds, this time for actually too long, and then behind the camera you hear a crash. The screen snaps to black. Roll credits.

And that's why May hadn't talked to Abee in eight or nine days.

~~~~~~

But today May's hoarding of space and time had to come to an end. Today was the solstice. The one day she couldn't afford to have any time or space between them. This year was going to feel different. They'd hop from 2025 to 1997 at 7:41 p.m. on June 20, and they'd hop back from 1997 to 2025 at 1:19 a.m. on June 21. It was technically no different from the past two years, but somehow the fact that their time in the past would bridge from one day into the next scared her a little.

May's mind couldn't quite make sense of how everything got to be lined up so perfectly. Surely there were some years where the solstice in the past would have happened before the one in the future, making it impossible to use the five and half-ish hour window they had been given so far. But somehow they were in the perfect loop, the perfect sequence of years where that was never the case.

A good hop was when the solstice in their present happened before the solstice in the year they were hopping to. A bad hop would be one where in their present the solstice happened after the one in the past, meaning that if they went to the past it would be a whole year before they'd have the chance to get back to the future. She had done the math over and over, not wanting to get stuck in the past for a whole year, and sure enough the stars were aligned with this pattern. 2023 to 1995, a good hop. 2024 to 1996, a good hop. 2025 to 1997, assuming that's where they were headed, would be a good hop. And the pattern continued for over another decade. And more mind-bending, she and her mom were always the same age in this pattern of years. Fifteen, sixteen, and as of today they were both seventeen. But when she would sit and stare at her spreadsheets, there was always one line she avoided looking at...2035 to 2007. Ten years from now. It would be a good hop, of course it would be, and if her assumptions were correct, it might be the last one, because 2007 was the year her mom died.

~~~~~~

Tonight, once they hopped, they'd have to hurry to make the most of their time before it got too late, and they'd have a lot of dark time to contend with. It would not be a sunny afternoon on the beach like last year had been. How long could they pull off this "we show up out of nowhere one day a year" business?

The anxiety of everything that today might hold and the angst of having spent a week without Abee had her up early. So early that birthday breakfast was still at least an hour away. She knew what she should, no needed, to do. She needed to go and talk to Abee.

Abee's room was on the second floor of the Berenson house. His window worked nicely as a high-dive platform to jump down into the pool, but it was less helpful as an entry point. May would have to go through the house. Tal and Elise wouldn't care, if they were even up yet, but she felt exposed somehow. Everyone was very aware that she hadn't been talking to Abee.

May turned the handle of the door that led to the mudroom. She stepped over Elise's clogs. She stood still, listening, but the first floor was quiet. May was still in her slippers. She slid noiselessly across the slick terrazzo flooring of the kitchen. She felt her way through the darkness and up the stairs. Still no signs of life. She tip-toed down the hall to Abee's door. She paused. May could hear the heavy breathing of sleep on the other side. She pushed his door open, just wide enough to let herself slide through.

Out Abee's window May could see the sky had lightened by one shade, but the room was still dark. Her eyes tried to adjust between the two. She hadn't been in here since he'd been back. It was a mess, but it smelled like him, in a good way. May made her way across the room, toward his bed. From experience, she knew trying to wake him was no small job - lights, music, shaking - none of it had ever proved to be very effective, and she wasn't trying to wake the whole house. Maybe giants responded better to small voices.

She knelt down on the floor next to his bed. Her right knee clunked against something hard on the floor. It was a book. She picked it up and squinted to read the cover in the graying darkness of the room. She leaned back down and pulled up another. There was a whole stash of time travel related literature spilling out from under the bed, a mix of hard and soft covers and even some loose papers, a mix of fiction, physics, philosophy. A few names she recognized, Einstein, L'Engle, Sagan, and Hawking. But most, she didn't. Her arm reached further and further under the bed as she tried to grab hold of a slick covered book. She pulled out a MHS yearbook from 1994-95. It had a shiny black cover with teal writing. She hadn't seen this one yet. 94-95 would have been Amy and Tal's freshmen year. This volume was missing from her mom's stuff. Her fingers ran across the stamped word *Aquarius*. That had been the publication name of the yearbook back then, back when yearbooks were thought of as a serious and necessary publication worthy of an established title. Aquarius, the Water Bearer. Everything in Malibu pointed back to the water or the sun or both. This must be Tal's copy. Before she could wonder what Abee was doing with it, his arm swung down and thunked her on the head. Right, she was here to talk to him, not just dig through his stuff.

"Abee. Abee," May whisper-hissed. "Abee, when did you turn into a mad scientist? Or for that matter, when did you start reading?" She knew he couldn't hear her yet. "And have you heard of this thing called the internet? You don't have to have all of the actual books on your shelf, or floor, anymore. You can read them on a computer." Abee didn't move but May could hear his breathing change. "I had to come ask why you stopped talking to me." She knew this question would get him. She could barely make out the slight shifting of the lines on his face. Abee was smiling. May leaned forward on the bed, putting her face just a few inches away from his, waiting for him to open his eyes.

"No need to apologize," she teased. "Just promise you'll still travel through time with me today?" His smile grew. He still wasn't opening his eyes, though. "It is my birthday after all."

May took a long breath before going on. "Do you really think all of this is pointless? Are we just stuck in some loop? I thought you were *the future is open, the past is malleable, anything is possible*, guy. But maybe you're not that guy anymore.

And that scares me." May paused again. "And it scares me that Meredith might know you better than I do."

Abee's smile drooped, but he finally spoke. "I try not to philosophize this early in the morning, but if it means we are talking again, I'll make an exception." He opened his eyes. "So you know about the Sisyphean Loop?" Abee yawned as he talked, but it sounded more like a roar or like a bear breaking out of hibernation. May nodded. She knew enough—maybe. He went on, "Well, what if there is a solution for Sisyphus? What if he can redeem himself and get out of the loop? What if every time he gets to the top of the mountain, before he turns around to follow his doomed rock back down, he just stops and puts one pebble from the top of the mountain in his pocket, then deposits that pebble at the bottom of the mountain? Given enough time, he'd make the ground level. It would all even out and he'd be free. He's stuck in a loop, but if he's smart enough to make the loop work in his favor, he won't be stuck forever."

May tried to get what he had just said to soak into her brain.

"So, you think I can actually help my mom?"

"I think given enough time, Mays, you can do anything."

May was looking directly into his ocean eyes.

"I'm sorry," May confessed.

"I know you are." Abee's smile was back.

May's smile was back, too. And then they were just smiling at each other. May suddenly, awkwardly became aware of the moment. She should go. She didn't want to go.

"I should go get ready for breakfast."

Counter to everything her body was telling her, she stood up and headed for the door. May glanced back at him. The morning light filled the room now. Why'd he have to be so handsome? Abee looked up and saw her, still staring. She looked down, deflecting. The hoard of books was spilling out from under his bed. She remembered something.

"Hey, why do you have a yearbook from the 90's?"

Abee's face didn't move. It wasn't that he reacted slowly; it was weirder than that. His reaction was to freeze. Finally, he shook his head, like he'd been somewhere else.

"I'm not sure. I must have accidentally picked it up somewhere."

~~~~~~

Birthday breakfast was over. They were May and Abee again, mostly. The canvas tote was packed and ready to go. It held the old clothes and the old money and the new small hope that moving pebbles wasn't futile work.

Listen: "multiverse"
by Maya Manuela
Featuring Pembroke

SEVEN

~~~~~~~~~~

JUNE 1997 CE

The sun had set. The board was stashed in the cave. They each had on new-old clothes. They were headed toward the stairs and then straight up to Duck's. It was after 8:00 p.m. by the time they got there. In sync, they each pulled open one of the familiar front doors. May could see back into the Humpback room and over into the Redwoods room. Most people were at the point in the night where at another restaurant you might pretend that you didn't want dessert, but at Duck's there was none of that charade. Everyone got the pineapple cake.

Each table glowed with three creamy taper candles. Three candles at every table, every night, Nonna Gloria would not budge on this extravagance, or so May had heard. It was protocol Shep and Tal and Louis still held to. It was beautiful, and heartbreakingly ironic, May thought. From room to room, the thing that tied all of the California kitsch together was fire.

The hostess station was empty. May peeked down at the book that lay open on the stand. It was June 20, 1997 and everyone with a reservation for that evening had been successfully seated, except for the Mitchell Party, who had bailed on the Hollywood room. May waved at Abee to come see the proof for himself. It had happened, again. This was really happening, and it was really happening to them.

"Well, aren't you two just right on time!" They didn't see Gloria coming around the corner, and at the sound of her voice they both jumped back as if they'd been caught with their hands in the cookie jar. May couldn't find her words, but Abee was immediately chatting as if they were long lost friends. Yes, Gloria remembered them. Yes, she was glad to see them. Any chance of awkwardness was nipped in the bud when Gloria called them by their names without any hesitation, Josh and Mel, the names Amy would have used when she told her mom about them. If Gloria remembered that May had introduced herself as *May* two years ago, she didn't show it. It was easier this way, but May felt a twinge of loss at not being able to hear her Nonna say her real name.

Gloria apologized profusely that Tal and Amy were out of town. They were spending a few weeks out east this summer with Tal's cousin. It was a trial run of sorts, they were seeing if New York City could be the place for them after they graduated next year. Gloria's eyes moistened in a way that said they all knew the verdict of the trial was never up for grabs. Tal and Amy would love it there. Gloria said to make up for it, tonight was on her, and they were getting the royal treatment, and don't try to stop her.

She led them back to the Hollywood room. Abee did a decent job of remembering to act like he didn't already know every inch of the place. They both oohed and ahhed appropriately as Gloria took them through the maze of rooms. As they stepped into Hollywoodland, the breeze swept in, picking up Gloria's signature scent and carrying it throughout the room. Grandpa Gene wasn't crazy after all. Jimmy stared at them from the middle of the table. He was shinier than May had ever seen him.

Gloria stopped short; turning back to them, the mistiness in her eyes had been replaced with magic. "I have someone I want you both to meet." Gloria gestured toward the table and slid a chair out for May. Then she quickly turned and headed toward the open French doors.

"Isaac, the two kids I was telling you about are here. Come in, I'll introduce you."

~~~~~~

Dr. Isaac Berenson was probably a few inches on the underside of six feet tall. But what he lacked in height (compared to Abee), he made up for in girth. May smiled as she took him in, not quite realizing why exactly at first. But as he stepped into the light of the room, May was able to confirm what she had anticipated from the shadows. A big bushy white mustache that hid any evidence of his lips, black full-rimmed circular glasses that sat atop plump cheeks, and wispy gray fuzz that speckled but didn't cover a liver spotted head. This man was a harbor seal come to life. Then, much to May's delight, out popped a stiff arm, like a flipper. The flipper was first offered to May and then to Abee. May had to stop herself from standing up and hugging him. Abee had to stop himself from saying *Zayde*. Grandfather.

His colleagues and patients called him Dr. Bere. Yes, like Bear, he said. He spoke slowly, and his voice was warm and sturdy. May imagined that this seal of a man smelled of fish and salt, but as he took the seat next to her, she caught an air of books and antiseptic instead. It would be years before anyone would call him Zayde, but even now he seemed grandfatherly. May guessed he was in his 50's, or maybe the years had just been hard on him. Maybe he had gotten into it with an orca or two.

"Gloria tells me you two are travelers."

"That's right," May nodded. "We stumbled upon this place a few years ago," that was one way to describe it, "and we keep finding our way back every summer."

"And where do you go from here?"

May hesitated, "Wherever the wind takes us I guess."

Zayde Berenson gave her a small knowing nod. May relaxed. There would be no prying questions from this man.

"As long as the journey is your destination, you'll always end up right where you're meant to be." He said it more to the cloud of witnesses plastering the walls of the room, than directly to May and Abee. May nodded shyly, not sure how to respond to his proverb.

Gloria popped back in with two Dr. Peppers and one sparkling water with lime. May and Abee almost never drank soda, but they figured it was what you were supposed to drink when you were in 1997. On the other hand, Isaac almost always drank sparkling water with lime; he figured it was what you were supposed to drink when what you really wanted was a gin and tonic.

Zayde Berenson shifted, focusing his big round lenses on Abee. "How has the road treated you on your journey thus far?"

The kindness of this question was not lost on May. Any other adult might have hounded them about what school they went to, or what their parents did, or why in the world they were allowed this yearly road trip. May didn't want to spend the night churning out lies, and it was almost as if Zayde Berenson didn't want them to have to do that either. May could see Abee start to relax as well.

"It's been amazing—" Abee hesitated, not wanting to accidentally call him Zayde, not feeling right about calling him Isaac, he settled on, "—sir." Abee continued, "The world is so much more than I knew it could be."

Zayde Berenson offered another one of his small nods and a soft, "Hold on to that, my boy."

Before anyone could say more, Gloria was back with bowls of split pea soup and the suggestion that Isaac tell them about his work and research. "It's fascinating," Gloria insisted. "He's brilliant," she boasted.

Gloria looked right at May. "He's changing the world," she promised.

~~~~~~

May knew that Zayde Berenson had been a doctor and a professor. She wasn't sure in which order. Tal and Elise often went to events and galas at USC having to do with his work or his old colleagues. It all had something to do with women's health and reproductive technologies, but she'd never thought to ask more than the cursory info she picked up from the programs and fundraising brochures that they often left on the counter.

Zayde Berenson gave Gloria an appreciative nod, for her words and the steaming soup. He delicately lifted a spoonful of milky green mush to his mustache-covered mouth. After a slow swallow, he dabbed his whiskers with his napkin, and then he started talking. Tal had apparently gotten his knack for prolonged storytelling from his father, because Isaac started at the beginning.

~~~~~~

In November of 1944, when the war in Europe seemed to be rattling out its last dying breaths, Isaac Eber Bereson miraculously took his first.

As Rachel Berenson was forced out onto Király Street, in the heart of Budapest, the other women struggling to help her stand, she felt the initial pangs of what was to come. The frigid air sliced into Rachel's lungs. She meant to scream, but found that she couldn't. No time to scream. No air to scream. Move, the men said. March, the men said.

Yes, March, that was when Rachel's world had ended. Back in March the end had finally come. It had taken Zeke outright; it was taking her more slowly. When Rachel had first gone into the closet, *closet* was easier to wrap her mind around than *hole*, she hadn't known that she carried another life with her. By the time she felt the first flutters, her mind had become so frozen in darkness that she imagined one of the rats had found its way inside of her. Being slowly eaten from the inside out seemed much more probable than a new life finding its way through this nightmare.

Now as Rachel slipped and stumbled down Dohány, she could no longer ignore what her body had been doing apart from her mind the past eight months. She was two. Where were they taking them? To the Synagogue? Something wet leaked from her body. Was it blood, urine, the waters? No matter. It was warm for a brief moment.

Why was there a fence here now? The wood and the wire. The soldiers in green uniforms, badges displaying two crossed arrows, blood red. They weren't supposed to be here. They were yelling in Hungarian. They were Hungarian. Rachel had been confused ever since the world started to crack apart some five years ago. But now, now the world had become incomprehensible.

Rachel and Zeke had not been unaware; they were not naive. They knew what was happening in Germany, Poland, and France. They knew of the camps. They knew that some people went to the camps and worked; they were being used as slaves. And they knew that some people went to the camps and disappeared; they were being murdered. Rachel and Zeke were terrified, they were heartbroken, and they were haunted, because their own country was in bed with the devil. Hungary had sided with Hitler. They were sickened by the evil; they were ashamed of the complicity. But they were still alive.

While their brothers and sisters throughout Europe disappeared into the cracks, life in Budapest had gone on. And somehow it had gone on well enough. In Hungary there were hundreds of thousands of Jews living openly and freely; some were even able to offer refuge to others who were escaping the horrors that gripped their own homelands. In Budapest they kept working their jobs; they went to synagogue; their children went to school. And while Zeke and Rachel knew the devil was notorious for making bad deals, by 1944 they made the mistake of wondering if the devil had perhaps forgotten about them. Perhaps? The Allies were gaining and the Nazis were gasping. It looked like the end was near. Were they ridiculous for hoping—hoping they might actually make it through?

Hope is never ridiculous, but it is often dashed. And as a bedmate, Hungary was still well within the Reich's dying reach. The complicit Hungarian government had tried to quietly make a run for it; they had tried to slide out of bed and cozy up to the Allies. Hitler's Third Reich would have none of it. Heads rolled, and new, more amenable governing partners were brought in to rule Hungary. Don't mind the blood on the sheets, we will get along just fine, the Reich seemed to say. And tragically they did. The fascist Arrow Cross Party, hungry for power, happily slid in with the Third Reich and happily went about the work of exterminating their Jewish neighbors. Their own countrymen. It turns out the devil's memory is long and deep.

Normandy had been stormed. Paris had been liberated, and yet on November 29, 1944 Rachel Berenson was locked behind the makeshift walls of the Budapest Ghetto. Hell had come for her at last.

Collapsing and shivering against the cold porcelain of an empty bathtub that wasn't her own, she fought to keep the baby in. All that she could offer was inside of her. She knew there would not be enough milk, would not be enough warmth once this life inside of her crossed over. But despite her best efforts to stop it, her muscles took control and she started to push.

Rachel wrapped the boy in her shawl. A woman she had never seen before appeared with a small candle, a pair of scissors, and a length of twine. The woman said there was no running water here. Maybe the water would come back on in the morning. Rachel heard the woman speaking, but not really. Her head, her whole body was buzzing, and Rachel's hungry eyes raced to take in the face that was staring up at her. The baby looked like Zeke. The woman said she would go find a blanket and a basket. Just keep the child quiet, the woman said. For all of us, keep the child quiet. Neither the mother nor the child had it in them to say anything back. The woman left with her little light.

The room was unbearably dark now. Instinctively, Rachel undid the buttons on her dress and brought the child to her breast. She'd share whatever she had to give. She let the fingers of one hand cradle themselves under the not quite round head that was thick with hair. She let the fingers of her other hand try to discern what her eyes could no longer tell her. An arm, a hand, five fingers, a leg, a heel, five toes, and miraculously the other side told the same story. And for the first time in eight months, Rachel laughed. A baby, here. She caught the laugh and pulled it back almost as quickly as it had escaped. But the damage was done; Rachel had started to hope again.

Isaac knew the story well. His mother told and retold him year after year. Never forget, Isaac. We must never forget. Rachel had chosen *Isaac* because it meant *laughter*. She had chosen *Eber* because it meant *to cross over*. Rachel couldn't bear to give him his father's name. Ezekiel. Her heart only had room for one Zeke. But Zeke's name was always on her tongue, and Isaac grew up feeling convinced of his father's love. Rachel never told Isaac that Zeke had been taken away before they even knew she was pregnant. It was one of the truths of her life that she chose to reject. Zeke knew about his son, of course he knew.

Isaac came to understand that in some macabre way the ghetto had saved them. In hiding, a newborn would have had no chance. At best his mother would have had to send him down the river, like Moses. But the Danube was already swirling with blood and Pharaoh's daughter was nowhere to be seen. Mercifully though, camouflaged in the filth of the ghetto, Rachel and Isaac were able to survive on one small miracle of kindness after the other.

Every day, more people disappeared. Rachel heard the soldiers bemoaning their orders to better dispose of the bodies. The Reich said it was unseemly to have corpses floating down the river and piling up on the streets en masse. And yet, every day, Rachel and Isaac were spared. There was no food for her, and yet she would find bread crusts in her pocket. There was no food for him, and yet not quite empty cans of powdered milk would find their way into his basket.

And then one day—Rachel wouldn't find out it was January 17 of 1945 until much later—new soldiers were there. Russian soldiers. The Arrow Cross soldiers were gone. Rachel had seen too much to need to wonder if these were the good guys or bad guys. They were all bad guys. But these particular bad guys weren't trying to kill her or her son, yet.

~~~~~~

Isaac spent the first thirteen years of his life in Hungary, in Budapest, less than a mile away from the borrowed bathtub in which he was born. The ghetto had been reclaimed and the wood planks and barbed wire were long gone, but Rachel would walk the old perimeter of the place, over and over, day after day, like it was a prayer. And it was. Rachel had survived, and so she prayed with every step that Zeke had survived, too.

Rachel was, and would always be devastatingly optimistic. What if, just what if Zeke came back? She couldn't leave Budapest. Over the years, Isaac watched his mother fight to find the truth, and then fight to forget when it was all too much to bear. There were documents showing that in the spring of 1944 Zeke had been held in Hungary for three months, and then there was a passenger log from June 21, 1944. That was the day Zeke was forced onto a train headed for Auschwitz-Birkenau. And that was the end of what they knew for sure.

Isaac, who always had a brain for numbers, had come to assume that his father's journey ended inside of Auschwitz, just as it had for 99.995% of the people who entered through its hellish gates. Those who were tasked with unearthing and documenting what had happened in the concentration and extermination camps eventually let the world know the terrible truth. Based on the physical evidence and the surviving documents (which were not plentiful) they believed that approximately

1,300,000 people were brought to Auschwitz during the course of the war. When the camp was liberated on January 27, 1945, approximately 7,000 of those prisoners were still present and alive. Isaac was too logical to let a 0.005% chance feel like hope.

And then in October of 1956, the Danube again filled with blood. A revolution was coming. Hungary could finally rid itself of its Russian overlords. But even though many fought and died in the hope of securing that freedom, the Soviets would not budge. Finally, Rachel saw that it was time to go.

And so not long after his thirteenth birthday, Isaac Berenson stared up in wonder at the giant coppery-green statue who was ushering them into a new world. Back under the warm glow of the desk lamps at the National Széchényi Library, Isaac had read about de Laboulaye's gift to the Americans and his vision of *Liberty Enlightening the World*. Before the revolution Rachel had worked as a page at the library, and when Isaac wasn't at school, she would tuck her young son into a seat at one of the sturdy wooden desks. She would bring him book after book as she worked the stacks and came across volumes she deemed necessary for his education.

Now, far from the warm library, Isaac stepped up onto the railing of the ship, hoping that these few extra inches would put him in view of the green lady's feet. He wanted to see that shackle and that chain he had read about. These instruments of slavery, broken under the force of the lady's presence. De Laboulaye had placed them there to remind the world what was at stake. Isaac wanted, needed, to believe they had found a place that was truly free. He felt sure the chain and shackle were up there, smashed to bits, just like he had read, but no matter how tall he stretched, he couldn't see them.

~~~~~~

May realized she hadn't moved, maybe hadn't even blinked. At some point Gloria brought in dessert, but no one had noticed at the time. Zayde Berenson cleared his throat and took a sip of his sparkling water.

"My dears, please forgive me for stealing your evening with my stories. I didn't mean to hold you so long, or bore you so thoroughly."

Abee reached forward before May could move or speak. He clasped his grandfather's hands in his own. "Thank you. I needed to hear all of that," Abee said gently.

Zayde Berenson nodded slowly, betraying a slight look of surprise. "I didn't even get close to telling you what I believe Gloria hoped I would get to share with you.

Perhaps you can indulge me with another story time in the future."

When May glanced at her wrist, it was only 12:15; they could spare a few more minutes. She looked at Abee. Every second, every word with Isaac felt precious. "I am afraid we are the ones who have asked too much of you tonight, but I really want to hear more. What's the gist of the work you're doing right now?"

"Well, the technical term for it is oocyte and embryo cryopreservation. But the layman's term is egg and embryo freezing, as in preserving a human egg or embryo, by freezing it. However, if I'm being very honest, I'd tell you that what it really should be called—is time travel." He paused, waiting for them to react to his joke. When no one cracked a smile, he continued.

"Initially, it means that women who have a type of cancer which requires chemo or radiation have options and opportunities if they want to have children later. We can retrieve eggs before they are ever exposed to any treatment or before a woman has to have her reproductive organs removed all together. And then someday these options, these opportunities will be available to all women, for all sorts of reasons. Maybe you have heard of the baby from Australia. No of course you haven't. But she was the first, an embryo frozen for two months, and now she is, well she must be thirteen now. She was born April 11 of 1984, but technically, if not for the cryopreservation, perhaps her birthday would have been February 11. But now we are looking at years, even years upon years of viable preservation. The science fiction movies love to freeze old men so they can come back later for their money, but the science of that experiment is nowhere near even being tested. But we know that what we are doing works, and it's working exponentially better all the time, and for exponentially better reasons." His mustache rose with his smile.

A chill started at the very crown of May's head and slowly spread down her whole body until it reached her Converse covered toes. Zayde Berenson wasn't just changing the world. He was building a new world. A world that had room in it for her.

DUCK DIVE

Listen: "When We Are Together"
by The 1975

EIGHT

~~~~~~~~~

JUNE 2025 CE

The sun poured in May's windows. When they came in last night, closing the shutters had been the last thing on her mind. Her left hip and shoulder felt frozen and her arm and leg tingled with sleep. But surprisingly her head and neck felt comfortable, propped at exactly the right angle. Something was soft against her cheek, but sticky. As she started to roll to her back and attempt to shake the life into her limbs, her head turned toward the ceiling and she felt the distinct sensation of sticky skin separating from sticky skin. She slowly sat up and then rolled to her stomach to take in the situation. A small pool of what she could only assume was her own drool shone in the triangular dip of flesh that was hemmed in by his collarbone, shoulder, and chest. Abee was there. He had been the soft stick against her. She gently, but quickly, wiped the drool away with the corner of her blanket.

This was a new, and not unwelcome scenario. They had slept in generally the same place a million times before, but never with quite so much skin on skin. And certainly never with quite so much drool.

"Abee, I want to learn to surf this summer."

He opened his eyes more quickly than she had anticipated. Shoot. Maybe he had felt the drool. Maybe he had felt her head pressing into his chest, not totally unaware of where she was or what she was doing.

"Well I think we can do your first lesson right here; there's enough water." Abee teasingly wiped off his chest. May pulled her still tingly hand back to punch his shoulder. He intercepted her jab, pulling her back down, and back into him.

~~~~~~~~~~~~~~~~~~~~~~~~~~~~~~~~~~~~~~

With only six weeks before Abee headed back east, they quickly fell into a new rhythm, up at 7:00 and on the beach by 7:15. In the water, every day, for as long as they could put off doing anything else. That was the curriculum. It was all new to May and it wasn't. She had watched other people surf her whole life. She technically knew how to do it, but her body didn't believe her yet. Abee knew it would take a summer's worth of thrashings to get her mind and body on the same page. And it did. Paddle out, turn the board, wait, and wait some more, paddle into the wave, pop up, wipeout, repeat. With each wipeout May got a little more confident, and Abee felt the tension in his chest a little more sharply. He was so proud of her for doing the thing she had managed *not* to do her entire life. Abee wanted to cheer every time she even got up. But at the same time he wanted to yell at her to paddle in and never come back out.

This fall's good-bye was harder than the first one. There was no pretending this year. Abee knew exactly how much he would miss May now. Before he left, he made her promise to never surf alone. When he said it, her freckled nose wrinkled the way it did when she was trying to dam up her tears. A few managed to spill over despite her efforts.

Everyone was downstairs waiting for Abee. Some of his books were packed in his bags, some he was leaving behind. They were neatly stacked on his desk now, not strewn under the bed. For the first time in years his room was completely clean and in order. He had made a point of letting his mom know that he had washed his sheets and blankets so she didn't have to do it.

Abee knew he didn't need to look again; he had already looked ten times that morning, but he couldn't help it. He lifted the corner of his mattress. He lifted it just high enough to see the length of the spine. He could just barely make out the turquoise letters that read, MHS *Aquarius* 94-95.

Satisfied the book was in place, he lowered the mattress and stepped back to take a final look, to make sure the bed didn't also bulge to betray its secrets. He still didn't really understand what he had in his possession, even though he had been keeping it, and keeping it a secret for seven years now. But he couldn't imagine May having it either, not yet. What if it was too much? Too much to process? Too much of everything all at once? He hadn't intended on lying to May. But he had to, right?

They stood out by the pool while Tal changed out of his running clothes and looked for his keys. Elise had already squeezed Abee good-bye a dozen times and then hurried back to the kitchen. Abee kissed May on the forehead and then softly on the mouth. It wasn't awkward, it wasn't forced, it wasn't rushed. It was them. May felt light headed and heavy footed at the same time.

"We've got to go! There's a wreck at Topanga. Down to one lane for a few miles," Tal called out from the driveway. Abee gripped May's hand, running his thumb across the scar on her palm, and then he was gone.

Fifteen minutes later, May was lying on her board, alone. The water was suspiciously calm. In the distance she could see a plane sweep out over the Pacific and then turn back toward the east. The next one pointed west and never stopped. May hadn't intended on lying to Abee. She had to, right? A set was coming, finally. She was up; she caught it; she didn't wipeout.

Phase Three

FIRST QUARTER

YEAR	DATE	TIME
1998	21-Jun	7:02 AM PDT

YEAR	DATE	TIME
2026	21-Jun	1:24 AM PDT

Listen: "When U Love Somebody"
by Fruit Bats

ONE

~~~~~~~~~~

JUNE 1998 CE

Tal knew it was silly. He and Amy were about to move to the other side of the country. She wouldn't be able to take it with her, but he felt like he had to make it all the same. He would have asked Amy to marry him right then. She probably would have even said yes, but he knew they were just eighteen. He knew there was plenty of time. Tal knew that Amy was his person and he was hers. So for now, a surfboard would do.

Isaac let Tal have the garage as his workshop. He started with a 9'1" blank. Amy was great on a shortboard, but she was at home on a longboard. Tal carved each curve and rise to fit just her hands, just her torso, just her stance.

Years ago Isaac had found a root-branch of a great banyan washed up on the beach. Isaac had seen banyans in a few botanical gardens nearby, but there was no reason their branches would be washing up at El Matador. This root-branch had come from somewhere far away. Isaac could feel it. He took it home and sat it on the railing of his deck. He never told Tal or anyone else, but every morning he would run his hand over the smooth wood and remind himself that the end of one thing is always the beginning of another thing. Its work as a root and then as a trunk was done, but Isaac always knew it had another purpose still yet to serve. When Tal started making Amy's board almost a decade later, it was obvious what the wood had been waiting for. Tal ran a strip of sacred banyan wood down the center of the board.

Amy loved those magic moments when the water and the sky were the same color of blue. So Tal sprayed the foam with just the right shade of azul and then made the resin with a dash of opalescence. After the hot coat was set, he hand painted a fluorescent pink heart on the nose, and in his best cursive he wrote *Mon Amie* through the center of the heart.

Gene called Amy, *Aimée*, pronounced e-MAY; in French it meant "beloved." It was a precious word between father and daughter. And so half in jest, half out of respect, even as kids Tal had always called Amy *Mon Amie*, pronounced ah-MEE, "my friend". Now that they were more than friends, the nickname felt even sweeter. It was their joke, and it was their promise.

Not many people could duck dive a longboard, but thanks to Gene, Amy had perfected the angle, the pressure, and the speed necessary to get the board under the wave. Then, the same buoyancy and mass that took so much skill to contend with under water would propel her like a jet as she came up out of the water, leaving Tal in her literal wake. Amy was proof that in surfing technical skill mattered more than strength.

This board would be almost invisible under her feet. It would look like she was walking on water, or in those moments where the sea and sky melted together, she'd be flying.

DUCK DIVE

Listen: "I Wish I Was"
by The Avett Brothers

TWO

~~~~~~~~~~

JUNE 2026 CE

May's Senior year was done even though she hadn't really done it. She was graduating and all, but she hadn't been mentally—or sometimes even physically—present. What she had been, was surfing and reading. May wanted to read everything that Abee was reading about time travel. Abee would send her recommendations or mail her the actual books after he had read them. She loved how he scribbled through paragraphs and wrote down the margins with his sharp black pen. May preferred a yellow highlighter and a blue pen for notes. By the time they'd both been through one it looked more like an artist's sketchbook than a textbook.

They talked a lot, but mostly just about what they were reading. May always tried to dry her hair before they talked. She kept her board—now it was actually boards plural—out of view. When Abee commented about how tan she was getting, she changed the subject. But he was coming home—tonight. Abee would want to go surfing. He would see her toned arms. He would spot the ease of her paddle and the length of her rides. He would know that she had been surfing a lot, and that meant she had been surfing alone. He would know that she had been keeping it from him. He would start to wonder what else she kept from him.

It turned out that May had been keeping a lot—from everyone. As far as Shep, and Tal, and Elise, and Abee knew, she was headed to Hyde Park, two hours up from New York City, where she'd do the full bachelor's program at the Culinary Institute of America. They would refine her skills as a chef, and she'd get all the business side too. The stuff that thus far she had resisted letting Tal and Shep train her on. Tal loved to quote her, *I don't want to learn about taxes–I'm only fifteen,* speech every April when he was elbow deep in receipts.

Paris had been her dream once upon a time, but after the geopolitical and health stressors of the last few years, living abroad now posed logistical difficulties that Shep wasn't ready to let her navigate at eighteen, and if she was honest, the allure had dimmed for her as well. Not filling out the application back in October had actually been a pivotal moment. As she sat there staring into her laptop, realizing she actually agreed with her dad, something started to crack. If she could just let go of that version of the dream, maybe she could set it all down. Maybe she could pick up a new one. What if her future wasn't what she had always assumed it had to be? What if all these books that she had been pouring herself into were just the beginning? Literature, philosophy, physics, ethics—what if the whole world was open to her? She wasn't sure how to tell her dad that she suspected time was more of a loop than a line and that somehow generational trauma was making time fold in on itself in a way that allowed her to be physically present in what she had once thought of as the past.

May wasn't sure how to say that, so she just filled out applications to Harvard, Yale, and Columbia without saying a thing. The internet said they had the top philosophy programs. She paid the fees on her own. She wrote some pretty dope essays. She figured the admissions staff didn't often get time-travel fiction woven into the "You're teaching a new class at Yale, what is it?" essay question. In hindsight, maybe she had gone too weird with that one. Harvard and Yale were both *no*. But Columbia—Columbia somehow was a *yes*. And if May wanted to keep her spot, she had to send them more money by tomorrow.

May had gone rogue this year, and she liked it.

~~~~~~

Shep was confused. Everyone was confused. May liked to read something besides recipes? May wanted to do a version of school where all you did was read and write? May's grades and scores were good enough to get into an Ivy? They all stared at each other. Elise shrugged when Shep caught her eye. *I didn't know either*, her shoulders said back to his wide-eyed stare. Abee wasn't surprised by May's "new" interests, but why hadn't she told him?

May hadn't told Abee because going to Columbia meant she was going to be in New York City. The city where he also was going to be. May had not forgotten his drug-store-shot-clock-break-down, and she knew that the minute they switched from being childhood best friends who grew up in Malibu and who had loose benefits to being adults who lived in New York City; the shot clock would have to start ticking.

Shep had never pressured May to take up his passions. He had just always made a point of inviting her into what he loved. But he wouldn't lie, it was nice when she seemed to like it, too. May grew up in his kitchen. Her wooden step stool was still under Shep's prep table, even though she hadn't needed it in over a decade. Shep was no stranger to holding things loosely. Shep reminded himself that he loved his daughter more than any dream he had for her, and so he sat next to May that night as she typed his credit card number into the payment screen.

"I love you my Pad-May. I'm already proud of you."

And just like that, her future changed.

THREE

~~~~~~~~~~

JUNE 2026 CE

"So the hop is at 1:24 a.m. and then we come back at 7:02 a.m. What are we going to do for five and half hours in the middle of the night? Go knock on your grandpa's door? Do you think every year has its own mission? Or is it all just layer upon layer of a bigger story? Like what if we don't *do* anything in particular this jump? What if we can't do anything? Are we wasting the power of the universe?"

They hadn't really talked about what they needed to talk about yet, and so May kept trying to stuff as many other words between them as she could. Abee was fully aware of what she was doing, and he didn't hate watching her squirm.

"I think we still have to go. Just to make ourselves available to possibility. I wonder if not going is even a thing?" This certainly wasn't the first time Abee had pondered this question, but he was no closer to answering it than he'd ever been. What if they were just in their rooms? What if they weren't touching the board? What if they weren't together? Would they still hop?

"I think we walk up into town, see if anyone is around, and then if nothing else we go sleep on the beach in 1998."

~~~~~~

JUNE 1998 CE

In 2026, it was warm and clear, and half of the moon glowed in the sky. When their watches clicked to 1:24 the sky filled with low, thick clouds and even though the temperature couldn't have been that much different, May felt herself shiver. It was 1998.

The beach was empty. The streets were empty. But across the intersection they could see a light shining from the back room of the sprawling bungalow that was part restaurant and part residence. A shadow passed by the window. Amy was up.

"Tell me I shouldn't go knock on the window," May whispered.

"You should definitely go knock on the window," Abee whispered back. But May was already crossing the street before he could finish his sentence. "This is all you," Abee called out just loud enough for her to hear. "Just don't fall asleep. Meet back on the beach by 6:30."

In the light of the street lamp Abee could see May check her watch and then nod in agreement. May held his gaze for just a second and then slipped through the back gate.

~~~~~~

"We got a late start heading out, so Josh is taking a cat nap in the van. We don't have to hitchhike this year; we have a car," May added quickly, realizing her story was getting cumbersome. "But I was walking around, saw your light on, and decided to be the weirdo who pops in at 1:30 in the morning." Lying like this felt gross, but she had to. May was sitting cross-legged on Amy's orange shag rug. She was actually sitting on more clothes than shag, but there were clothes covering most surfaces in the room.

"Sorry it's such a disaster in here. I'm trying to pack and clean stuff out. Tal is going to be working for a cousin's uncle's friend or something like that as a cater-waiter, so we're going out early. Oh right, I skipped the main part of that story; we're moving to New York!"

May had to stop herself from saying, *me too!* Being that honest would complicate things unnecessarily. So instead, May made a jittery motion with her hands and said, "I had a Red Bull on the way here." She really had. She also had been very lucky. Red Bull only started being widely distributed in the States in 1997, Amy had heard of it, but never tried it. "So, I'm pretty wired. Can I help?"

"You're a lifesaver," Amy sighed. "How do you feel about folding clothes?"

For the next two hours May systematically turned the piles into folded and sorted stacks. Amy worked on filtering the not-clothing items out of the hoard. The whole time they chatted and sang along to the softly playing radio. May knew enough of the songs that she didn't look like a total dweeb. They talked about Tal and Josh. May found it was fun to talk about kissing Josh and how much she liked him, even though things were still very gray between them. She wondered if it would be as easy to talk about it all if she was saying his real name. But it was easy. It was normal. And May was painfully aware of how quickly the minutes were ticking away.

Amy told her about how she had gotten into an Interior Design program at Parsons. May tried not to act surprised. She hadn't known her mom was studying design when she lived in New York. Tal was going to be doing some sort of business degree at NYU. Isaac had stopped requesting brochures from med schools a long time ago, but he had expectations; he wasn't ready to let his son just be a hippie-rock-and-roller. Amy did air quotes around his words as she said them.

"Do you want to just crash here for a bit?" Amy offered after catching May yawning for the tenth time. May wanted to curl up in her bed almost more than anything she'd ever wanted, but it was too risky. What if she overslept? May declined. She needed to head out. It was almost 4:00 a.m.

Amy stopped, surveying May in her GAP t-shirt and color blocked Bonjour shorts. May knew the look skewed more early 90's, but she preferred this aesthetic to the current low-rise, halter-top, butterfly-bedazzled situation. "It's drizzling outside now. At least take one of my jackets if you're leaving." Amy headed for her closet, which had just recently become accessible again. She flipped the light switch on the wall before entering and was back in a few seconds, cropped Levi's denim jacket in hand. May heard herself gasp. Amy mistook the gasp as a protest.

"It's really fine, I was going to get rid of it anyways. It has a blood stain on it. Sorry, that's gross isn't it?" She laughed at herself. "Let me get you something else." She turned to go back into the closet.

"No!" May blurted out, too loudly. She lowered her voice. "I mean, this jacket is great. If you're going to get rid of it anyways. What's a little blood between friends?" May bit her lip. She hadn't meant to say friends.

"You know, I've always said that." Amy smiled and let the jacket slide off the hanger. She handed it over to May. May slid it on. Just like she had two years ago. Just like she had countless times before and since then.

"It's kind of perfect for you to have it. I swear this jacket has been trying to live a different life for a while now. It disappeared a few years ago, and then Tal found it out on the beach. He brought it back just because he thought I'd like it. He didn't know it was my jacket. We pick up all sorts of stuff the tourists leave behind. I didn't even realize it was mine at first, but it's always had this stain on the cuff from when I busted trying to do a stupid trick on my skateboard one time. My hands were full of asphalt. So all that to say, it will be happy to go on a new adventure with you."

"Thank you," May whispered, and before she knew what she was doing, she was hugging her mom. Maybe because it was four o'clock in the morning, or maybe because she really wanted to, Amy hugged her back.

"Will you come back for the summers?" May asked as they mutually released each other from the embrace.

"Oh for sure! I can't imagine not spending the summer here. Come knock on my window, no matter what time."

May blinked fast to disperse the tears.

"Sorry, I know you have to go. I'm really not trying to stall, but Mom would be mad if I didn't send you off with some food. We had some killer bolognese tonight. I think Mom even packed some up, just in case you guys came to visit. Hold tight, I'll just be two seconds." Amy quietly slipped out into the hallway and May was left alone with the jacket burning into her skin.

Now would be a really great time to have some clarity on how the hell this all worked. Could she take it with her back to the future? What if she tried, and it disappeared in transit? Could there be two of them? She couldn't take it. She just couldn't. She started to feel panicky. She had to get out. She peeled the jacket off and set it on the desk, entrusting its fate to the unknown.

In an instant May was through the window, standing in the more than drizzling rain. She quickly stepped back to get under the shelter of the eaves. She felt her heel hit what she assumed was the side of the house, but the next instant something was falling, pushing her forward, and crashing to the ground. May stood up, wiping her increasingly wet hair out of her face. Flustered, May turned around and picked up the bright blue surfboard with a hot pink heart and set it back against the house. Only as she released her grip did the questions come flooding in. And then she ran.

May managed to navigate the death stairs. They were extra deadly in the rain. She was early. Abee might be down here already, or he might not.

"Abee! Abee!" She yelled into the rain. Luckily the beach wasn't completely dark. The clouds had a way of capturing light that would have otherwise escaped out into the universe. May found him tucked in the cave with half of the whole board she had just touched.

"Abee, my mom was going to get rid of the jacket and she has the board. The whole board. And I touched it. How is it here and there and if we just go bust it right now, then she can never ride it again, and then she can't die on it. But if she was going to get rid of the jacket then maybe she did get rid of it, but if she did, how did I ever still have it? Did I have it because this has always happened and will keep on happening and every move is just a game?!" May fell to her knees in a wet heap.

Abee pulled her in toward him. They sat with the busted board behind their backs, propped between them and the cold rock wall.

"If this is all just a game, I'm glad I get to play it with you."

~~~~~~

May's eyes flew open. She was still soggy and cold but it was bright around her now. She could see the water sparkling out past the sand. There wasn't a cloud or evidence of rain in sight. It was 7:03. They had slept through the second solstice, and it hadn't seemed to matter.

Listen: "If We Were Vampires" by Jason Isbell
and the 400 Unit

FOUR

~~~~~~~~~~

AUGUST 2026 CE

"I'm not going to be living in campus housing this year."

"What? I can't hear you," May yelled from inside the closet. The scene around the room was a copycat of what she had experienced in this same place just six weeks ago, or was it 28 years ago? Either way, it was just as much of a mess. May stuck her head out into the room to see what Abee wanted.

"It hadn't come up yet, so now I'm telling you, we're moving off campus." May nodded, not really comprehending what Abee was saying. There were so many details she had to figure out for herself, she hadn't asked *him* many questions lately. She had just assumed he would be in his same dorm. Housing was so insane in the city, a lot of people lived in campus housing even as graduate students. May dropped her armful of hangered clothes and plopped down on the bed next to Abee.

"Okay, start over. What?"

"My suite, we all really like each other, and they had a connection to a townhouse, and so we're moving."

My suite. We. They. Abee was being vague. May should call his bluff.

"So, Meredith has a rich uncle who is letting her bring you and Jake and Alexis to come live in his townhouse while he works in London for a few years. His VC firm just merged with a group in the UK and it's all perfect timing since Alexis graduated and Meredith is traveling back and forth to LA more than she's actually doing school." She smiled, proud of her improv guess slash burn.

"Umm, it's her aunt and the merger isn't final yet. But shit May, you nailed it." Her smile fell. "Really?"

"Really. We'll both be on the Upper West Side now. We will practically be neighbors." Abee had friends. That was good. She would have friends—probably—

eventually. And she had to live on campus for at least two years anyways. This was all good. This was all normal. She didn't hate Meredith. She didn't like her. But she didn't hate her. She would try and remember that.

Listen: "Pink Moon"
by Nick Drake

FIVE

~~~~~~~~~~

OCTOBER 1998 CE

August in New York City was gross. September was a slight improvement. But October. October was why people moved to this city. Who knew that a place known for its buildings actually had so many trees. Amy realized she sounded like a tourist, but she genuinely couldn't stop talking about the colors. It was like each leaf had somehow seen to the other side of the country and captured the Malibu sunset in its cells.

The past two months had been filled with the best days of her life, but she did miss her parents. She hadn't expected to even think twice about them, but here she was, staring at the Washington Square Arch, Tal asleep on the blanket next to her, and she was wondering how her mom was managing to bake and frost all the cakes without her.

"Hey I'm getting hungry," Amy nudged Tal in the ribs. "Can you swipe me into your dining hall? I'm out of meals for the week already."

Gene would do anything for his Aimée, but the idea of paying luxury prices for buffet style food was too much for him. *Eat that food if you have to, but mon Aimée, don't settle for lazy cooking.* Amy could feel his eyes on her when she grabbed an untoasted bagel and a green banana because she was already late for class. The illegal hot plate and the ridiculous set of French cast iron pots her dad sent her were still in their boxes. She missed cooking with her mom, but she didn't actually miss cooking.

Thankfully, Isaac had no such hang-ups when it came to Tal's dining situation. Amy wasn't sure what it was called, but in her mind when Tal swiped his pretty plastic card, the hair-netted person on the other side of the register must have seen it flash GOLD - DIAMOND - UNLIMITED PLAN. Tal never ran out of meals.

The hall was oddly busy for a Thursday evening. There was finally enough chill in the air to keep people from sitting on the patio. Amy spotted Tal in the soft-serve line, per usual. She jostled her way though a group of still wet swim team members and slid up next to him just in time for him to hand her a cup of chocolate-vanilla twist, topped with chocolate jimmies.

"There aren't any open tables," Tal commented, surveying the crowd. "Looks like someone gets to be our new friend."

When they spotted her she didn't look like she wanted any friends—new or old. And that's exactly why Tal chose her table.

~~~~~~

Elise had friends. She had plenty of friends. She just wasn't the kind of person who needed to be around them all of the time. She was a sophomore, part of the inaugural class of NYU's newly founded Food Studies Program. She was obviously put out when they first sat down, but Tal started talking about some cousin's-cousin who he had been catering with. She knew him too; of course she knew him, she said. And by the time she finished her slice of pizza she knew she'd be seeing these two Californians again, whether she liked it or not.

The guy, Talmai, was obviously cute. But he was also, obviously, in love with the girl, Amy. No need to waste any time on him. Amy though. Amy was interesting. She was kind, but not overly sweet. She had a weird beachy-punk vibe, and she admitted to watching the new creek show that had started on the CW earlier that year. Elise didn't know anyone their age who admitted to that. Maybe she hadn't been totally honest. Maybe she could use another friend after all.

DUCK DIVE

Listen: "I Remember Everything"
by John Prine

SIX

~~~~~~~~~~~

OCTOBER 1998 CE

Amy was on the other side of the country, but the blanket on the end of her bed still needed to be straightened—one day an inch to the right, the next day an inch to the left. The slats on the shutters still needed to be opened every morning and closed every night. The fresh air still needed to be let in to do its work and then needed to be shut out when it got carried away with itself. Gloria tended to each of these duties, knowing full well she was the only one who really needed these things.

One afternoon a storm blew in. Gloria didn't make it across the yard in time to close the windows. A shutter blew open, knocking over a lamp, pushing over a book, dislodging another book. And that's how Gloria found the Malibu High School *Aquarius* yearbook from 1994-1995, open on the orange shag rug.

A ping of recognition ran through Gloria's hand, up into her arm, and tickled her brain as she picked up the yearbook. An idea grabbed Gloria's mind and so she grabbed a scrap of paper from Amy's desk and jotted down the first thing that came to her. A poem that had been growing inside of her.

> If only my life were a story.
> But my morning glory,
> what would it even be?
> Because lives aren't told,
> they are lived, not sold
> in cold pages.
> History is a story and
> that's no way to
> to spend your days.
> Not when right now has
> coffee to drink

and strawberries to pick
and hair to brush
and walks to take
and faces to kiss
and hands to hold.
The only story to be told,
is that I lived.
I lived hand in hand
with you.

This was just how Gloria's brain worked. Sometimes she felt compelled by words, ideas, or were they memories, or visions? She wasn't sure. When she gave May that first poem, she wasn't sure why; she just knew she needed to tell her something. And she knew in this moment that she still had more to tell her. Gloria closed her eyes and tried to get it straight in her mind, but all she could see was a circle. She flipped forward in the yearbook to find the perfect pages where she could tuck in her message. This book seemed like as good a place as any to try and connect the past and the present and the present and the future. She flipped some more and landed in the freshmen section. Her eyes scanned the two pages open in front of her. *N-O-P-Q-R-S*. And there was her beautiful red-headed ray of sunshine—*Amy Rousseau*—her freshman year of highschool. In the box to the right of Amy was Sam Samuels. It was one of Amy's great joys in life, always getting to be next to the boy so nice they named him twice. Amy and Sam had gone to school together ever since kindergarten. The box to the left of Amy's picture then caught Gloria's eye. It was a solid gray box that said *No Portrait Available*. Who had missed picture day? Gloria followed the row to the edge of the page where the names were listed.

Brit Raymond
Steven Reynolds
Lola Rossi
Amy Rousseau
Sam Samuels

The gray no portrait box was the third one in and corresponded to the name *Lola Rossi*. The name felt very familiar, but Gloria couldn't place it. Amy didn't have any friends in her class named Lola. But somehow Gloria knew the girl. She looked again. Gloria shook her head, as she often did, and then she tucked the poem in the yearbook and closed the pages. She latched the shutter. Picked up the lamp. Put the books back in line on the desk and shook her head one last time.

FIRST QUARTER

Listen: "Midnight Rain"
by Taylor Swift

SEVEN

~~~~~~~~~~

OCTOBER 2026 CE

Abee had downplayed the quality of his living situation. Some words he left out—limestone, five stories, roof deck, Central Park West. And oh yeah, *Architectural Digest* shot the house last year for bonus content in the June digital edition. His suitemates, turned housemates, all had their own rooms. Actually they had their own floors.

May pulled her knees up into her sweater. It was finally getting chilly. The rooftop was hemmed in on three sides by yew topiaries, but the front looked straight out over the park.

"You know you're gorgeous, right?"

May could feel herself flinch. This was only her second time hanging out with Meredith, and she wasn't convinced that she could handle it. Overt compliments weren't helping the situation. Abee caught her eye and hit her with a *please just try to be nice* stare.

"That's what all the boys tell me." May looked at Meredith as she said it, but Abee knew he was the intended recipient of that message. May was no stranger to the hot girl vs. obviously not *as* hot girl dynamic, and when an objectively beautiful person comments on the looks of a person who is at best, unconventionally attractive, it's always going to skew patronizing.

"Have you done any acting? You're so fun to look at. I could shoot a whole scene just tight on your face."

May couldn't. She started to answer with something about being done acting like she liked her, but she caught Abee's stare again and froze, and then awkwardly pretended like she never heard Meredith's question. May slipped her knees out of her sweatshirt and stood up to look out over the park. Some students, or maybe they were professors or maybe they were TA's—that was one of the most confusing parts of university life; every one looked like they could be an unkempt mad-genius or a hung-over freshmen who was late for class, and you couldn't immediately tell which was which. But whoever they were, they were unearthing a new section of the archeological site in the park down below. Their white tents hid their progress, but a few days ago May had stopped to watch a muddy kneed genius or hung-over freshman filter a bucket of soil through a mesh screen.

"People lie. People can write books full of lies. But the ground doesn't lie, does it?" May looked over her shoulder, not convinced he was talking to her. He was.

"To be honest, I've never understood the difference between lay and lie, so I'm not sure what it does."

He smiled. A fellow ginger, making a grammar joke. He was into it. He was into her.

"How do you know you're not just writing a story into the ground?"

Now he was really into her.

"We have to continually ask ourselves that question, that's how. We dig one millimeter at a time, we obsessively measure, we record everything, and if we've done our job well enough, the story tells itself through the data."

"But what if something is out of place? What if somehow the layers got disturbed? How do you know the datas not all confused and telling a confused story?"

"Cause data-s a lie." He smiled, proud of his yes-and to her grammar joke. May stared at him blankly. Uh oh, he had nerded too hard.

"It's just that the plural is data not—" His already red face flushed even redder. He felt like an ass. This outcome was inevitable when he made the mistake of thinking he could flirt, but he decided to press on through the redness. "Yeah, sometimes it's not at all in the order or layers you'd expect, but that's kind of the point I guess. The disrupting force is as much a part of it as the physical artifacts. The fact that they are disturbed is the story. And disruptions to the normal flow of things always leave some sort of mark, if you know what to look for—fires, earthquakes, droughts, floods, epidemics, wars, genocide—greed—they all leave specific breadcrumbs. We find the people and the animals and the stuff, and then we find the crazy shit that happened to the people and the animals and the stuff; it's all connected, and it's all right here under our feet."

She seemed interested, so he quickly went on, "You can tell when a bone was buried, uncovered, moved, and buried again in a new spot. The remains and the ground around the remains can tell us the story of *what* with 99.99% certainty. But the bone doesn't necessarily tell us *why* it was moved. A piece of wood can tell us where it grew, when it was harvested, that it was doused in fuel, and that it was burned. But it doesn't tell us why it was burned. And we have to be okay with that. Other people get the job of piecing together the why's, but my work is just unearthing the past and saying, here it is."

"Do you ever feel like you should just let it be, though? Just *let the past die*? Do you have to dig it *all* up?" Was this girl quoting *Star Wars?* Either way, he couldn't quite believe his luck. He knew he was smiling too much. But now May was the one who felt like an ass. How could she explain that she wasn't really asking about this sacred site, but about digging up a living past? She was sure she was going crazy. She had to stop trying to talk to strangers about time travel theories.

"Not dig up the past? I mean what if someone gave you the most interesting, compelling book that had ever been written and then told you to read only one chapter in the middle, and it's a chapter written by one old white man. You wouldn't want to flip the pages back and read at least a few of the first 99 chapters? You don't want to read the chapter written by these people?" He held up a delicately painted and only slightly faded shard of porcelain.

He thought he was convincing her of the value of archeology; he couldn't have guessed at the layers she was contemplating. "We have volunteer days if you ever want to come help, or we could go get something to eat."

Now May was the one blushing. It's not that she hadn't realized he was flirting, but she hadn't realized he meant it. Was she going on dates? Was Abee going on dates?

~~~~~~

His name was Jack, and he was actually very fun to go on dates with. May didn't go out of her way not to mention Jack to Abee, but she didn't mention Jack to Abee. It wasn't that hard to not do. She and Abee saw each other less than she'd imagined. It made sense; they were busy. But that wasn't exactly true, was it? Abee invited her to things all the time. They could have been busy together. They could have been busy in the same direction. But May couldn't fight the urge to find her own way.

DUCK DIVE

Listen: "Chinese Translation"
by M. Ward

EIGHT

~~~~~~~~~~

"How the hell are you done already?!" Jack wasn't bothered that May was often smarter, quicker, funnier, generally better than him at things. He was raised reading Emma Goldman, Simone de Beauvoir, and bell hooks. He was just genuinely confused how *anyone* could do it so quickly.

Since their earliest connection over grammar and the philosophy of archeology, things had only gotten more nerdy. They did normal sorts of things together—dinner, movies, schoolwork—but they also created a spreadsheet where they tracked the best dumplings in the city, and every day they competed for the best time on sudoku. The hard level. May always won. Always.

"What can I say? It's like a nine-sided Rubik's Cube. I can just see how it all fits together."

"So you hold the power of the enneract?"

May stared at him blankly. She might be smarter, but he was nerdier. There was a difference.

"It's what a nine-cube is called."

May continued to stare at him blankly. Finally, he realized she was teasing him. He didn't pick up on social cues very quickly.

"I actually have no idea what an enneract is, so I was only kind of joking with that look."

"It's a nine-dimensional hypercube that presents as a sphere in space."

"Coooooollll."

May leaned out of his reach, anticipating a playful squeeze to the side, or jab in the arm. She anticipated correctly. She dodged his first pass. Jack shifted on the couch, putting both his hands in reach of her rib cage. He tickled; she laughed. It was nice, sort of. May wasn't mad about it. But she wasn't ready for it to be more. She slid down to the floor. Time to deflect.

"Sorry, I'm really not making fun of you. I think *you think* that I'm smarter than I really am. But I just got smart like a year ago."

"There's no way that's true, but I'll indulge you. What happened a year ago that got you so smart?"

May squirmed. No one ever tells you how hard it is going to be not to talk about how you moonlight as a time traveler. "I don't know exactly. Abee and I just started reading a lot of stuff, and the more you read the more you want to read, and now here I am doing number puzzles and thinking about how sudoku is a great way to explain quantum entanglement."

Now Jack was the one staring blankly.

"I mean it is! It's like the puzzle exists; it is what it is, but it doesn't reveal itself till you start looking at it. Once you start observing, things show themselves to be in a definite arrangement, but also before you start looking, the same thing exists in an undefined state. A box is '6', but there is a period of time where it exists in this limbo state of being '6' or '2', and it's not until you observe '2' that '6' actually has to be '6' but at the same time it has always been '6'." Jack was tracking, more or less, but he still shook his head in amazement. Who was this girl?

"Do you know that there are over six sextillion possible solutions to a sudoku board, but the vast majority of those have symmetries, so it's really just around five billion unique solutions. That's so much less. That means most solutions have mirrors, twins, duplicates that are the same but flipped and turned. So then are the multitude of solutions just really about perspective? Like it just depends on how you look at it?" May was out of breath.

"You really do hold the power of the enneract."

She was about to dive into her thoughts about the minimum number of given clues necessary to solve a board—it was seventeen. Sixteen clues were not enough to lead the player to a definite outcome. It had to be at least seventeen clues. MIT had tried every possible way to use only sixteen clues, and it never worked. You had to have seventeen given clues to allow the player a chance to actually win. Less than that and there could be multiple right answers, and people don't generally like to play games which only allow you to sort of win.

But May stopped herself, because if she started talking about that, she would want to start talking about how she stayed awake at night wondering if she was working a definite puzzle, if she had enough clues, or if she was working with fewer than seventeen clues and therefore was working a puzzle with multiple right answers. Yeah, she stopped herself from saying more.

DUCK DIVE

Phase Four

WAXING GIBBOUS

YEAR	DATE	TIME
1999	21-Jun	12:49 PM PDT
2000	20-Jun	6:48 PM PDT

YEAR	DATE	TIME
2027	21-Jun	7:10 AM PDT
2028	20-Jun	1:00 PM PDT

Listen: "Einstein's Idea"
by Johnny Flynn

ONE

~~~~~~~~~

MAY 2027 CE

Abee started to get out of the car to go help May with her bags, but before he could open the door she was coming out of the front of her dorm with some guy following behind her. The *some guy* already had the bags. She was walking awkwardly, fast and then slow, and with the guy but ahead of the guy. The driver turned to ask if she was the other passenger. Abee nodded yes.

The driver popped the trunk and Abee watched as the guy offloaded her luggage and then went in for a hug. It was painful to watch. May half hugged back, half pushed him back, and then she was in the back seat with Abee, obviously flustered.

"I didn't know your dorm came with bell boys."

May punched Abee in the arm, and they both relaxed.

"It's my friend Jack. You've heard me talk about Jack." May knew he hadn't.

"Oh yes, Ol' James, how could I forget. Oh that's right, cause you've never mentioned him." Abee could play this game too.

May was going to snap back; she had her response ready before he even spoke. She knew what Abee was going to say, so him actually saying it was just slowing down the conversation she was having with herself at double speed. But May hadn't anticipated that Abee would say *Ol' James* in an English accent, and she hadn't anticipated that it would awaken such a visceral memory. They had spoken in English accents that whole summer, that summer when she first really realized he was her best friend.

What was she doing? Why was she being like this with Abee? May was going to apologize, she really was, but the car stopped again and another rider got in the front passenger seat. The driver took the car's full load as his sign to turn up the music, and before May could say anything, loud 90's rap was taking up every inch of talkable space in the car. She turned, anticipating that Abee would meet her gaze and they could at least share an eye roll. It was nine o'clock in the morning for heaven's sake. But Abee's eyes were locked straight ahead and he was mouthing every word of the song.

Alright. If this is what they were doing, they might as well do it all the way to JFK. May joined him, but out loud. The other passenger started singing too. The driver turned it up even louder. Abee started shout-singing. Ten minutes ago, she had almost had a panic attack, and now she was having a laughing attack. She could—no she would—tell Abee more about Jack later. As she mentally committed to this conversation that she'd been avoiding, she felt a thought, or a question, or a fear, zing across her brain. God. She hoped Abee didn't have something to tell her, too.

~~~~~~

They made it home. The world was warm and happy, and the Vitamin D soaked into May's bones and brain. Jack felt like a distant memory. No need to bring up old memories; they had enough of those to deal with.

Listen: "Chinatown"
by Shakey Graves

TWO

~~~~~~~~~~

JUNE 2027 CE

"Abee, we have to destroy the board. If I am going to stop my mom from dying, and she died when she was out on that board, then the most logical step to take is to get rid of the board."

"I think we've ventured beyond logic."

"Well, if not that, then what? Do I just say— *Hey Mom, I mean Amy, don't ask me how I know, but you're going to die. Could you please try not to do that?* There. Is that better than trying to break a surfboard? I've tried to take it slow. I've tried to move some pebbles, but this is about to be our fifth time Abee, and I don't think we've done anything except be like the time traveling equivalent of dark tourists. We have to make a big move before it's too late."

"May, you know that I agree with you. There's no way this is just random; there's a reason behind all of this, I guess. But what if it's not what we think? What if you don't have to save your mom? What if this is about something else? I've been thinking, and I've got it down to two questions. How do you know your life would be better if your mom was still alive? And what if saving her means that somehow you aren't you anymore? What if by keeping her alive you unalive yourself? We've danced around this question for years now. And we can't anymore. I can't anymore. I'm afraid that we are getting too close. Observing the past is one thing, but you're talking about deliberately altering the past. We've got to say what the worst case scenario is here."

"I think I'm already kind of living the worst case scenario."

"You've got to be kidding me." Abee shook his head in disbelief. "Cause I just, I disagree. People die, May; that's what happens. People die. They just do. That doesn't mean you have to give up your life."

"I know people die, Abee. Don't insult me. I think you're the one who doesn't understand that. You have both your parents. My mom is barely even my mom. But your mom isn't my mom either. I don't have a mom, Abee. She never even knew if I existed."

"That's my point, May. How in the world can we be sure that if you change the past, you will exist—or not?"

"I have to at least try."

"You don't, though. What if we just don't, anymore? What if we stop? Just because we can hop doesn't mean we should, right? We can just stop, May."

"Okay, well what if I don't want to stop? What if I want to try?"

"But why? You have so many people who love you. May, what if my worst-case scenario is losing you? May, what if I love you?"

The conversation had been escalating with every sentence. Now it was on a different plane. A different sonic frequency and she could hear the buzzer louder than ever. Had Abee said *I love you* before? Was he saying it now? May played this weird game with her brain where she pretended like she wasn't sure if he had or not, like she wasn't sure if this was a declaration or not. But she knew with one-hundred percent certainty that those words had never crossed his lips going in her direction before now. Only when the house was completely silent in the middle of the night did she ever let herself stare out into the darkness of her bedroom and imagine she was hearing these words—from him. Immediately her brain tried to rearrange, change his meaning. He loved her like a sister. That's what he meant.

And then Abee was kissing her—so not like a sister. May was kissing him back. It had been a while since they had kissed; she couldn't remember exactly how long. There was the game again. May knew exactly how long it had been, 503 days, or 504, depending on how you counted. Why the pretending? She shook her head to clear out the fog. But the kiss continued and the fog was trapped between them.

"May, I can't lose you."

"Abee, I just found her."

Listen: "If You Need To, Keep Time On Me - Solstice Version"
by Fleet Foxes

THREE

~~~~~~~~~~

JUNE 1999 CE

Abee reluctantly agreed to a plan. They would get to 1999 at 7:10 in the morning. If they knew their parents, which they increasingly did, this would be the perfect time to catch them surfing. Of course they weren't actually sure if Tal and Amy came back to Malibu for the summer of 1999, but if they weren't there for some reason, that might actually make it easier. Maybe they could steal the board and get rid of it, and no one would be the wiser. But that was Plan B. Plan A involved the assumption that they were going to have to create an accident in full view of their parents.

Tal and Amy had in fact come home for the summer and true to form they were out in the waves. They had been out since sunrise, and so by half past seven they were ready for a break. It all seemed too perfect. May could barely see the board under Amy as she rode in on a small set. Tal really had made it the perfect shade of blue. It might all work out better than they could have hoped.

This outcome is what May had been working towards over the past two years. Today, all those mornings, and afternoons, and evenings of surfing alone, when she had promised Abee she wasn't, it was going to pay off. May and Abee obviously didn't have boards with them, except for the magical busted one that was now stashed in the cave, so they'd have to borrow some—and that was the plan.

"We could keep time by you two!" Tal was coming toward them out of the water. The boys high-fived, the girls hugged, and then May dove in.

"Any chance you guys have boards we can borrow? We'll go out with you if you do."

"Heck yeah! We'll go grab 'em." Tal was high on saltwater and adrenaline. He motioned for Abee to come with him. May let out the breath she had been holding. The plan was in motion.

"You're surfing now, that's awesome!" Amy offered May some of the grapes she was snacking on. May politely shook her head no; her stomach was in knots.

"I took your advice on that, too. Definitely worth the risk."

~~~~~~

The boys were back. Abee had executed his part. He told Tal that May preferred a shortboard. And he, well he liked both, but today felt like a shortboard day for Abee, too. So they were back with two shortboards in tow.

Would Amy be pissed? Would Tal be pissed? Would it be hella awkward after May "accidentally" destroyed the board? Probably.

Tal moved to hand May the shortboard. May hesitated in accepting. It was all part of the plan. "I actually haven't ever gotten to spend much time on a longboard, but I'd like to—." May spoke with a slight tremble in her voice, partly intentional; she didn't want it to seem like she had rehearsed that line a hundred times, but partly it was an inevitable byproduct of the shakiness she felt inside. "So could I actually try out your board for a bit?" May looked at Amy. May knew it was a bold ask. Boards were very personal, this one more so than most. But May had to try.

Amy didn't hesitate. "Of course, it's all yours! Walk up that way with Tal. The waves will be better for you up there, and he can help you if you need it. We'll—" she nodded to Abee, "catch some of these on the south end, they are better for the shortboards."

The waves in 1999 broke in the same ways they did in 2027. Plan A was going, well, it was going according to plan.

FOUR

~~~~~~~~~~

JUNE 1999 CE

"What are the chances you two are actually twins, separated at birth?" The sand was still cool on their feet as they walked up the beach. Tal was making conversation.

"It does seem like it might be the most probable explanation, doesn't it?" Definitely more believable than time travel, May didn't add.

"I was actually a twin."

May stopped walking. She didn't know that about Tal. Of course Tal didn't expect Mel to know that, but why didn't *May* know that?

"I had a twin brother. He didn't make it. I never even knew him, technically. But I still miss him. I can still feel that he's gone. No one ever told me as much, but it must have been my fault. I think I was too much, too big."

May had never seen Tal so serious, so sad. Why was he telling her this, now? Tal tried to shake the pain off his face.

"All that to say," Tal regained his composure, "I've read a lot about twins over the years. I don't talk about it much; it's not like the coolest thing about me." He grinned sheepishly, as if to acknowledge the odd choice of bringing this up to her, here, now.

"There's no way that's your fault, like in any culpable sort of way." May's words sounded like something Abee would say. Tal shrugged.

"Being a secret nerd though, that definitely is my fault. My favorite twin story is the one about Castor and Pollux."

May shook her head; she didn't know it.

"The story of Gemini, the twins" Tal said, like that explained everything. Now May was the one to shrug. "Castor and Pollux were half-brothers, same mother but different fathers. No big deal, except that Zeus was the father of Pollux, making him immortal, and Castor just had a normal dad, meaning he was mortal. One day the two boys get in a dust up with Idas and Lynceus, and Castor gets mortally wounded. Pun intended. But before Castor gets slashed up too badly, he calls out and warns Pollux that their enemies are at hand. Despite the warning, and despite his immortality, the fight progresses and things aren't going well for Pollux either. At the last second Zeus swoops in with a thunderbolt and saves his son, Pollux. Pollux then runs to his dying brother and Zeus offers him a deal. Pollux can keep all of his immortality for himself and live forever on Mt. Olympus with the gods or he can give half of his immortality to his brother, and sort of keep him from dying."

May scrunched up her forehead.

"Yeah the details don't really make sense, but the point is, Pollux opts to share his immortality to save his dying brother and then he and Castor are forever linked. They spend half of their time in Hades, fulfilling Castor's mortal death obligations, and then they get to go spend half their time on Olympus being immortal."

May shook her head, not quite believing what she was hearing.

"I'm a Gemini," May blurted out.

"Of course you are." Tal smiled.

~~~~~~

"Another weird thing about me—" Tal called out over the waves, "is that I can't drown."

The waves had gotten bigger. May heard him, but barely.

"I came out with the amniotic sac still intact. I was born, but I was still in the water, just breathing away like a little fish. When that happens, legend says you can't ever drown. I like to remind myself of that legend on days like this."

What he was saying felt important. But navigating these big waves with this big board felt more important.

"You okay over there?" Tal called out.

May responded, but he couldn't hear her. They were following an imaginary arc as they paddled out. Swimming straight would have been suicide. The bulging curve of the shore and the natural rocky break that jutted out to the north, created giant waves which seemed to come in diagonally, though it was really just a matter of perspective, May reminded herself. But nonetheless May had learned that you had to swim around the waves and get behind them to have any chance of riding them, hence the paddling out in what felt like a circuitous route. May knew exactly how to do it, but she followed behind Tal as if he was showing her the way.

Once in position, behind the breaks, they sat and waited, noses pointed toward the rocks. It was unnerving every time she did this maneuver. It looked like you planned to surf into the mouth of a dragon, and if you didn't have control of your board, you just might. But executed correctly, you could catch a wave that simultaneously took you in and away from the rocks.

"You take the next one," Tal shouted.

"I'd rather watch you do it first," May shouted back.

Tal said something that May couldn't quite hear, but his gestures told her that he was protesting. She waved her arms for him to go on anyway. Tal squared his shoulders, eyes on the waves that were building to his left, and then he was off, and up, and an ocean away.

May didn't like lying to him, so she did her best to watch him, like she said she would, not that he'd ever know one way or the other. As May watched, she also worked her way to the back of the board and deftly unattached the end of the leash from the plug. She wasn't connected to the board anymore, but if anyone was watching, all they would see was the leash still strapped to her ankle, just like it should be, and the cord dangling down into the water, just like it always was.

May let a few waves pass. They weren't big enough. She needed one that could throw the most power possible at this board. But if she waited much longer, he would be back out and would be too close. May had to go. She paddled; the wave was bigger than she'd even hoped for. She was up. She had to make it look spontaneous, accidental, unfortunate. She had to make a jump look like a wipeout. May couldn't see him; she hoped he couldn't see her. She moved forward, almost imperceptibly, forcing the nose to catch and buck. As May jumped, she pushed the board back in the direction of the rocks.

In a normal bail or wipeout, the leash would catch within two seconds, and while you'd be shook, you and your board could live to surf again. But with no rider to maneuver the thing and no leash to catch the thing, the board would almost certainly find its way to the rocks where it would be bashed over and over again. And you can't surf a board that ends up in ten different pieces, and you can't die on a board you can't surf.

Listen: "Hell N Back"
by Bakar

FIVE

~~~~~~~~~

JUNE 1999 CE

The board was gone, but May was stuck in a bad set. Just as soon as she figured out which way was up and managed to take a breath, the next wave was on top of her, pulling her back and down. And then repeat. The board, the only thing May had been able to think about for so long, was now completely out of her mind. All she could think of was how to get unstuck. There was a rip current in the mix, complicating things even more. On a normal stretch of beach you just have to swim parallel to the shore to get out of the flow of the invisible river. But here, stuck in the curves and chaos, it was almost impossible to discern which way to go, not that she had much strength left to make it happen anyway. This had not been part of the plan. She'd be happy to let the rip take her farther out. She could regroup and at least breathe, but this particular iteration had mushed big barrels on top of the strong outward pull, and she was losing ground. And then, showing up like a thunderbolt from the heavens, a strong arm pulled her out of the chaos.

~~~~~~

The sand was warm now. Or maybe it was just that May felt so cold. She opened her eyes. They were all there. Abee looked terrified. Tal looked shocked. Amy looked like a mom, concerned but present, and warm, and capable. May had some gashes on her legs; she was shaking, but her eyes were open and she was breathing clearly. Abee wrapped her in a towel. Amy held her hand. Tal kept apologizing. Then they all sat in silence for a while, maybe two minutes, maybe ten.

Finally, May broke in. "I am so sorry you guys. I did not mean for that to happen." The board was still gone from her mind, so she was genuine in her apology. She did not mean to almost drown. "And Tal, you don't need to apologize at all. None of that was your fault. You rescued me. I don't even know what to say. Thank you doesn't seem like enough."

There was a pause, and then Tal spoke slowly and softly. "That wasn't me."

~~~~~~

Some twerps had been hogging the waves at the south end of Zuma. Amy said they should bail and go see how the other two were doing. Abee tried to dissuade her. Part of the plan was to keep Amy away, the fewer eyes on the incident the better. But Amy was in no mood to put up with a crew of annoying thirteen-year-old boys. Abee tried to stall, but she didn't seem to care how fast he was or wasn't going. By the time they got close enough to see, the aftermath had begun.

Tal was stuck in the chaos of the rocks. He had put his eyes on May, he really had, and he had judged that she was fine; she just had to take the waves in, no big deal. And then he put his eyes on the board; it was headed for the rocks; it wasn't fine; he had to try and save it. Before he got to it, the rocks had taken a bite out of the tail, and the fins were smashed, but the board was in one piece, more or less. He didn't recognize he had misjudged the situation until it was too late.

Abee and Amy went for May. Abee was a strong swimmer, but Amy was fast and lithe and swam at an almost supernatural speed. Amy assessed the direction of the rip, watched the rhythm of the waves, and then dove in like a deus ex machina and pulled May out of the water.

~~~~~~

Tal ran his fingers over the jagged break. He wanted to take a hammer to it and finish the job. It mocked him. He was so embarrassed, ashamed. Someone had almost died because he had gone after this piece of junk. If Amy hadn't been there, well he couldn't even think about that. No one ever said they blamed him. People rarely came out and said those sorts of things, but Tal felt it.

Tal was only repairing the board because Amy had begged him to. It was a symbol of resilience and teamwork; that's how she tried to spin it. He'd fix it because that's what Amy wanted, and he would do anything for her, but he didn't feel good about it.

Tal sanded and filled the holes and dings, rebuilt the tail, put on new fins. Fixing it took almost as much time as when he first built it. Maybe if he hadn't been so angry with himself, or maybe if he had just had a few more years of experience, he would have been able to feel the minute stress crack about half-way down the board. Or if he had managed to take the board out in the water himself he would have been able to feel the way the now over extended stringer left the board feeling dead. But he couldn't feel it, and he couldn't imagine taking it out again, and so no one knew that he had just patched a ticking time bomb.

~~~~~~

Abee couldn't believe he had let himself be talked into such a ridiculous plan. Hadn't they decided one small move at a time was the best way forward? Wasn't that how you got out of the loop? Abee was beginning to wonder if May was really trying to find a way out or just a way to blow it all up.

Listen: "August (Acoustic)"
by flipturn

SIX

~~~~~~~~~~

EXHIBIT "C"

Computer Scientists had been aware of the looming issue since the 1950's, and then in 1971 someone finally felt confident enough to speak about it publicly. They were being short sighted in their computer programming. Yes, everyone understood the practical limitations, storing four digits worth of information took up a lot more memory than just storing two digits. In the computing world, memory is money, so why make the computer remember *1978* when *78* works too, and it's cheaper. Well, because that plan only works until it doesn't.

The Y2K scare, the year 2000 problem, the millennium bug, there were lots of clever names for it. But the fear was real. When the clocks switched from 11:59 p.m. on December 31, 1999 to 12:00 a.m. on January 1, 2000, would the computers understand correctly what year it was? Or would the computers interpret that 00 as 1900? Would automatically generated daily bus schedules be thrown back to a time when buses didn't even exist? Would banking systems try to calculate a hundred years of interest in reverse? Would the war machines that kept missiles, nuclear plants, and defense systems in check, go on the fritz and unleash violence upon the world?

What if the computers insisted it was 1900? Could you blame them if that was what they had been programmed to understand? Is there some possible dystopian future in which humans have to bend to the will of the computers and accept time as whatever the computers say it is? Isn't that kind of what was already happening, but just swap *computer* for *Emperor* or *Pope*?

Maybe.

But Y2K came and went, and the world didn't explode. Some people say a catastrophe was diverted by the hundreds of billions of dollars that were thrown at the problem in the last few years of the twentieth century. Others speculate that the hype was manufactured for the benefit of those who took in the hundreds of billions of dollars.

Maybe.

Amy watched the hype build with mild interest, but she had the growing sense that the years mattered a lot less than the days. There was the day when the moon was gone from the sky, and then there was the day when the small fingernail of it came back, and then it grew, every night. The moon never got tired, and then before you knew it, it was as big as it could possibly be. Amy knew it wasn't one of her better tendencies, but sometimes she would look at the full moon and she'd feel sad, because she knew that tomorrow it would start shrinking. It had worked so hard to get there, full of light, but it never got to stay that way.

Listen: "Astrovan"
by Mt. Joy

SEVEN

~~~~~~~~~~

JUNE 2028 CE

"When I'm ready to get a real job, I can get a real job." Abee was yelling from the bathroom. May felt annoyed, with the fact that he was talking to her while he was going to the bathroom and with his glib declaration of privilege, but she knew he was right, so the anger felt wasted. At the very least there would always be Duck's. They both had that privilege.

Abee walked back into her room, still drying his hands on his pants as he talked. "Did you know that every five years the number of living Holocaust survivors decreases by half? My Zayde was born in the last days of the war, and if he were still alive he'd be in his mid 80's. In the next fifteen years or maybe twenty at the absolute most, they will all be gone. We've got to make one last big effort to get all of the stories. Meredith is the auteur and the technical genius, but she's not Jewish, May. She needs me."

May knew Abee wanted her to act excited for him, and she was, in theory. She just couldn't believe they were still here, unsure of what they were or weren't, still talking about Meredith. At least they didn't need to talk about Jack any more. May had avoided that conversation with Abee, the one she promised herself she would have a year ago. She had avoided it by slowly but surely avoiding Jack, and Jack wasn't stupid. As much as Jack liked May, and as much as he was afraid that he'd never meet someone else quite like her, or another girl who would put up with someone quite like him, Jack finally had the courage to call it like he saw it. May was in love with someone else.

"I don't have to head out until July, so I won't miss, well you know." Even after all these years they fumbled through what to call it. Every word or phrase they tried always sounded weirder than the one before.

~~~~~~

JUNE 2000 CE

May was worried. After the debacle of last year's plan, she was back to having no idea what to do—about any of it. They left abruptly last year. Everyone had been cordial at the time, but maybe with the benefit of a year to ponder the weird day, Amy and Tal might feel less warm about it all. This year was an afternoon hop; it was the perfect timing, but the gloom still hung thick—in both years. No one was there to greet them on the beach. No one was really there at all. May and Abee walked up the stairs and headed to Duck's, without even saying it.

Then there was someone yelling at them, in the parking lot, from a bright yellow VW Bug. She was calling out to them, more than actually yelling, but the effect was the same. They turned. Gloria was waving them over.

"Any chance you two travelers want to go for a ride today?"

Abee and May exchanged an apprehensive glance.

"It's just that my two sous-chefs are out of town and we've got a big wedding coming up."

May and Abee exchanged another apprehensive glance.

"Oh no no no, it's not them getting married. Not yet. We don't know these people, and I can't tell you their names, but I can say that she's a really good *friend*, and the guy, well he has two *rules* about his club." Gloria winked. May got the first reference, Abee got the second; together, they understood the gist of what she was getting at. This was a big wedding.

"Alright, well we're here for the afternoon. What can we do to help?" May offered with a shrug. Gloria's warmth was starting to make them both feel better.

"I've got to go talk to our lobster guy, and I wouldn't hate having some company."

"How long will it take?"

"Tuesday afternoon getting to San Pedro...probably an hour there, an hour haggling with the guy, and an hour back?"

May and Abee shared a third apprehensive glance. They had never left the area during a hop. It should be fine, but what if there was a bubble they weren't supposed to pop? This time Abee shrugged and they both hopped in the car. Abee and his long legs up front, May and her not so long legs in the back.

Five hours and two-hundred negotiated lobsters later, they were in Malibu again. Abee's shirt was soaked through. May no longer had any fingernails. They had a stressful, wonderful time. Gloria sensed they didn't have time to come up for dinner. She could also sense the gloom that seemed stuck to them today.

"It's such a treat to spend time with you two, I really mean it. Thank you for coming with me." Gloria paused, not a pause of hesitation, but a pause for effect. "Not that you asked for my advice, but be good to each other; be patient with each other; it'll all be okay. You know what they say: everything's okay in the end, and if it's not okay—"

Abee interrupted, "that's okay."

Listen: "Goodbye Mr. Blue"
by Father John Misty

EIGHT

~~~~~~~~~~

DECEMBER 2000 CE

Gloria always called the summer months *fast time* and the winter months *slow time*. She despised slow time, aka standard time, aka sad time. On the west coast, in the depths of the winter season—not that you would ever know it was winter from the weather—without an assist from daylight-saving time, the sun sets as early as 4:50 p.m. There is no evening; there is just day and night. And the nights move slowly.

Gloria always asked what good it was to have a beachfront view if the sun couldn't come out to play. It was too much darkness for Gloria. And it was on one of those dark nights, about a week before Christmas, that Gloria felt the first lump. The restaurant had been packed that night, as it always was around the holidays. She had been helping the food runners. Her arms were tired and sore now as she sank back into the bathtub. But this lump—it was in her armpit, edging toward her left breast, she pressed its edges with her index and middle finger—this was not a strained muscle.

Gloria always assumed this day would come, but she still wanted more time.

DUCK DIVE

Phase Five

FULL

YEAR	DATE	TIME
2001	21-Jun	12:38 AM PDT

YEAR	DATE	TIME
2029	20-Jun	6:47 PM PDT

DUCK DIVE

Listen: "The Wind Cries Mary"
by Jimi Hendrix

ONE

~~~~~~~~~~

EXHIBIT "D"

Kalanchoe delagoensis, commonly known as Mother of Millions, is a fast growing succulent plant. It replicates through the prolific development of small plantlets along its leaf edges. The plantlets drop from the mother plant and begin their journey to becoming mothers themselves in the soil at the borders of her reach. Or for some little plantlets, a strong gust of wind or a wandering passerby might take them farther away from their mother than they ever could have imagined.

A human female fetus develops reproductive organs by twenty weeks in utero. At this early stage of development the fetus has six to seven million unmatured eggs inside of her. There is the mother, there is the female fetus in utero, and then there are six to seven million eggs inside the growing fetus. Mother, daughter, and the possibility of millions—three generations occupying the same body, at the same moment. Like a mother—or grandmother—of millions.

At birth, a baby girl's reproductive system has already absorbed most of the six to seven million eggs that were initially present, and one million immature eggs remain. The female body continues pruning and absorbing the lot, and by the time a young girl has her first period there are around 400,000 left. In the 30-50 years that a female has between first menstruation and the final pause of menstruation, between 300 and 500 of those 400,000 eggs will actually have a chance to make the journey from the ovary, into the fallopian tube, and then to the uterus. What fate awaits the egg in the uterus is a whole other story.

Seven million — one million — 400,000 — 500 — and in the 21st century the average female in America will give birth to one or two children.

There was a moment where your mother's mother held the possibility of you inside of her. And for 40 weeks, give or take, what happened to your grandmother, happened to your mother, happened to you.

There were some things about her Nonna that May needed to figure out.

FULL

Listen: "Santa Monica"
by Everclear

TWO

~~~~~~~~~

JUNE 2001 CE

Gloria didn't tell Gene right away. She wanted to know what she was dealing with before she worried him. But the doctor only told her what she already knew. It was cancer, and it was spreading—quickly. Some of the words the doctor said sounded vaguely familiar—metastatic, chemotherapy, stage IV, mastectomy—some words were new—Breast Cancer Gene 1, Breast Cancer Gene 2, positive—none of it was a surprise, but she wasn't sure why.

Isaac knew the best doctors—*his colleagues.* He knew the right questions to ask— *did Gloria have a family history of breast cancer?* Isaac knew it wouldn't go on for long—*a couple of years, probably not more than five.* Isaac owed Gene and Gloria his life. He would do anything for them, but he couldn't stop this from happening to them. They didn't tell Amy and Tal—not yet. No need to disrupt their semester. They'd be home soon enough.

Gloria was tough. No one ever dreamed of saying differently. But she felt what was happening in her body. The treatment was good at getting rid of her hair, but not the cancer. Fighting was the last thing she wanted now. She wanted to be soft and slow with herself. She wore a bright yellow beanie when the house was drafty, or a green paisley scarf when the sun was bright. But in the mornings when it wasn't too cold or too hot, and the beach wasn't too dark or too sunny, she walked up and down shore and let the salty air sink into her bare skin.

She was out on one of these walks when the kids came home. They'd taken a red-eye. Isaac poured them coffee. Gene started to explain. Isaac took over when Gene couldn't say anymore. As far as Tal was concerned, Gloria was his mother too, but he let Amy go to her first. Amy found Gloria out on the beach. They stood at the spot where the water just barely licks at the sand, and their feet slowly sank in, deeper and deeper. Amy hadn't held her mother's hand in years. It hadn't seemed necessary. Now, she forced her fingers through her mother's and only let go when their feet got deep enough and the waves got bold enough to knock them over.

Everyone wanted to believe that *years* was a real possibility, but Gloria knew it was *months*. And Gloria wanted to go out with a bang. Gene and Amy begged her not to talk that way, but she got the party she wanted all the same—a solstice bonfire. Duck's closed for the day. Amy put a sign on the door inviting everyone down to the beach.

Calling all Ducks
Dive on in
We bake the clams
You bring the drinks
The sun makes the magic
Today June 20
Zuma Beach

Gene got the fires going as soon as the sun was up. By lunch the potluck-picnic to end all potluck-picnics filled the space between the water and the cliffs. Gloria worked the beach like it was a reverse receiving line. She visited each blanket, and every umbrella, played frisbee, and jumped in the waves. Her thin body, expertly tied scarf, and flattened chest told the beginning of a story, but her joy finished it. No one felt sorry for Gloria that day; she was writing a good ending. The only sadness came with the thought of going on without her.

Gloria hadn't worked out exactly *when* they were coming from, but it seemed like they always showed up about five or six hours before the solstice. Solstice was going to be a few minutes past 12:30 tonight. The sun would be long gone by that point. It felt perfectly poetic. She had chased the sun as far as she could. Now it was time to let it go.

Gloria hadn't ever worked out exactly *where* they were coming from either, but it seemed like they came from around El Matador and made their way along the coast to get to Point Dume. That's why she asked for the party to be at Zuma. They wouldn't be able to miss them.

A little before 7:30 that evening, May, or Mel as the others called her, and Josh came walking down the beach. Gloria knew to call him Josh. But she also knew that obviously wasn't his real name. What was obvious was that he was Talmai's son. He was also obviously *not* Amy's child. There were some chapters coming that Gloria didn't understand and couldn't even guess at. It was probably best that way.

Gloria had set back two heaping bowls for them. Gloria hugged them tighter than she ever had before. They tucked in around one of the fires. Amy and Tal would be back in a few minutes, she said. May spotted them walking in tandem, a three-tier-bright-yellow-sunburst of a pineapple cake between them. They held it in front of Gloria. Tal lit three sparklers that started shooting out of the top of the cake like it was a beautiful volcano. May couldn't tell if it was planned or spontaneous, but Grandpa Gene took Gloria's hands and started singing their wedding song. May wondered why he had never told her this part of the story.

May worked it over in her head a million times. Gloria would be gone by Christmas. This was it. But this had always been it. May had loved her Nonna before she even knew her. Now she knew her and loved her even more. May had found some old doctor's reports in Grandpa Gene's files. Combined with a few details from Elise, May pieced together the severity of the situation. The doctors did everything they could with the knowledge and technology available to them at the time, but it wasn't enough. If it had been 20 years later, they would have known more; they would have had more options, but sometimes the time really just is the time it is, and there is no getting around it. There was nothing to warn her about; Gloria knew as well as May did what was going to happen next. And short of dropping a stack of studies in Isaac's lap—about developments in triple-negative breast cancer therapies, along with an explanation of what triple-negative even meant, and how you determined it—years or even decades before he would learn this information otherwise, May had to accept that it was going to happen. As May ate the cake and stared into the fire, she kept thinking, on repeat, *this is the part where Gloria dies.*

Had she moved any pebbles in Gloria's life? Or Amy's for that matter? It felt like the mountain was as big as it ever was. What if Gloria knew about Amy—that once Gloria died, the clock would start ticking on what was coming for Amy? In any universe could that ending be helpful for a mother to know? May wasn't sure about any universe, but in this one, she didn't have it in her to say it.

Gloria didn't ask any questions when May and Josh said they had to leave about 30 minutes before the group was going to ring in solstice with a few more fireworks. Gloria knew it would take them a while to walk back up to Broad or El Matador, whatever secluded spot they were coming from. Gloria considered following them. Maybe if she could see it with her own eyes, maybe she could learn something about something and it would make some sort of difference, but the night was deeply dark. The sky was giving birth to a new moon. *It's funny,* Gloria thought as she watched them disappear into the veil of darkness, *new life starts out looking like death.*

Listen: "Change"
by Big Thief

THREE

~~~~~~~~~~

The next morning, while Amy was showering off the day before, Gloria slipped into her room and placed one last message in between the pages of the *Aquarius*. Well actually two—one from her and one she wanted to pass on.

Whatever the early parts of her life had been, the haze surrounding them never cleared. If anything, as time went on, the fog started to sink into areas that she knew she used to be sure of. She remembered there was a Diedre in the life she had before she met Gene. But now the name Diedre was just a remembrance of a kind voice, but not a face, and she must have been a kind friend, but now she was gone. Gloria remembered her in essence, but not in fullness, and even the essence was starting to fade.

June 20, 2001
My Darling May,

I barely understand my own story. I won't presume to understand yours. But I'm thankful our stories have become intertwined. I'll spare you the platitudes; there's no time for that, but I do need you to know two things; you are loved and you are not alone—except for those times when you want to be. We all get to just sit with ourselves sometimes.

And one more thing—we are so so proud of you. Close your eyes and feel that in your chest. Your mother and I are right there, and we are so proud of you. You are the best of us. We live on in you, and that's all we need. The next page is a letter from someone very dear to me, and now I pass it to you.

See you in the sun,
Gloria Lahaina Rossi
P.S. I didn't know I'd get to choose my grandma name this soon, but I think I'd like to be Nonna Lola.

FULL

Listen: "God Is Just the Universe"
by Corey Kilgannon

FOUR

~~~~~~~~~~

AUGUST 2001 CE

Amy scooped up a handful of sand and then let it trickle out between her fingers. It was a quintessential Malibu day. Tal was sprawled out on a towel next to her, wetsuit pulled down to his waist, his chest soaking up the last bits of summer's sun.

"You know I love you right?" Amy wiped her hand on his towel. Tal flipped his head to look at her. Why'd he have to be so handsome? She'd better say it quickly. "I want to stay here. I can't go back. I need to be where she is."

Tal sat up—using only his abs, Amy noticed. Then, he shifted so that he was kneeling, but like a giant in child's pose. He leaned forward to cup her face between his hands. "Then, I'll stay too."

Amy was shaking her head *no* before she even knew she was doing it. His hands moved with her. The shaking made the tears zig-zag across her face. His hands caught them as they tried to fall.

"Tal, I don't want you to stop your world. I want you to go back and keep studying and making friends and living your life. I need you to keep going so that when I'm ready to come back, there's something to come back to. I need you to make a new life for us, a life that can keep me from getting sucked into the black hole that's going to come when she—is gone."

Tal was shaking his whole body *no.* "You don't have to do this alone. I love her too."

"I know you do. But she's not your mom, Tal."

Tal pulled back. Amy froze. She hadn't meant for that to come out.

DUCK DIVE

Listen: "I'm Not My Season - Solstice Version"
by Fleet Foxes

FIVE

~~~~~~~~~~

OCTOBER 2001 CE

Gloria spent that fall getting ready. She filled the freezer with trays of meatballs, they were Gene's favorite, and cinnamon rolls, they were Amy's favorite. Gloria went through every picture she could find and wrote notes on the backs, trying to solidify anything she knew for sure about what her life had been. She marked up her poetry books one last time, and every evening she sat on the shore and watched Amy surf. When it got too dark they'd go home and drink coffee that kept them up too late. The doctors told her to watch her caffeine intake. She didn't listen. They didn't watch tv anymore, not after the towers fell. But they did puzzles and they listened to records, and when Gloria had to start keeping to her bed, Amy read to her.

Listen: "La Lune"
by Billie Marten

SIX

~~~~~~~~~~

NOVEMBER 2029 CE

May threw the blankets off like they were attacking her and sat up straight and stiff, trying to catch her breath. She had heard a crack or a rip, not a bang though; it was different from the bangs that filled life here. Were there earthquakes in New York? Surely not. A thunderstorm in November? That felt ominous. May slid off the end of her lofted bed, carefully navigating the puzzle which was her miniature dorm room. She pulled the blinds back and stuck her head right up against the window. She couldn't see any stars—you never could—but it was unquestionably a clear night. No storm. Even more ominous. May looked at her phone. 4:44 a.m. And there it was again, but it wasn't a sound; it was a sense. Crack. Break. Rip.

Maybe it was just because she knew that Gloria had died 28 years ago today, but she had always known that, and she'd never felt it before. November 13, 2001 in the early hours of the morning, or the middle of the night. Grandpa Gene had been in bed next to her. He cried every time he told the story. He wasn't exactly sure when she had passed, but when he woke up, her fingers were woven between his and she was gone.

If May had to guess, she'd probably say Gloria must have passed at 1:44 a.m., on the west coast that is. Gloria was gone, but she was more present with May than ever.

~~~~~~

NOVEMBER 2001 CE

It was a cool November morning when Tal got the call. Gloria surely would have preferred a summer's day, but she didn't get a say in the matter this time. Tal flew home three days later. He could only stay for the weekend, though; his professors offered make-up tests if there was an emergency involving an immediate family member. Immediate family member—no exceptions. But what if your mom left and the lady from next door raised you? He needed someone to explain what that relationship qualified as, because apparently it wasn't what he thought.

The morning of the service Tal washed Amy's hair in the sink. He helped her get into her dress. Gloria didn't want anyone wearing boring dark colors, so she bought a sunflower print shift for Amy and matching yellow linen shirts for Gene, Isaac, and Tal. It was a good idea in theory, but the attempt at happiness looked ridiculous on them.

Tal went back to New York on Sunday night and kept working to make a life for Amy, but they both underestimated the voracity of the black hole that came for her after all.

FULL

SEVEN

~~~~~~~~~~

DECEMBER 2029 CE

The car was warm, but not too warm. Just the kind of warm that makes you want to push the seat back and take a nap. But the seats in the bus didn't recline, so it was mostly just warm.

"The first time I came to LA, it was your mom who picked us up. Believe it or not, driving around here was even crazier back then. But there was your mom, driving your Nonna's old yellow bug, and it was the most California thing I could ever have imagined. Until today, that is." Elise gave May something between a smile and a smirk.

Elise was very aware of what was going on. Abee and Meredith could have gotten a car from the airport, but May had come up with a story about how Shep needed her to go get some things at the commercial supply store in El Segundo anyway. The supply store delivered; it had for over twenty years, but Elise didn't argue. And they could have come in Elise's brand new G Wagen, with literal massage chairs for seats, but here they were in the 1973 Saturn yellow bus with no air conditioning. Meredith would be on May's turf from the moment she entered their world. Elise wasn't stupid.

"Abee tells me they're just friends...coworkers even—" Elise purposely let her statement hang, unfinished, to see what May might add. May didn't bite. Elise tried again. "What does he tell you?" Elise waited.

"She doesn't come up much."

"I wonder why that is?"

May wasn't stupid either, she knew these weren't just casual cell-phone lot ponderings. The springs in her seat creaked under her as she shifted to look directly at Elise. May was slightly annoyed, but mostly glad that they could talk like this.

"To answer your real question...I'm not sure, probably because he's not my brother, but sometimes he is. He's not my boyfriend, but sometimes he is. He's not mine, but sometimes I want him to be." May paused. "Okay, most of the time I want him to be." May paused again. "But it wouldn't ever really work, would it?

How would we ever know if we really loved each other because we wanted to or just because we always have?"

Now Elise paused for a moment. "I don't think that's how love works, May. If love is obligatory, it's not love. I think that's called duty. Are you two bound by duty or love? Sure, there is duty in love, and love can flow out of duty, but whichever comes first tints it all. And if it's love, if it's love first, May, well then a long love is the best kind."

A long love sounded nice.

"What if we try? What if we jump all in and really try, like make it an official sort of trying, but we mess it up? What then?"

Elise ignored the second part of her question. "I don't think you'd have to try that hard."

But he had; May knew that Abee had been trying for years, trying to figure out who he was to her. He had been so patient, maybe too patient. Abee had tried to tell her about the shot clock, and May had just shut him up with a kiss and then kept him at a comfortable distance. She wasn't a child anymore, and the time for excuses was done. It was time to stop pretending like it would just magically happen someday. And if May was really honest with herself, she had to recognize that they'd actually had quite a bit of magic dropped in their laps already. If May was waiting for a sign from the universe, she was lying to herself, because the signs had been in neon and they had been everywhere. May had been stalling. She had been asking for extra time-outs. She had been hogging the ball. Whatever, she didn't know basketball, but she knew the ball was in her court. It had been for a long time. But it wasn't too late. The game wasn't over.

Their phones buzzed simultaneously.

On the curb.

~~~~~~

The bus was not a subtle machine. It was loud, in every sense of the world. But Abee and Meredith didn't seem to notice. Their eyes and ears and hands and mouths were—distracted.

Elise took in a sharp breath.

May let out a low groan.

It sounded like a buzzer.

Time was up.

FULL

Listen: "I Contain Multitudes"
by Bob Dylan

EIGHT

~~~~~~~~~~

DECEMBER 2001 CE

Gene drank his martini in one gulp and then stared at Jimmy's face. It was generally frowned upon to just stare at another person's face. But you could get away with it if the person was the love of your life or a statue. He had always loved to stare at Gloria's face. But now there was just Jimmy left. He was beautiful and his eyes were sad. Was he eternally looking to the horizon, longing for his mother, or Pier, or Marlon? Maybe all three.

The gin found its way to the spot in his chest that ached, and Gene relaxed just a bit, but not enough. He pulled a flask from his jacket pocket, and then he relaxed a lot. Gene leaned forward and stared more deeply into the dark bronze eyes; he knew them so well. If eyes really were the window to the soul, then these eyes contained multitudes. And all of a sudden he was pushing himself back and away from the table. Whether it was the recognition of the shape, or the recognition of the distant sadness, he was never quite sure, but in that moment Gene realized he was staring into Gloria's own eyes. Of course she had formed herself into this creation. For 28 years Gene had stared into her eyes, and now to realize they weren't gone, not really. He might never leave this room.

It wasn't uncommon to have strangers wander into his house and his kitchen back in the day. But Gloria wasn't like the other strangers. She had come up next to him at the stove, swiped her finger through the chowder, and declared correctly that the roux had split. Gene knew it had, but he didn't know how to fix it, and he couldn't afford to start over with a hoard of hungry and high hippies waiting out on the deck. But Gloria did know how to fix it. Somehow she always knew how to make things better. What in the world was he going to do without her?

There was no falling in love for Gene. It just was. Gloria wasn't there, and then she was, and he loved her. Gloria was never reluctant with him. She wasn't hiding anything; that much was clear, but that was about all that was clear. Gloria had lived in Malibu in the past; she swore it, and she had a best friend named Diedre.

But Diedre was nowhere to be found, and one day on their way back from Market Basket, when Gloria told Gene to take a quick right, and then another right, and then a left, and when they got to the spot where she said to pull over, a dirt lot was all that the side quest had to offer them. Gloria sat there and just stared at the patch of earth, at it, and beyond it. She shook her head. She said that she knew the place, she knew she did, she had lived here. *Lived here, in an empty field*, Gene asked. She must have been confused, she decided. And that was the first time Gene saw it in her eyes. Gloria knew things that she'd never be able to tell him about. He knew from the very beginning that this was part of the deal.

But what Gene hadn't known was that in the deepest parts of the night—those hours when you swear the whole world has stopped and the darkness and the delirium are thick—that in those parts of the night all deals were abandoned. Gloria laughed and moaned and cried. She talked to Diedre and she cried out for Diedre. She fought off a known but unnamed abuser, and then she surrendered and quietly wept as the blows came, one after the other. Gene tried to wake her, to save her from the torment. But when she opened her dark eyes, she had no sense of why he was waking her. And as soon as she returned to sleep, the strange world would return with her. So when her dream world shifted from light to dark, Gene learned to just take her hand and hold it through the night. Gloria loved waking up every morning to find their hands intertwined. She never asked why, afraid of the answer, and Gene never told her.

That last night, Gloria's last night, the nightmares had never come. Gene's cue to take her hand had never come. When he realized he was awake simply because the sun was dancing across his face, a panic gripped his chest. Like the mother of a newborn waking from a much needed sleep only to be immediately afraid of why she was given such an unimaginable gift. As the adrenaline turned on all of his senses, all at once, he immediately heard and felt the truth of the morning. The small whistle of her nose was silent; the puff of her cheeks was void. And then Gene felt her fingers, locked around his own. Gloria had found her way to him, but now her hand was cold.

Phase Six

WANING GIBBOUS

YEAR	DATE	TIME
2002	21-Jun	6:24 AM PDT
2003	21-Jun	12:10 PM PDT

YEAR	DATE	TIME
2030	21-Jun	12:30 AM PDT
2031	21-Jun	6:16 AM PDT

DUCK DIVE

Listen: "the sum of the in-between"
by Maria Kelly

ONE

~~~~~~~~~~

JUNE 2030 CE

May's phone buzzed in her back pocket. It better be him. It was Meredith.

> *Hey, it's actually me*
> *Abee I mean*

Alright, still annoying though.

> *My phone is just freaking out*
> *Got delayed out of Amsterdam*
> *At JFK now*
> *customs is slow*
> *I should still have plenty of time*
> *See ya tonight*
> *Moon emoji*
> *Clock emoji*

This was the new normal. Learning how to do life when your person gets a new person. May believed in having an abundance mindset, she really did. Life didn't have to be a zero-sum game; one person's gain didn't have to mean another person's loss. But Abee was just one person, and one person can only be in one place at one time—right? However it worked, his physical person was increasingly with Meredith, Meredith's gain, which meant he wasn't with May, May's loss. May told him he didn't have to come back this year. Abee rolled his eyes. He said he'd be cutting it close, but he promised he'd be there. She hadn't completely lost him.

~~~~~~

May left this year's clothes out on his bed for him, and she scribbled on a scrap piece of paper that she would be down on the beach. Shopping for clothes from the 90's had felt exotic, but as they were inching toward a world they recognized as their own, the thrill was diminishing. And not just because the clothes were generally horrible, but mostly because the illusion of the game was starting to wear off. In the summer of 2002 Gloria would be gone and Amy would be living back at home with Grandpa Gene. That meant May might get to see her, but it also meant that Amy was 22, living at home with her widowed father. May's heart ached.

This year was another middle of the night jump. 12:30 a.m. to be exact. Five minutes to go. No sign of Abee yet. She'd count to one hundred and then she'd head out. Maybe she had to do this on her own now. 97-98-99-100. With the board firmly in her grasp, May walked out into the water. She wanted to close her eyes, but she couldn't stop looking at the moon. The waves were loud. The light was entrancing. May didn't hear him coming until his hand was on her back and his other hand was on the board. Abee was there; in an instant the moon flashed from just over half full to almost completely full, and the magic found them again.

Listen: "Growing Season"
by Love You Later

TWO

~~~~~~~~~~

JUNE 2002 CE

They literally ran into her. Was Amy there waiting on them? Or was she just there?

"Mo—I mean, Amy? Is that you?"

Amy didn't move, except for a slight shiver that made her seem like she was a little blurry around the edges.

"Hey, it's, it's us. Hey. You okay?" Abee put his jacket around Amy's shoulders. Amy was there, but she was somewhere else. May bent down next to her. May's touch seemed to call her back.

"I miss my mom. She's not here anymore. She's not here."

May wrapped her arms around her own mother. She knew exactly how she felt. They sat with her until the sun rose.

WANING GIBBOUS

Listen: "You're Gonna Live Forever In Me"
by John Mayer

THREE

~~~~~~~~~~

JUNE 2003 CE

The minute Elise stepped out through the sliding doors and into the concrete fume bath of LAX, she knew she was home. She would grow to love the palm trees and ocean breezes and avocados, but it was the smell of cigarette smoke and gasoline that first convinced her she could make a life here in this strange sunny world.

Her left shoulder relaxed as Tal lifted her bag out of her hand. With one arm he carried his duffle and her satchel, and with his other he grabbed her now free left hand. Maybe it wasn't just the fumes that were making her convincingly lightheaded.

"My dad doesn't have texting on his phone yet, and he won't answer while he's driving, so who knows if he's here circling or still an hour away."

Elise started to make a comment about how ridiculous it was that the city didn't just have better mass transit, but decided it would be best to drop the New York comparisons before she even got started. "So, what kind of car are we looking for?"

Before Tal could say *a goldish-tan maybe, not big, but not too little, not too old, but not new, Subaru, I guess...*a banana-yellow convertible Volkswagen Bug pulled up to the curb and honked its little clown car honk at them. Tal jumped back. It was Gloria's car. Obviously it was not Gloria driving Gloria's car, but maybe not so obviously, there sat Amy.

"Amy!" Elise chirped excitedly. Before Tal could move, Elise hopped over the passenger side door and had Amy locked in a twisted up tangle of a hug. From over Elise's shoulder, Amy looked up at Tal and gave him a crinkle of her nose and a squinting of her eyes that somehow said *welcome home* and *don't get too close* all at once. Tal nodded in agreement.

Elise had insisted on being the one to call Amy. They weren't expecting to get her blessing, but they had to tell her. It had been a year and a half since Gloria died, 503 days to be exact. Tal had done the calculations over and over again in his head, hoping and praying that 503 days was long enough between one heartbreak and the next.

165

The spring after Gloria died, Amy said she was just taking another semester off. She had already missed the fall, might as well just make a gap year out of it. Tal called all the time, but Amy never remembered to charge her cell, and she never felt like getting out of bed to go answer the phone in the kitchen. Sometimes Gene answered. For every word Amy refused to give to Tal, Gene was glad to give him a double share. Gene had lots of words for his grief, and he was ready to say them to whoever would listen. Amy just had two words. Two words that banged around in her head and her heart and her body all day long. Two words that she never said to anybody, except herself.

Fuck you.

Tal felt guilty the first time he logged into Amy's email. But he had created it for her, and she had never changed the password, so he didn't actually feel that guilty. He just needed to know if she was at least getting his emails. She was. But she wasn't reading them. Tal deleted months worth of spam, hungry just to feel like he was doing something for her. He hesitated but then clicked open a message from the Registrar. Amy's withdrawal had been processed, and they wished her all the best in her next endeavors. Amy never actually told Tal that she wasn't coming back to New York.

Tal offered to come home that summer and help Gene with the restaurant. But Gene had already talked to Isaac and had heard the good news that Tal had gotten a summer job with a recording label. If you asked Isaac, Tal was going to be busy signing the hottest bands of the new millenia; it's what Isaac needed to tell himself. What Tal really did the summer of 2002 was drive a van and set up merch and tell greasy-haired kids that the label wasn't accepting unsolicited demos anymore. Yes, he was sure, and no, he'd never met Liz Phair. Tal stopped calling Amy that summer. Not that he didn't want to talk to her—he did. But it didn't matter what he wanted; maybe it never had.

Gene loved his Aimée as well and as deeply as he ever had, but he was too close. His love felt too much like the love that was gone. Her father's love reminded her of her mother's love and that created an ache on top of an ache. And so Amy had to push her father away too. That meant Isaac was the last man standing in Amy's life, and Isaac was a man of his word. He was bound to do for Amy what Gloria had done for his boy. Amy had always liked Isaac well enough. He was the smartest person she knew. She suspected he might be the smartest person anyone knew. He didn't use too many words and the words he did use were delivered with a gentle confidence. Isaac helped Gene at Duck's in the evenings when he wasn't on call, and he discovered that Amy would wander out of her room on Saturday mornings when he brought over fresh milk, eggs, and donuts. Most of the time Isaac had to pour last week's carton of milk down the drain, but it wasn't really about the milk anyways.

During their first few Saturday mornings together, Isaac did his best to keep a poker face without seeming cold. He knew Gloria would be worried for her girl. He was worried. One week Amy stayed long enough to watch him do his crossword puzzle. The next week Isaac bought two copies of *The New York Times*, arranged four donuts on a plate, and set it all out on the patio table. Amy hungrily dove into the crossword, and by the time she was done she had absentmindedly eaten two donuts. 600 calories and 90 minutes in the sun. It was a start.

Isaac didn't feel good about tricking her, but he had to find a way to get Amy talking. After he finished his second donut, he asked her if she had heard about the seals and sea lions that were dying and washing up on shore. Mother seals were seen miscarrying their pups in convulsive fits; even pelicans were falling out of the sky. If anyone else had been listening, they would have thought Isaac cruel for giving Amy the news so bluntly, almost as if he was unaware of her own loss, but it was because he knew her pain so acutely that he told her the way he did.

And the carnage down on the beach was no trick. Getting Amy to care about another creature besides herself, that was the trick. Some people in town were saying it was dog poop that was infecting the sea life. They were trying to get dogs banned from the beach. Isaac didn't have a dog in the fight, or even a dog for that matter, but he cared about the scientific truth of it all, and he knew it wasn't dog feces causing the trouble. A toxic algae bloom called *Pseudo-nitzschia* was poisoning the local shellfish. The seals, sea lions, and birds were eating the contaminated shellfish, inadvertently ingesting the neurotoxins from the algae, and then seizing to death.

If Amy was willing to help him get some samples, he could run the tests at his lab and prove the dog-haters wrong. He just needed an extra pair of hands. They spent two hours at the beach that day. They talked about what they observed in the animals and how sad it was to watch innocent creatures suffer. They talked about how morally neutral happenings (say an algae bloom) had the power to make humans feel like an evil had occurred. But the algae wasn't evil, was it? No. But the loss was still tragic, wasn't it? Yes. Are seal pups a more valuable life form than an algae spore? Objectively, no. Subjectively, of course. When Amy got back to the house later that afternoon, she didn't realize that it had been six hours since she'd cried. She didn't even realize she felt better. But she knew she didn't feel worse and that was a start.

Isaac had extra funding that his Department Head approved to use for hiring additional personnel. Or at least that's what Isaac told Amy. He really did need some help; for all of his genius, he was classically inept at organizing his paperwork. But there was no extra funding. The envelope of cash that Amy got every other week came out of Isaac's own pocket. In the right thinking part of her brain Amy knew that people who worked at universities didn't get paid in cash, but she wasn't in her right brain, and so she didn't think much of it. Isaac would mention Tal in the normal ways a father would talk about a child to a coworker, but he never brought up Tal in relation to Amy. Amy never brought up Tal at all.

Amy started out organizing, copying, shredding, repeat. She made quick work of Isaac's mess. She asked him if any of it was confidential or if there were things she shouldn't read. Isaac said she was welcome to look through any of it. He would often find Amy leaning against a newly organized banker's box, intently reading through research papers or copies of his published pieces. And when a participant in Isaac's latest trial called with concerns of bleeding, it was natural that he would ask Amy to go pick up Tal and Elise in his stead. Amy didn't hesitate to say yes, but she did sit in the parking lot for ten minutes trying to work up the courage to start the car.

WANING GIBBOUS

Listen: "In the Morning - Solstice Version"
by Fleet Foxes

FOUR

~~~~~~~~~~

After that first meal together in the cafeteria, the friendship had come about almost effortlessly, which was a completely new experience for Elise. Elise had never had that one person, that one other person with whom she could be completely herself—unhinged, untethered, unserious, unjudged, unobjective, unafraid, unlonely—a best friend.

Elise lived in a small studio, that was really just a closet, off campus. She was determined to become the best pastry chef in the city. On weekends Elise volunteered at a small organic farm upstate. The first one to get to class she would realize at some point that she was squinting to read her notes in the dark because class was over and the professor had turned the lights off. Elise believed better food would build a better world, and she needed to believe there was something, anything, that could make the world even just a little bit better.

The effortlessness of the friendship came with a few more chance encounters in the cafeteria. After half a dozen meals together Elise found herself scanning the tables for Amy and Tal every night and then feeling disappointed if they had apparently gone somewhere else for dinner. But to Elise's great relief, most nights they did show up. And one evening, as they were all scraping off their trays, Amy asked Elise if she wanted to go to a movie. *She's All That,* surely you've seen the ads, Amy said. Elise hadn't. So of course Elise had no idea that she could have been twins with the protagonist, the nerd turned hottie, Laney. And while not an exact match, Tal looked enough like Freddie Prinze Jr. that the resemblance was bound to plant a seed of an idea in Elise's mind. Zack and Laney made a much better couple than Zack and Taylor. It was kind of the whole point of the movie. Elise buried the thought. She felt gross for thinking it. But burying seeds has a way of making them grow.

The story line was incredibly offensive anyways. All Laney had to do was take off her glasses, and the whole world suddenly cared about her. The better story would have been the one in which Laney and Taylor became best friends and left all the asshole, superficial boys to deal with the crumbling patriarchy. But that's not where the story went and Elise had the stupid song stuck in her head for the next week. Kiss me. Kiss me. Kiss me. Kiss me.

Amy was the first person Elise talked to about her parents. People back home and extended family knew of course, but in her new life, the life she had to build for herself, Elise hadn't talked to anyone about it. Amy was the first person that Elise trusted not to pity her or look at her like the orphan she was.

On the third anniversary of the accident Elise asked Amy to go back to Amherst with her. It was four hours on the bus, or six hours on the train. They opted for the train. They stayed with Elise's aunt and uncle. They borrowed their car, and Amy drove them the fifteen minutes up to Shutesbury where an idyllic green patch of earth held Elise's past life. The cemetery was tucked in on three sides by giant northern red oaks, sprawling eastern hemlocks, and magical smooth alders. The remaining side welcomed visitors—or kept in the permanent residents—with a waist high iron fence and a wide wooden archway. The Magen David had been fashioned out of iron and was hung on the outward facing side of the arch. Elise said the star had first belonged to a Jewish community in Poland. Their cemetery was desecrated at some point during WWII, but inexplicably the star had remained. As survivors made their way to America, hoping to start new stories, they brought parts of their past with them. So now the star remained here, with the remains of Elise's parents.

Amy waited outside the gates as Elise went in and knelt next to the stones. Elise pulled a towel out of her backpack and then a bottle of water. Amy watched as Elise gently but thoroughly cleared the dirt that had gathered in the indentions of their names. With the towel over the end of her index finger she traced out their memory and then poured water over them. She did it with the care of a mother washing her newborn baby, or a priest wiping away the sins of the past. Over the breeze Amy could hear bits of a prayer, or a poem, or a plea.

"Each day tells its story to the next. I hear the story and I remember them."

Amy felt transported as she watched this motherly priest go about her work. Life could be cruel, but it didn't have to make you cruel.

"The sun wakes the world from its cold slumber. I wake up, shaking the frost and I remember them."

At that moment Amy had no idea that within a year her own mother's name would also exist in letters but not in body. Amy had no idea how hard it would be to make such generous acts look so effortless.

"I live because of them and they live on in me. Every day I wake is a day I remember them."

~~~~~~

Elise had never stopped calling, even though Amy had never answered her calls either. For 503 days Elise hadn't given up. Not that she had called every one of those days, she wasn't a stalker. But Elise eventually fell into the rhythm of thinking of Amy every Saturday night, when the three stars came out, signaling the end of Shabbat. Every Saturday night, Elise would call her best friend, who never called her back. So on that 503rd day when there was a voice on the other end, it took a minute for Elise to find the words she had to say.

DUCK DIVE

Listen: "True Blue"
by boygenius, Julien Baker

FIVE

~~~~~~~~~

JUNE 2003 CE

It was Saturday morning, but it wasn't a normal Saturday morning. Amy didn't expect Isaac to come over. Not with everything there was to do today. Amy wasn't sure what made her answer the phone that specific Saturday back in April. Maybe it was the way Isaac seemed to be waiting for her to acknowledge something, or maybe it was that on that 503rd day she felt that she finally had more than just the two words to say, or maybe it was because all of a sudden her heart seemed to have a bit of margin, a bit of space to miss more than just one person. But for whatever reason, Amy did answer, and that was the day she learned that grief doesn't stop time in equal measures. Her two best friends were in love. Of course they were. What did she expect?

What Amy didn't expect was for Isaac and Elise to be sitting on her patio with donuts and three copies of the *New York Times*, but there they were. Amy hadn't been able to decide if she would go or not. But as she ate her cherry-glazed old-fashioned and talked about a four-letter word for "treads lightly" that starts with a "p", she decided she could do it. The only dress that still kind of fit was the sunflower print, but even it hung on her like a flour sack.

Isaac, the only parent in attendance, walked Elise down the aisle and then took his place on the front row—alone. Isaac would have loved to have had Gene and Amy next to him; they were family. But family is complicated, even when they aren't blood.

In real life no one ever asked if there was any reason a couple shouldn't be joined in holy matrimony; that was just for movies as far as Amy could tell, and so she sat through the ceremony knowing her only option was to forever hold her peace. It wouldn't be that hard. It wasn't like she had much to hold anyways.

~~~~~~

"Amy, Amy." Elise gently shook her by the shoulder. Amy hadn't meant to doze off, but she still wasn't sleeping well at night, and the warm sun and the soft deck chair had worked some unintended magic on her nervous system. "I have someone I want you to meet. My friend—my friend from school that I told you about."

If Amy had gone back to New York, she would have met this friend two years ago. But if she had gone back to New York, she also wouldn't be passed out on her dad's deck at three in the afternoon, being woken up by her ex-boyfriend's new wife, who also happened to be her best friend—maybe? She was still feeling out who she and Elise were to each other.

Amy opened her eyes, but with the bright sun in her face all she saw was orange for a few seconds. As Amy blinked the world into focus, she saw the outline of a man standing next to Elise. Recently, part of Amy's expanding duties in the fertility department, which were still very much off the books, included watching another doctor's five-year-old daughter two days a week. The little girl brought a house, a car, a camper, a pool, and a whole village of dolls with her on those afternoons, and so Amy was increasingly familiar with the beautiful dolls and their whole extended group of family and friends. Whether her dreams were creeping in on her real life, or vise-versa, this man standing next to Elise was the spitting image of one of those dolls.

As Amy blinked a few more times, the details of the man filled out, and she realized he was most definitely the best friend doll. He was the lovable everyman character who was meant to balance out the more handsome lead, while still being able to share clothes. Amy was always in charge of the supporting characters when they played dolls. She pretended to complain, but she liked it that way. So, maybe it was just because Amy's brain associated this new man with the best friend doll that she actually preferred, or maybe there was a genuine spark, but either way, Amy didn't want to go back to sleep.

His name was Shepherd Thomas, or just Shep as Elise called him, and he was in town for a meeting with a fancy French restaurant. Shep had been working in New York at another fancy French restaurant, and apparently if you knew anything about anything, which Amy didn't, you knew that the New York restaurant was not going to be around much longer, and so it was time for Shep to take some meetings with other chefs. For Amy, it wasn't love at first sight. It was more like the first ray of sunshine after a long cold winter, and that little bit of warmth felt nice.

DUCK DIVE

Listen: "Deep In Love"
by Bonny Light Horseman, Eric D. Johnson,
Josh Kaufman, Anaïs Mitchell

SIX

~~~~~~~~~

JUNE 2031 CE

"Okay, let's go over the timeline of what we know about your parents."

"Why don't you remind me about what we know."

As smart as Abee was, timelines were not his strong suit. All the months that started with *J* were basically the same to him and years were interchangeable. That actually kind of made sense given their circumstances though.

Meredith had stayed in Paris for the summer. Elise joked that she was too scared of May to come visit again. They all knew it wasn't really a joke. And they were all glad for time with Abee, without her there too.

May and Abee were out for a drive in the bus. May was a year into her graduate work; Abee was several years into his documentary work with Meredith. May felt surprisingly nostalgic about this moment, the warm air, the ancient bus, him. Her lingering hopes in regards to him. But that's not what this part of the story called for. It wasn't time for the future, yet. They still had to figure out the past.

"Okay, so your parents got married on June 7, 2003. Your mom started working with Grandpa Gene at Duck's that same summer, your dad was still working with the label, and they lived with your Zayde until you were born in 2006, and maybe even a while after. I'm not sure about that detail."

"Things change really fast, don't they? Back then, and now. Two years ago Gloria was still alive, our parents were together, and our other parents were nowhere to be seen."

"Yeah, things change—"

~~~~~~

JUNE 2003 CE

One downside of growing up in paradise is that visiting another paradise has the potential to be an underwhelming experience. But Maui was not just another paradise; it was another planet. And there was no disappointment. And Tal would go to any planet to be with Elise. Tal missed Amy. Sure. But he was happy. Tal was so happy with Elise. Elise wanted him to be her family. Elise wanted to build a family with Tal. They wanted each other.

Tal and Amy had needed each other. Once upon a time Tal had thought that need was the strongest kind of bond you could have, but need is too primal a force to be relied upon. If your needs change one day, if all of a sudden all you need is to learn how to breathe again, then everything else, everyone else, can just disappear. Tal wanted someone who wanted him and who would keep choosing to want him. Elise wanted him.

The doors between the bedroom and the lanai were open. He could hear the steady hum of Elise's breath. But his own mother hadn't needed *or* wanted him. How did that work? Maybe he didn't know anything about anything. Maybe he was just trying to piece together a life in which he felt loved and safe. Maybe that's all anyone was doing.

Tal looked over the paper that had come with the breakfast tray. The resort was hosting a solstice party. It was the longest day of the year. Tal put his cup of coffee back on the tray and in two long bounds he was on the bed, next to her. Elise smelled like home.

"Hey, have I ever told you about these kids who would show up out of nowhere at the restaurant every year? But only once a year, during the summer solstice."

Elise blinked open her big dark eyes.

"Coffee."

Tal left and was back with a cup before she'd even sat up.

"Good morning." Elise pushed herself up against the headboard. "Okay, start again."

"Today is the solstice, and it just reminded me that back home, there were these kids, I mean they were our age, but they would just magically appear every year on solstice. They said they hitchhiked around in the summer."

"But you'd only ever see them that one day a year?"

"Just one day."

Elise took a long sip.

"It's okay to talk about her. You don't have to filter her out of your memories or your stories."

Tal smiled. This is why he loved Elise.

"I know. I don't. Or I won't. I mean I know I don't have to. I hope they find her today, that's all."

Elise reached over and squeezed his hand.

"I know. I worry about her too."

~~~~~~

JUNE 2003 CE

Isaac and Amy were sitting on the patio. They each held a small section of newspaper that had been folded down to about quarter size. Abee and May could see them through the spires of the fence. But the old seal and the troubled mermaid were distracted with their papers and pens. It looked like Isaac had gotten into it with another orca or two, but he'd won. Amy didn't look like she was winning her fights.

May grabbed Abee's hand out of habit and whispered, "What do we actually do here today? How do we help? She doesn't look any better. One day at a time is never going to be enough."

"One day at a time is all anyone ever gets, Mays."

May couldn't let go of Abee's hand. Were you supposed to knock on an iron gate? What was the best way to just show up in someone's backyard? Abee opened the gate and stepped in. He always knew what to do. Isaac and Amy said that they were at their Saturday morning routine early because they had to go into the lab. It would be a quick trip on a Saturday morning. Did the two travelers want to come see what Isaac—and Amy—were working on?

May looked at Abee. They had left the bubble before and nothing had exploded then. Should they try it again? Isaac assured them they could be back by 11:30, in plenty of time for the odd lunch meeting that Mel and Josh said they had to go to. What sort of lunch meeting would two hitchhiking kids have? But Isaac didn't press them on it.

The lab looked like how Isaac smelled. Sterile and studious. For a minute May wondered if they had hopped to the future, not the past. Everything was so bright, and white, and glassy, and well—scientific looking. On the drive there Amy had been friendly, but absent. Now here in the lab, she came to life, at least just a little. Microscopes, fancy ones. Petri dishes. Giant computers. Freezers—vitrification chambers—vitrification? Amy clarified—flash freezing. She went on to explain. It was a process that happened so fast it was as if the ovum had turned to glass, frozen in time without any change to the structure of the cell. Gradual freezing allowed crystals to form, a process which would forever and irreversibly alter the egg. Eggs had to be frozen without creating any change in the system. Time had to be frozen in an instant.

Amy and Isaac were like a perfectly odd couple, not in a romantic way, but like two old buddies who had been through war together. They finished each other's sentences and anticipated each other's smallest movements. It wasn't like Amy was magically unsad here, but May could tell that Amy had a purpose and place here, and maybe that's just another way of describing happiness.

May spotted a wall calendar hanging at Isaac's workstation. Tal and Elise would be home from their honeymoon in three days.

DUCK DIVE

Listen: "Love is Tall"
by Oshima Brothers

SEVEN

~~~~~~~~~~

SEPTEMBER 2003 CE

Elise hadn't done it on purpose. She really hadn't. Shep was genuinely a good friend, and a fantastic chef. He needed a job, Gene needed the help, and Amy needed, well Amy needed a companion who wasn't on the other side of middle-aged. Shep was the oil to their squeaky door; he was the grease to their wheel, he was the butter to their sad and dry bread. For a while, before Shep found his own place, Isaac's house was full—Talmai, Elise, and Shep. Two boys and a beautiful strong woman sat around the table with him, and they all did their best to share the small kitchen, and they all tried to be as quiet as they could because the walls in Isaac's little cottage by sea were terribly thin.

Miriam had been gone for 15 years. Isaac still missed her. But his grief didn't feel like an end anymore. It had been a beginning. The beginning of a new story, a story that he was actually quite fond of now.

Listen: "Microwave Dinner"
by Petey

EIGHT

~~~~~~~~~~

SEPTEMBER 2031 CE

Abee wanted to call and tell May; he really did. She was the first person he wanted to tell. But it was still just 4:00 a.m. in New York, six hours behind Poland, and it had been a few weeks since they'd talked. They'd have to go through the awkward apologies and assurances, and it all combined in his brain to one big excuse and promise that he'd call her later.

Ezekiel Berenson. Abee's grandfather's father. His great-grandfather. The man who was arrested in Budapest in the literal last days of the war and taken to Auschwitz-Birkenau. The man Rachel and Isaac tried to find for thirteen years. The man they never stopped hoping for. The man that had surely died in the camp. Abee had finally found him.

~~~~~~

Rachel Berenson and her infant son were freed from the Budapest ghetto on January 17, 1945. On the very same day, some 650 kilometers away, as the crow flies, Ezekiel Bereson, Zeke as his wife always called him, walked out through the gates of Auschwitz-Birkenau for the last time.

The working prisoners passed through the gates two times every day, once in the morning as they went out to work, and once as they passed back in for the night. But Zeke knew today was different. The hell that he had come to know over the past six months was in a unique state of chaos on January 17. The prisoners weren't going to work today; they were getting moved. He looked back at the sign that hung over the gates—*Arbeit Macht Frei*. Work will set you free. Work will set you free, through crematory number three. That was the rhyme the prisoners had made up.

In these six months Zeke had learned that when you're in hell, any act of resistance matters—no matter how small. *Through crematory number three. Through crematory number three. Through crematory number three.* Even if it was just a few words, hummed silently in his head, it mattered. It only took a few words to help you remember that you were still human. And your body might be completely broken, and your brain might be mostly broken, but a few words could remind you that a sliver of you still stood against the evil. Words could still be resistance.

Hell, one letter could be resistance. Years ago, prisoners had been forced to make the iron sign—*Arbeit Macht Frei.* They had no choice but to make the sign, but with one daring flip they reminded everyone who walked through those gates that resistance was still possible. A simple upside down B. The top lobe of the B, always slightly smaller, like a head atop a larger more bulbous body, was on the bottom. It was still obviously a B, but it was off. It was resistance.

Zeke knew it was the last time he would see that upside-down B. There was no emotion attached to that realization—no fear, no hope. He was too exhausted for either of those. It was just a fact. He would die soon, no doubt, but it wouldn't be here, and it might not even be today.

The death marches—one final whim of evil. Some 56,000 prisoners were moved out of Auschwitz and other nearby camps. Evil had many faces, but Zeke decided the most frequent face that evil put on had to be greed. Greed couldn't even let people die in the hell they had come to know. It forced them out into the bitter winter to die in the middle of a muddy road. More chaos, more pain, more death—that was what greed wanted. What it required. If people walked too slowly, they were shot in the head. If people fell to the ground, they were shot in the head—just to make sure they never got up again. Some prisoners were marched due west, others more to the north. Each small town that the marches pushed through absorbed a part of the story, because death literally found its way to their doorsteps.

One town had 36, one 14, another 63. Humans they didn't know, humans they had no way of knowing. Some towns put up stones or plaques, memorializing the number of people and the date and the fact that it was the Hitlerites who had done it. A few towns kept track of the tattooed numbers they found on the stiff left forearms. They didn't know what the numbers meant, but they figured someday, someone just might.

Not many documents from Auschwitz survived to the end of the war. The SS knew the Soviets were coming—and quickly. They had to try to destroy an infrastructure which in a matter of just four years had imprisoned and tortured over one million people, the majority of whom were ultimately murdered. They burned as much evidence as they could, just like they had burned the people.

But in the fall of 1944, just a few months after Zeke's arrival at Auschwitz, while his intake paperwork was still near the top of the pile, and the Newcomer's List with his name on it was still being duplicated and approved and signed off on by the officers in charge, the prisoners who were assigned to work in the admissions department started to sneak duplicates of the records out of the camp. Another small act of resistance. A small act of hope. Someday the evil would crumble and they would need a way to help people remember who they were, or at least a way to help people on the outside determine who they had been.

An officer took Zeke's information that first day back in June. Maybe it was because the officer suffered from chronic ear infections as a child, the kind where the doctor had to rupture his ear drums to release the puss—or maybe it was because the 42's were so loud—or maybe it was because even genocide gets boring after a million people, but whatever the reason, when Ezekiel Berenson gave his name that day, the officer didn't really hear, or care to hear, and wrote down June 21, 1944 — Ebeneezer Verson — Jew — Hungary.

Ebeneezer was assigned a number which was tattooed on his left forearm, and he became a new man that day. And for all those years, Rachel and Isaac had been looking and hoping for the wrong person.

~~~~~~

It wasn't a Eureka! moment. It was a slow and painstaking process of elimination. Hungarian census and police records, Nazi transport books, camp logs. Abee and Meredith poured over it all. The process felt like playing a game of sudoku with only 16 clues—but if this was this, then that had to be that, and this couldn't be that, and that couldn't be this, and finally they figured out that Ebeneezer Verson never existed before June 21, 1944, and Ezekiel Berenson ceased to exist on that same day.

And then Abee found Ebeneezer's prisoner number, and then he and Meredith drove from town to town, winding around systematically from the north to west, hoping that Ebeneezer had made it to a town that had honored and remembered the dead with a small slice of earth, and a stone, and that someone had taken the time to carve the numbers into that stone.

Ezekiel had made it 42 kilometers to the west. The boys playing soccer in the street pointed to a green door up the block. The old man there knew about the stone, they said. Once a quarter, their class tended to the grass and plants and washed up the stone, but that's all they knew. The old man could tell them more.

The old man hadn't always been old. He had only been ten years old in 1945. The town wasn't on the direct path of the death march because it was tucked up and around the corner of a mountain valley. Their stone held only one set of numbers, because only one man had made it to their doorstep. The man hadn't died on January 17 or January 18; against all odds he had made it to January 19. The boy had been out hunting rabbits when he found the man propped up against a black alder. At first the boy had panicked, afraid he had been the one to shoot him, but as he got closer he became sickeningly relieved to realize that this man's wounds were not new. The man wasn't dead yet, but he didn't seem alive either. The boy started to run to get help, but the skeleton of the man called him back. Tell my boy I love him, the skeleton pleaded. My baby boy.

The boy came back with his own father, but it was too late. The man had passed on. The town used to have a special plot, a Jewish cemetery, but their Jewish neighbors were long gone, and in their greed the Nazis had even destroyed the memory of their dead. The boy watched as his father carved the numbers into the rock, he said he carved them extra deep so that no one could ever forget. They etched the Magen David—like the one that had once hung over the cemetery— and they finally etched the other things they knew for sure—a man, the date, killed by the Hitlerites, and a final epitaph. The old man said the epitaph translated to something like "a father's love lives on." Since the Jewish cemetery was gone, they set his stone under the alder tree.

Phase Seven

THIRD QUARTER

YEAR	DATE	TIME
2004	20-Jun	5:57 PM PDT

YEAR	DATE	TIME
2032	20-Jun	12:08 PM PDT

DUCK DIVE

Listen: "Nancy From Now On"
by Father John Misty

ONE

~~~~~~~~~~

JUNE 2004 CE

Shep took Amy to the pier for their first date. "Carousel or ferris wheel," he asked? Amy stopped for a minute, overwhelmed by the deja vu of it all. Had it really been nine, ten years? Shep assumed she was just seriously contemplating the options. She was remembering how Tal never brought her back here. They had gone on lots of other dates over the years, but they never came back here after the wheel opened again. It was their first broken promise.

"The ferris wheel," Amy told him confidently.

Amy had been feeling better. Well, maybe that wasn't true. She had felt like she wanted to feel better, and that did feel better. But she was still too thin; her appetite was non-existent. And the uneven ground which was her never ending loop of anxiety and depression felt more untenable than ever. Were her problems mental? Was something physical going on? How did you even know where one stopped and one started?

This was only the second first date she had ever been on. She shook her head. She couldn't decide if that fact bothered her because she thought it would be more or because she had been sure it would only be the one. Either way, this one felt oddly similar to her first first date at the pier. She might have hit her head again, or maybe not, but however it started, this date ended with her slumped down in the bottom of a swinging metal basket. Had she fainted or passed out? She wasn't sure if there was a difference. Shep was alternating between yelling at the guy on the controls to bring them down and checking on her. Checking her pulse, checking her breath, holding her hand. Amy wasn't getting better, but she was glad to have Shep there with her.

184

Listen: "Till the End of Days"
by Bermuda Triangle

TWO

~~~~~~~~~

JUNE 2004 CE

Restaurants didn't get to close just because one person was sick. Gene and Elise and Shep were coming back and forth as often as they could, but there were certain times of the day where they all had to be in the kitchen. Isaac was Amy's most constant companion, but even he had times when he had to attend to the duties of life that still ticked on. And it was for those gaps that this strange little family elected Tal to be the fill in. It's not that Tal didn't want to. Of course he wanted to be there for Amy, but it would have been easier not to be.

Amy asked Isaac to watch for them. Isaac had been planning on it, even before she mentioned it. Isaac found Mel and Josh heading into Duck's around lunch time. He explained that Amy was spending a few days in the hospital, and she'd love to see them, if they had time. He called the hospital room, Tal answered, Isaac said he was on his way with the twins. That's what Isaac had started calling them. He wasn't shocked by it anymore, but the resemblances were increasingly unmistakable. Who were these two people who looked so much like his own family?

Isaac wasn't Amy's doctor—yet, but he knew the doctors and he was constantly talking with the doctors. Cancer wasn't her problem—yet. Anxiety, depression, anemia, dehydration, depression, depression, depression. That's what Amy needed help with right now. But since she was here, and since this was Isaac's world, and since he had promises to keep, they ran some tests. Genetic tests. Isaac had been wanting to do them for a while, but Amy hadn't been ready. Now was the time.

Isaac saw the results that morning. He wasn't surprised. Gloria had the same mutations. The time caught up with Gloria before Isaac could help her, but it wasn't too late for Amy. Even though he'd been on the front lines of this technology for almost a decade, it still amazed him. It was like a crystal ball, a look into the future. But once you saw the future, you had to decide what to do about it. Isaac would tell Amy tomorrow, after the twins were gone. The girl twin, Mel, quickly slipped into the room when they got to the hospital. But the boy, Josh, put his hand on Isaac's shoulder and pulled him back into the hall.

"Dr. Berenson, I'm sorry to pry, but will she be okay?"

As Isaac thought about what to say, he scrunched his nose. His glasses lifted up toward his forehead. "I think right now Amy's mind and body need to come to an agreement about how to go on. I think a part of her has given up, even though part of her wants to go on. I'm just afraid that by the time her mind is willing, her body will object."

Abee nodded. He understood, but he didn't. Isaac nodded in return and started again for the door. Abee stopped him one more time. He thought he would just tell him, but on the car ride over he decided he couldn't. So he found a piece of paper and a pen in the seat-back pocket. He scribbled out a note. He hoped it was the right thing to do. Abee just couldn't imagine a world where his grandfather wouldn't want to know.

Ebeneezer Verson
Rudziński, Poland
the stone by the alder tree

Listen: "Blue is the Eye"
by Ye Vagabonds

THREE

~~~~~~~~~~

DECEMBER 2004 CE

Shep could see a middle-aged woman a few rows back who was not subtle with her stares. It made sense. He probably would have stared too. They did not immediately make sense as a group. Two men in their fifties but who looked older, either because of too much sun or not enough sun, and then four people in their twenties whose relationships were not immediately clear. Were they friends, siblings, partners, or all of the above?

Shep closed the overhead compartment, took his seat next to Amy, and squeezed her hand. Joining a family and a family restaurant at the same time was not without its complexities, but he had never worked in a kitchen that had the ability or willingness to shut down for two weeks so the family could go on a trip. Gene had never worked in a kitchen like that either. But if the last few years had taught him anything, if Gloria had taught him anything, it was that the old ways didn't have to be the new ways. His Aimée needed some new ways.

Isaac had been in contact with a nice young person in the wojt's office in Rudziński who spoke English, and one day back in September he opened an email that slowly loaded an attachment, and the attachment slowly revealed itself to be a picture of a stone next to a tree. The picture was slightly blurry, and the engraving was not clear. So it wasn't until Isaac saw the epitaph with his own eyes that he understood. Their guide paused for a moment to think about the best way to say the words in English. It means, *a father's love lasts,* or maybe *a father's love lives on.* Isaac's father had been thinking of him; of course he had.

DUCK DIVE

Listen: "Cold Water Swimming"
by Quiet Houses

FOUR

~~~~~~~~~~

JANUARY 2005 CE

Amy had come to know every inch of this office over the last few years. She spent more time in this room than Isaac did. Isaac preferred his work station in the lab, but Amy would come and tuck herself in on his velvety golden couch and read and read and read some more. It was funny that they had all come here to have this conversation. They could have had it around the kitchen table or on the patio. But maybe Isaac knew that this kind of conversation needed to happen in some place you wouldn't have to still eat and sleep and live in everyday.

Shep sat next to her on the couch, Gene sat in an armchair across from Isaac. Shep asked to be there. Not that Amy didn't want him to be there, it was just a lot. She already felt like the guilt might crush her. Isaac tried to remind her that none of this was her fault; she hadn't done anything wrong. But Amy was putting her dad through this again, and that sure felt like it was her fault. It was already too much. She couldn't imagine bringing Shep into it as well, but he promised her that he wanted to be there, and he was.

Amy smoothed the nap of the velvet back and forth a few times before settling on pushing it all forward. Then she started talking. Amy had two specific genetic mutations. Isaac nodded along as she talked. He could have legitimately hired her as a research assistant in his lab at this point, but this was not the time for real jobs. Amy explained that statistically her chances of developing cancer were so high that to not take decisive action now would basically mean she was agreeing to let the cancer take decisive action later. Isaac watched in awe as she spoke. Amy wasn't giving up.

In Poland, Amy stood next to Isaac under the alder tree. The sun was setting, but he couldn't leave. Isaac whispered into the silence that surrounded them. "It's not possible that my father knew about me." Amy leaned in to hear him better. Her eyes urged him to go on. "My mother always told me about how excited he was when they learned she was pregnant. But it would have been at least a month after he was arrested before she had any indication that she was with child. I've always had a mind for numbers," Isaac grinned, "but in her version of the story, she swore that he knew. And somehow he really did." Isaac let his fingers drift across the epitaph.

And it was standing there next to Isaac and next to the stone that Amy remembered how good it was to be alive. Amy believed the research supported doing two separate surgeries, rather than trying to do it all at once. Double mastectomy and bilateral oophorectomy—removing both breasts and then the ovaries and the fallopian tubes. She'd be a lot less likely to get breast or ovarian cancer if her breasts and ovaries weren't there. It was as straightforward and terrible as that. But there were still more words that needed to be said. Because Amy needed to decide if someday, whether in the near or distant future, she would still want to have a child.

Listen: "Secrets from a Girl (Who's Seen it All)"
by Lorde

FIVE

~~~~~~~~~~

APRIL 2005 CE

The house was too quiet. This was not how Amy had imagined this day. There was no eccentric wedding planner busting into rooms to manage slash create chaos. There was no adorable little brother wandering around. There was no overly sentimental dad trying to act like he wasn't losing his mind over losing his baby girl. And there was no mother, obviously, but that was uniquely her problem, not Annie's. Amy had watched George, Nina, Matty, and Annie navigate the big day a hundred times over the years. She had actually worn out the VHS. Amy felt weirdly disappointed that she and her dad hadn't played basketball last night. But they didn't even have a basketball hoop, and never had.

Everything was happening fast now. Maybe that was a consequence of seeing the future. Everything was rushing toward a known point. Could she change the future by the time they got to that point? That's what she had to figure out. Shep said he wanted to figure it out with her. Shep really, genuinely loved her. Amy suspected that he really liked trying to fix people too. But at this point she was in no position to begrudge anyone else's neurosis.

Amy hadn't worn earrings in—years? The post went in the front of her ear but then seemed to get lost. She scooted closer to the mirror, trying awkwardly and unsuccessfully to look out the side of her eye to see what was happening on the back of her ear. The hole must have closed up. She'd have to just push through it. Amy closed her eyes and took a breath. She'd count to three. One—two—knock knock.

Amy hadn't known how to ask Elise, things were okay between them, but it all still felt tender. Like a bruise that was still healing. They just needed some more time before it was all the way okay. Amy tried to not think about how sometimes bruises aren't just bruises but evidence of a broken bone or—cancer.

It had been easier, less complicated, to keep the wedding simple. Just Amy and Shep and Maggie from down the street who was a potter and an ordained priest. But

Amy wished she had asked Elise to stand next to her. It would have been nice to have Elise next to her today.

Again the knock. Amy realized she hadn't responded. Elise slowly opened the door anyway. Amy handed Elise the small pearl stud. It went right in. It wasn't closed up. The path out had been there all along; she just needed someone else to help her see it.

SIX

~~~~~~~~~~

Over time as cells in our bodies grow old they start to die and new cells are birthed to take their place. But sometimes this orderly process breaks down and where there should be healthy new cells there are actually abnormally mutated cells. Bodies have mechanisms to suppress and rid themselves of these abnormally mutated cells, but sometimes the mechanisms fail or the mutation is too prolific and destructive for the body to keep up its defenses.

If all body cells are susceptible to this degradation, it would seem to follow that a large body with a long lifespan would be particularly at risk for cancer.

EXHIBIT "E"

If a 30-pound beagle who lives 15 years is prone to cancer, how much more so for a 6-ton elephant who lives 70 years? Or a 35-ton humpback who lives to 50? But that assumption has turned out to be false. As scientists study African elephants and humpback whales, they've found it's the opposite of what they'd expected. These giant creatures not only *don't* have increased instances of cancer, they actually have similar and sometimes even fewer occurrences than smaller species.

Amy read the abstract and then the whole paper before she ever showed it to Isaac. It came in a thick manila envelope from a research group working on Maui in the Auau Channel. What was happening at the genetic level in humpbacks which made them so good at suppressing cancerous mutations, even in such large bodies over such long spans of time? This group was working to figure that puzzle out, and they wanted Dr. Berenson's input and review. Amy read and reread the paper.

It would be years of work and research, Amy had been in this world long enough to figure that out, but this Dr. Phillips and her team in Hawaii were putting together the pieces, bit by bit.

THIRD QUARTER

Listen: "Fall With Me"
by The Wild Reeds

SEVEN

~~~~~~~~~~

MAY 2005 CE

They were back in Isaac's office. Another day of the future rushing straight at them. Pushing the velvet forward had become a bit of obsessive behavior for Amy. Harvesting and preserving. Harvesting and preserving. Were they talking about babies or beans? Yes, for the culture at large it was still a new idea, new processes, but Isaac had been working on this for years. This was not new to him. If Amy and Shep wanted to preserve even the idea of having biological children in the future, they had to decide now. But how were you supposed to know what you were going to want in ten years, or five years, or even just tomorrow for that matter?

A series of shots would push Amy's body to speed up the development of multiple eggs within her ovaries. The plan, and hope, was to retrieve at least 20 mature eggs, and then the best of those eggs could be fertilized and frozen as embryos, or they could be frozen before fertilization. The success rates were higher for eggs that were fertilized before freezing.

This part was always hard to say. If you only have so many eggs, are you sure your current partner is the man you want to fertilize all of them? It was an awkward, but necessary question. Isaac was a proponent of covering multiple bases. Freeze some embryos with your partner. Freeze some eggs unfertilized, just in case. Options were freedom. They didn't have to decide immediately, but soon.

The doctors would leave Amy's uterus alone for now. Her situation indicated that removing the ovaries and breast tissue would be enough. It was possible, Isaac's eyes glimmered with tears and hope, that Amy could carry her own child some day, but it would be a long shot, and lots of actual shots, but it wasn't impossible.

But it also wasn't very probable, so they needed to know that a surrogate might be necessary. Shep and Amy might ultimately need someone else to carry their baby.

Listen: "Where Sky Becomes Sea"
by Palace

EIGHT

~~~~~~~~~

MAY 2033 CE

May created an exhibit to go along with her dissertation. Her advisor laughed at her when she first brought up the idea. Most students were struggling to finish their dissertations by the end of their sixth graduate year, but May was going to have her PhD in four and create an interactive exhibit to help prove her heady ideas were of some grounded use.

May rented a warehouse space in Brooklyn that was between tenants. She spent forever trying to decide what to call it—*The Wormhole of You* and *You are the Wormhole* were effective but sounded way too dramatic. She finally landed on *You in Time* with the tagline of *A Space Exploration.* May knew the tag bordered on cheesy, but it made her smile.

May used the structures of old hoop houses from a farm upstate to create a tunnel which serpentined through the space. One time around the tunnel took about 15 minutes—if you walked at a contemplative pace. She used projection from multiple angles to cast images on the insides of the tunnel. Participants had to enter the tunnel one at a time and were separated by at least one minute intervals. The images started with an infant; as you walked, the baby walked with you, literally growing up as you moved through the space. About five minutes into the tunnel you started to experience the child becoming a young adult, and then you saw that the young adult was pregnant, and now the abdomen of the person grew as you walked. Then the tunnel took a sharp curve into darkness, but the darkness was dotted with spots of light. Stars? Holes in the fabric? Yes. And in the dappled darkness you walked for a short while until a single projector showed another infant on the side of the tunnel and the journey started over again—infant to adult to infant. The child's features were different from but similar to the first. The cycle of images had three iterations, three journeys.

The tunnel wound in a way that was meant to prevent the participants from tracking where they were in the larger space, and so when the end actually morphed back into the beginning and the adult gave birth to an infant, participants would not be aware that they had literally started over again. They were also given the freedom to switch directions, turn around at any point, presumably heading back on a linear course, but unknowingly still participating in the loop. They were told to walk the tunnel as long as they wanted, and when they were ready to exit, the panels on the sides of the dark sections would give way.

As participants waited to enter the tunnel, a curator stood by and whispered a simple question to everyone who passed through.

Is time travel impossible?

May wasn't interested in arguing that time travel was possible. Somehow, knowing it was, made that a less interesting proposition. But if she could present, with a strong degree of intellectual integrity that it wasn't impossible, then things could get fun. The intellectual integrity was the work of her actual dissertation, but the work of this exhibit was purely imagination. In May's experience, saying that something was not impossible required a lot more imagination than the certainty of saying it was possible. And she still hoped that the universe bent in favor of imagining the impossible.

After all these years, May wasn't certain that her presence in what she called the past was affecting anything. She had the growing suspicion that there was nothing new. But she was still fighting to believe that at least, maybe, it wasn't impossible.

~~~~~~

Shep, Elise, and Tal flew out for the first weekend. May was prepared for them to be generously positive, no matter what they really thought of it all. May was not prepared for them to be genuinely shook. Tal was the one who found her first. He looked like he'd seen a ghost. He could barely get the words out. "It's not impossible is it, M—" he paused, like he had forgotten her name. He shook his head. That Etch A Sketch motion again. "May. It's not impossible."

~~~~~~

The space was empty. May was just about to walk the tunnel one more time to make sure nothing or no one had been left behind for the night. She felt her phone vibrate in her back pocket. It glowed like a torch in the darkness as she pulled it out. The sight of his name made her heart hurt, in a good way.

Am I too late?

Depends where you are?

What if I'm right outside?

May was trying to think of something quippy to text back, but she was walking too fast to properly focus on coming up with a clever response. She was going to be so mad if he was joking. Not mad. Sad. She hadn't seen Abee in almost a year. She didn't know how much she missed him until the possibility of seeing him was possibly right in front of her. Her screen glowed again.

Loading dock.

This was too specific to be a joke. May unhooked the chain from the wall, pulled hand over hand, and started to lift the door. She could see his white sneakers first, and then somehow, somehow, in the middle of Brooklyn the scent of eucalyptus and sea salt came wafting in. Abee was older. In a good way. Everything about him looked to be more on purpose. He was holding a bouquet of peach and coral ranunculus in one hand, a pizza box in the other hand, and he was alone. Thank God, he was alone. He started to scoop her up in a hug, but she already had her arms and legs wrapped around him.

Abee pulled two glass bottles out of his back pockets, twisted off the tops, and they sat on the cold concrete floor with the pizza box between them. He said he had some news. May said she did, too. He made her go first.

"I've been offered an assistant professorship at USC." She had accepted, she was glowing. May was going home. His heart sank. Abee always knew May would get back to California, but he had imagined they might go home together.

"I'm not with Meredith anymore."

May tried to look surprised, but if he thought his announcement was news, then he was more disconnected than she had imagined. From Meredith's posts over the past week, it was obvious that she was not in any sort of relationship, except with herself. And if Abee didn't realize that the pipeline between him, Elise, and May was a straight shot with no filters, well then he just wasn't paying attention.

"My mom already told you, didn't she?"

May smiled; he wasn't totally clueless. "When they were here last weekend, it came up." May tried not to look too happy. She reached for his hand. "Are you okay?" She genuinely wanted to know.

"I—am." Abee said it like he was surprised by it. "I am now. It was time. Time for us to go our separate ways, personally and in our work." Abee lifted his chin and looked May straight in the eyes. She had half of a slice stuffed in her mouth. "Mays, are we waiting around for each other?"

May stopped, mid chew. Just kidding, he was clueless. "Ummm yes. That's obviously what's happening here." May felt like a barbell was being lifted off her chest as she said each word. "You're my person. You always have been. You've just been hopping around the world like you forgot that maybe."

"I never forgot."

"If we wait much longer, Abee, I'm afraid I will."

He held her gaze. "I've been offered a role."

"A roll of what?"

"Not of. In. In a movie. A real studio movie."

May shook her head. She felt confused. "Say more."

"I've met a lot of people the past few years, and I guess some of them were impressed with my on-camera documentary work, and I got an audition. And then another, and another, and I got cast, May. In a real movie. It seemed like such a long shot, I asked my mom not to tell anyone—not even you. I didn't want to make it a big deal. But it's kind of a big deal. It's just a buddy role, but it's the buddy of a superhero."

May couldn't tell if her words were coming out fast or slow now. Of course Abee was going to be in a superhero movie. In some world she had always known this was coming. For now she'd let him pretend that he wasn't going to tell her every single secret thing about this movie, but they both knew he would.

"Will you wait on me just a little bit longer, May?"

"I'm not going anywhere—well I'm going back to LA, but you know what I mean."

He kicked the pizza box out of the way and scooted toward her. She had really missed kissing him.

Phase Eight

WANING CRESCENT

YEAR	DATE	TIME
2005	20-Jun	11:46 PM PDT
2006	21-Jun	5:26 AM PDT

YEAR	DATE	TIME
2033	20-Jun	6:00 PM PDT
2034	20-Jun	11:43 PM PDT

ONE

~~~~~~~~~~

JUNE 2033 CE

"Have you ever told your therapist?"

Abee looked at May like she was crazy.

"No, I'm not trying to get committed. Have you?"

"No, but she for sure thinks I'm crazier than I really am. Sometimes I forget to talk about my mom like she's dead."

Abee let his hand rest on her leg. "Amy wasn't doing well last year, Mays. And I know you know this, but I need you to hear me say it; maybe we don't save her. Maybe we can't. You've spent your whole adult life now trying to figure this out, and you put on a very academic face about it, but I know it's your heart, and it's your heart that's on the line, and I know you've figured out more than you want to admit. Lay it all out, you're not gonna scare me. We are a decade into this. What's the next move, Mays?"

Abee and May had flown into LAX last night. He'd get to spend a few months doing costuming, scans, prosthetics, and martial arts training in LA, and then he'd be off to Romania—for six, seven months? After he gave May the news, it took less than an hour for May to get him to tell her the name of the movie and the top three names on the call sheet.

They had meant to drive home, to Malibu, when they got back last night. But then they were stuck in traffic on the 1 through Santa Monica, and then they were going past the pier, and then there was the Miramar, all glamorous and exciting, and then he squeezed her hand, and asked if she was okay with a detour. Then by the time they were about to pass the next sexy looking hotel, he told the driver they actually needed to cut their ride short. Somehow, with all the insane things they'd been through, walking in and paying a thousand dollars for a room on the spot felt like the craziest. They bought stupidly expensive designer swimsuits in the boutique, jumped in the pool, and giggled and hung on each other like they were drunk. And they were. And May let herself soak up the magic of him.

May adjusted the pillow under her head as she stared at Abee. "The next move is your dad." It sounded way creepier than she meant, but it was true. They needed Tal's help. Or more accurately said, they needed Tal to fall for a lie.

DUCK DIVE

Listen: "Across the Universe"
by The Beatles

TWO

~~~~~~~~~~

JUNE 2005 CE

Abee spotted him first. "I think that's my dad out there." They watched as Tal waited for a wave that never came. It was weird to see him surfing alone.

May felt like she hadn't let go of Abee's hand in four days. They waited for Tal to see them, and then eventually paddle himself in, with no assist from a wave. Tal greeted them like the long lost friends that they were. Tal said they had to meet Elise. He said Elise wasn't convinced that Josh and Mel actually existed. He laughed and said that at times he wasn't even sure if they actually existed. But here they were, and they absolutely had to come meet Elise.

All these years, May and Abee had been interacting with their parents, or one of their parents, and the universe hadn't melted, but for some reason the thought of being with Elise felt like too much. Abee could imagine a world where in the future his dad forgot about this twin of a kid who used to show up every June, but not his mom. There was no world where once Elise saw him, she would ever forget him. Abee knew it made zero logical sense, but it totally made sense. They couldn't go meet Elise.

May jumped in. "This is probably so weird, but before we go up to Duck's, can we get your help with something?" May explained and apologized that this was so long in coming, but they wanted to do something to make up for the board that she thrashed a few years ago. May watched Tal cringe as the words came out of her mouth. May asked if there was any way she could see the board, to measure it. May said that she knew Amy had been having a rough time since Gloria passed, and they wanted to get her a new one. Maybe a fresh board could inspire her to get back out in the water. The image of Amy in the hospital bed, so frail looking, was almost always front and center in May's mind now.

Tal shrugged. What he wanted to tell them was that he had tried. He had tried everything. And if he couldn't get through to Amy, then who could? But he didn't say that. Maybe he misjudged his role, his importance in her life, whether past, present, or future. Would he ever stop feeling protective over Amy? Jealous for her? Things didn't seem to be going in that direction. Without being unhelpful, Tal tried to make it clear that it was kind of weird for him to dig around in their shed, looking for a board that was more than just a board—for all people involved. May could tell Tal wasn't stoked about this request, but she pressed in all the same; she needed to get her hands on it, again.

May and Abee had to remember to act like they hadn't been in this shed a million times over the years. Tal tugged open the rusty door, but a rise in the ground stopped it from opening all the way. It always did that. He kicked at the grass, making a divot. It swung open. It was just dark enough outside that it was hard to see what was what inside the shed. Tal actually really hated this shed, for the memories and the spiders. May hated it for one of those same reasons. Tal said he'd be back in a minute; he was going to get a flashlight.

As the gate closed behind Tal, May went into the dark shed. This was her chance. This might be easier than she'd anticipated. All she had to do was kick the board, kick it hard, maybe a few times, but if no one had used it in a while, they'd have no idea how or when it happened, and surely this time it would be damaged beyond repair. Abee put his hand on May's shoulder, stopping her. Telling her he would do it, without actually saying those words. May squeezed his hand and smiled, saying she had to be the one to do it, without actually saying those words.

May stepped in, waiting just a few seconds for her eyes to adjust, but there wasn't time to let them fully get their bearings. She pressed forward. May could feel webs catching in her hair, but there wasn't time to worry about those either. She pushed and pulled at some boxes, beach chairs, umbrellas, bikes. Grandpa Gene had always been a bit of a hoarder. Her hand felt it before she saw it. She pried it free and slid it out into the small walkway which she'd created in the hoard.

She hadn't seen it since Tal had repaired it. It almost glowed. Maybe she was just being sentimental, but she could almost see the love radiating from it. She hated what she was about to do. She tried to kick it, but there was such a small area of free space around her that her first attempt was pitifully ineffective. She had barely tapped it. She was going to have to get it out of here and quick. She wrestled it free from the last bits of entanglement and started to turn toward the door. But in the same instant a beam of soft yellow glowed from the porch, it spread across the yard, through the door, and landed on May's right hand.

Someone had turned on the patio lights. It was just enough light to see the situation clearly.

May's right hand was covered in small translucent brown dots, which almost looked like sand. But the sand was moving—up her arm. There was no thought process after that; everything else was instinct. May was screaming and shaking, and then she was out in the yard again. They were so miniscule, Abee couldn't immediately see them on her hand or in the air as she flung them around. They were never sure exactly when Amy had appeared; she must have been the one who turned on the patio lights, but Amy was there, and before May knew it, the warm water of a garden hose was soaking her body, head to toe to hand.

Amy said she hadn't known what the problem was, but she could see Mel had something on her that she didn't want to be on her, maybe chemical, maybe creature, and she just instinctively grabbed the hose. The baby spiders melted away into the grass or air, or back into the shed, but it was weeks before May stopped feeling small tickles up her arm and on the back of her neck.

They decided it must have been a spider sack. Black widows? Probably. They'd seen black widows in the shed before. Amy said the babies and the males weren't poisonous. The stuff of nightmares no doubt, but even if they had bitten her, the babies were not a threat. Only the mature females could do real harm.

Tal came back with his flashlight and lots of questions. May had shed her wet clothes and was down to her swimsuit. May heard herself saying it before she even knew she was. "This backyard could really use a pool." She'd always said that.

In the chaos of the spiders, no one had asked why they had been in the shed, and they didn't offer any explanation. Amy offered to go get Mel some dry clothes. May didn't know what to agree to or hope for anymore. So she just said what she wanted. "Actually, can we go for a swim down at the beach? I just want to make sure they're all off of me."

It was awkward, just the four of them together, May, Abee, Tal, Amy. But no one objected. It wasn't completely dark; the sky still glowed in one thin layer. They didn't take any boards. The ocean was warm. May held herself under the water for as long as she possibly could, imagining any lingering dots floating off of and away from her body. When May came up out of the water, it had started to rain, but just softly, perfectly.

WANING CRESCENT

Listen: "Palm of My Hand"
by May Erlewine, Woody Goss

THREE

~~~~~~~~~~

AUGUST 2005 CE

Amy needed Elise's help. She used the nail of her ring finger to flick the sand out from under her thumb nail. Then she used her thumb nail to clean out the sand under the nail of her middle finger. How do you ask someone to have your baby for you?

Amy looked up from her lap. Elise was already looking back. She would say yes. Amy knew Elise would say yes. Amy wanted her to say yes, she wanted it for Shep, she wanted it for herself. But she didn't want to have to ask her. She didn't want this to be the answer. Amy hated herself for having to ask it.

"Els, I might need your help. I have eggs. I have ovaries with good eggs, but not for much longer. I thought I had time, and I don't. But we can steal some time I think. I think we can steal some back, but someday I might need your help. Isaac says we can freeze them. We can even fertilize the eggs, and then freeze them. We can stop time. He says it's like time travel. And then someday, Shep and I could still have a baby, but we will probably need help. I probably won't be able to do it on my own, Els."

Isaac had knocked on the door to Tal and Elise's room that morning. He was a man of facts and science. But he was also a man who knew how hard the facts could hit you, and he always had an eye to softening particularly hard blows. Isaac told Elise what Amy and Shep were up against. He told Elise what he suspected Amy might ask of her. Isaac knew Elise would need time to process it.

Amy said that Elise should obviously take some time to think about it and talk with Tal. Elise wasn't sure what to think. She had just taken the test yesterday. Her breasts were unusually tender, and then she realized she was late, just four days, but that wasn't like her. And then, the test was positive. Positive for pregnancy. For some reason as Elise stood at the sink staring at the stick and then back up at herself in the mirror, it struck her as a ridiculous way to say it. Positive. Positively pregnant and positively terrified.

Her—a mother? How was she supposed to become a mother, without her own mother there to help her? Elise had lost her mother again and again over the years. All the first holidays, her wedding day, those evenings when her inclination was still to call her just to say hello, but this felt like the most unbearable shade of grief yet.

"Amy. This feels like the absolute worst thing I could say right now. But I think I would regret not saying it. I haven't even told Tal yet. But I'm—I'm pregnant." The words hung in the air like an unexpected innocent verdict.

Amy never quite understood where the next moment came from, but if she had ever believed in God, it was here and now, because she didn't find herself recoiling. Amy was reaching toward Elise. There was no jealousy or fear. Just gladness.

Elise said she would still think about it. Amy waved her words away and told her not to give it a second thought. But they both gave it many more thoughts. Amy couldn't imagine a stranger carrying her child. Elise was having a hard time imagining having her own child, let alone carrying the weight of it for someone else. Elise didn't have to give them a yes or a no; they could just pretend that Amy had never asked, but in her heart Elise knew that if she did have to say something now, or maybe even later, the answer would be no.

Listen: "Don't Worry Baby"
by The Brook & The Bluff

FOUR

~~~~~~~~~~

APRIL 2006 CE

"Are we settled on Andraus? It means strong and manly. Isn't that a little on the nose for a boy who is probably going to be a giant?" Elise had a list of scribbled names and meanings in front of her.

"Yes, it's settled, in honor of your father. The middle name though, I'm not settled on that."

"Talmai, let me name our first boy after you. Is that too much to ask?" Elise tried to make her eyes big and round. It worked. Tal would do anything for her.

"If you want him to be Andraus Bartholomew—the son of Talmai—I won't stop you. But hear me out. What if we used my grandfather's name?"

"Ezekiel?"

"I was actually thinking the name from the camp—"

"Ebeneezer? Tal, I get it, but we can't. It's a little—macabre. And well it's just a lot of name for a kid."

"Not the full name, what about just Benee? Andraus Benee. It's part of our story. It will be his story too."

Elise smiled. She didn't hate Benee. "Could we call him Abee for short?"

Tal gently put his hand on her stomach.

"Always and forever."

Listen: "Ceilings"
by Lizzy McAlpine

FIVE

~~~~~~~~~~

MAY 2006 CE

Amy stared at the white ceiling. She couldn't move her eyes or her body. If she moved her eyes, the moisture that was collecting would spill out, and she couldn't cry anymore. If she moved her body, well she was too afraid to move her body. Shep was asleep in the chair next to her. The soft hum of his nose rattled in beat with the beep of the machine that was on the other side of her.

Amy wasn't just afraid to move her body though. She was afraid of her body. Was it on her side or working against her? It seemed like the verdict was still out. Had it been a year already? It was all a blur. Isaac had been able to retrieve sixteen eggs. Not a lot, but better than none. They opted to fertilize eight, and four of those eight made it to the blastocyst stage when they became ready for freezing. The other eight eggs were frozen immediately after retrieval. They had options. But all the options still broke Amy's heart.

Once the options were frozen in time, it was time for her undoing. And that's why she found herself here, now, staring up at the ceiling. Breasts, removed. Ovaries and fallopian tubes, now removed as well. No wonder it felt like she couldn't trust her body, could her body trust her? She was trying to trick it. She had to get to the tricky bits before the cancer could. It was like a game of hide and seek, with herself, but someone was sure to lose and since she was the only one playing, she didn't feel very optimistic about the outcome.

WANING CRESCENT

Listen: "When The World Stopped Moving"
by Lizzy McAlpine

SIX

~~~~~~~~~~

JUNE 2034 CE

May and Abee held the busted board between them like they had eleven times before. Once on accident, but ever since then, it had all been on purpose.

It was almost midnight. A sliver of moon hung in the sky and a sliver of moon rippled in the water. In 2034 it was a waxing crescent moon. It was 20.84% illuminated tonight and growing. In 2006 the moon would be a waning crescent, 20.75% illuminated and shrinking. Two completely different phases, but when they hopped, the amount of light would be the same; 0.09% would be an imperceptible change to the human eye. However, in a flash or a blur the illumination would move from the right side to the left side of the moon. It would be the same but different. May hadn't started out charting the moon; it hadn't even occurred to her the first few years. But the more she learned, the more she learned, and everything touched everything. It was all connected. It had to be.

May could see Abee to her right, but just dimly. She mainly knew he was there because of the balance of the board between them, the sound of his legs pushing through the water, the rhythm of his breath, and the smell of eucalyptus that was baked into him. She wouldn't have thought it was possible, but he was stronger, bigger, more of a presence after this year of pretending to be the best friend of a superhero.

The glow-in-the-dark hands on her watch pointed to 11:42. One minute to go. The third hand didn't glow, but she could feel it dutifully ticking away, moving the story forward. May wondered if it ever wanted a break. May squinted her eyes to try and see his face better across the darkness.

"Thanks for being here. I know it's more of a burden than ever. I love you for it."

"Mays, I think this might be the—"

May blinked; she must have blinked. The board was falling. She couldn't hold it. Why was it falling? May had no choice but to let it splash down into the water.

She had a picture in her mind, of herself staring up into the sky and trying to catch the moment when the light of the moon flashed from right to left. But all she could stare at right now was the void around her. The eucalyptus had vanished from the air. The waves pushed in, and there was no one next to her to push back. Abee was gone. She forgot all about the moon.

~~~~~~

"the end for me."

May was gone, and the board, and the magic was gone with her. But the moon was still there, so Abee talked to it. "I was born on April 20, 2006. I'm still there with you, Mays. Just as a less helpful two month old—I think." He smiled to himself. She'd be okay right? Sure, she had to be.

Abee slowly pushed through the water back up to the beach. They had been waiting on each other for a long time, hadn't they? He was happy to keep waiting, right here, as long as it took.

WANING CRESCENT

Listen: "Wordless Chorus"
by My Morning Jacket

SEVEN

~~~~~~~~~~

JUNE 2006 CE

Abee was gone and there was nothing May could do about it. She had never really worried about getting stuck in the past, because he had always been with her. If something went sideways, they could figure it out together, or at least that's what she had told herself. But now May felt deeply cold. She couldn't tell if it was fear or the weather. Maybe if it wasn't the middle of the night, maybe if even one other person was out on the beach, maybe it wouldn't have felt so overwhelming. But it was, and there wasn't, and it did. There was no reason to hurry. It was after midnight. They weren't eighteen anymore. Showing up at Amy's room wasn't really an option. And not just because she didn't live in that room anymore.

But what if Amy was awake? What if she *was* waiting? May stood and peered through the iron gate. All the lights in the house were off, but the patio lights were still on. The yellow glow triggered the wispy feeling of little legs crawling up her arm. May shook her hands, for the invisible spiders, and the visible stress. Her eyes adjusted to the darkness that was punctuated by the artificial yellow light. There was a big red board lying on the table. It looked like it had a piece of paper on it—a note.

May was through the gate and up on the patio. It was a note, and it was addressed to her—Mel. It was in her dad's handwriting, but written on behalf of her mom. Amy wasn't feeling well, or else she would have waited up, the note said. But Amy wanted Mel to have this board, as a thank you. A thank you for all the friendship over the years. It was a longboard, red, like the crayon a kid would use for a sunrise, or a fire, or a sunrise on fire. May wondered if Tal had ever told Amy the story about May wanting to get her a new board.

Prepared as always, May dug a pen out of her bag. She didn't let herself think about Abee's extra set of clothes that she had to rifle past to find the pen. He had just stayed in the future, right? He was fine, right? She'd see him in the morning, right?

211

The night was so still and quiet. Maybe her imagination got the best of her, but May thought she could hear a baby crying in the distance.

May flipped the note over, scribbled a few words of thanks. What was she going to do with the next five hours? The thought of shivering alone on the beach felt like too much. She just wanted to be in her bed. May pressed her face up against the widow of her room. The window was closed; she lightly pushed up on it, testing to see if it would budge. It would. It did. She pulled an old Coleman flashlight from her bag—never too prepared—especially after last year. The room was empty—of people. The stuff was still there though, like a time capsule of Amy's sadness over the past few years. It felt wrong to be there, but necessary. Was she trespassing? Breaking and entering? Coming home?

The beam of the flashlight swept over the room. She could just lie down for a while. The guest room, which became her parents room, and then just her dad's room, was on the other side of the sprawling house. Gene's room was upstairs. No one would even know she was there. This room was hers after all; she was just two years early. The flashlight illuminated the dust hanging in the air and clinging to the surfaces. The bed—dusty, the side table—dusty, the alarm clock—dusty, the dresser—dusty, the shag rug—well who could tell, the desk—dusty. The desk. May pointed the light back to the desk and walked closer. Amy's old high school yearbooks were still lined up on the desk. All four of them. May wasn't sure why she was drawn to them, well just the one, the one that she hadn't been able to find. The one from 94-95.

May touched the spine of the book with just the tip of her index finger, and a shiver ran down her own spine. She awkwardly held the flashlight with one hand and awkwardly tried to maneuver the book with the other hand. Nothing out of the ordinary on the first few pages. Then there was a scrap of paper, and a few pages over there was another one. May flipped back to the first one and pulled it out to read. It was a handwritten poem. The next scrap was the same, well a different poem, but the same idea. They were both in her Nonna's handwriting. But why in a yearbook? May flipped toward the middle, and the book opened itself to spill out two full-size sheets of paper.

June 20, 2001

My Darling May...

And then in an instant the flashlight wasn't necessary because the lights in the room were on, and a bleary eyed Gene was standing at the door. He moved toward May.

"Mon Aimée?"

May froze. Grandpa Gene said it again. He was confused. He was drunk. His martini was splashing out on his hand and dripping down into the shag.

"Mon Aimée? You look so, so well. How are you so well? Am I dreaming?"

There was only one thing May could do. She didn't speak, but she gently took the glass from him, put her arm through his, and helped him up the stairs to his room. He fell onto the bed. May pulled his shoes off, set them in his closet, and turned out the light.

"I love you grandpa," May whispered from the door.

"I love you too—" he must have slurred together *Mon Aimée*, but it really sounded like he said *My May*. May could hear him snoring before she even got to the stairs. She couldn't stay. She had to run. It was all getting too close. Too real. It was all coming painfully into focus. She had to get out. May grabbed the red board and went to spend the night shivering alone on the beach.

EIGHT

~~~~~~~~~~

Abee had meant to stay awake, to see what it looked like when it happened. But May was there next to him, talking to him, shaking him, and he had missed it.

"Abee! Abee?! Why do you have my mom's yearbook? I saw it, under your bed, years ago, but I didn't understand what or whose it was! What do you know? What haven't you told me? What's in it?"

Abee was so glad to see her, but he couldn't take in what she was saying. He tried to reach for her, but she pushed back. He shook his head, trying to catch up.

"I saw it, I saw it in Amy's room or my room, whatever. It's full of notes, but then my grandpa came in, and I had to leave. I was too freaked out. But you have it. You have it, don't you?"

"I found it. Years ago. I didn't mean to. You asked me to go to your room to find something, and it literally fell off the shelf and hit me. I don't know why I took it. I was worried, I guess."

"What do you mean, years ago?

"Remember when you cut your hand, on your tenth birthday? That many years ago."

May's mouth hung open.

"What's in it, Abee? What's in it? I saw my name. There was a letter to me. To me."

"I'm not sure to be honest. I never meant to lie to you. I was twelve. I just stuck it under my bed for a long time. It wasn't until, well all of this started happening that I even remembered I had it. I wanted to protect you at first, I think. And then I wanted to protect myself. I've always been afraid of losing you."

"What's in it, Abee?" May's eyes were full of fire.

"I'm being honest when I say I don't understand, but you're not the first person in your family to get to do this. Your Nonna—Gloria, I think she was from a different time."

Phase Nine or One

NEW

YEAR	DATE	TIME
2007	21-Jun	11:06 AM PDT

YEAR	DATE	TIME
2035	21-Jun	5:32 AM PDT

and

YEAR	DATE	TIME
1967	21-Jun	7:23 PM PDT

YEAR	DATE	TIME
1995	21-Jun	1:34 PM PDT

and

YEAR	DATE	TIME
1995	21-Jun	1:34 PM PDT

YEAR	DATE	TIME
2023	21-Jun	7:57 AM PDT

DUCK DIVE

Listen: "Last Time"
by Adam Melchor

ONE

~~~~~~~~~

JUNE 2007 CE

May's ears were ringing so loudly it made her feel nauseous. Or maybe the nausea was making her ears ring. She had hopped at 5:32 this morning. Thirteen times this had happened now. Thirteen times of standing on this beach, holding this busted board, surrendering herself to the weirdness of the universe. Thirteen moments of hoping she wasn't losing her mind. Thirteen moments of being sure she had. Thirteen chances to catch a glimpse of the women who created her. Thirteen chances to let them get a glimpse of her. And now here she was, with nothing to do but wait.

May understood why no one had ever told her. She couldn't imagine them having to say it. She couldn't imagine herself having to hear it. And she understood now that when you don't even know to ask the question, you're not going to ever get an answer. After all these years, who knew that one piece of paper accessible online, just dots and lines on a screen, could give her so much clarity.

Amy's body had been cremated. Not being particularly religious, Shep and Gene opted for a small gathering led by friends. It felt impossible to do it, but it felt impossible not to do it—they let her ashes out into the waves. Grandpa Gene told May about how Abee slept through the whole memorial, his curly black head smushed against Tal's chest. Grandpa Gene said that when Shep let the first handful of ashes down into the water, Abee laughed in his sleep. Grandpa Gene said it was just like his Aimée to come laugh at her own funeral.

May knew this story. It was nice to know and somehow it wasn't. It always made her feel separate from the rest of them. May assumed the disconnect was her problem, her insecurity. But maybe it was really that she had known, she had always known there was more that they weren't telling her.

Amy wouldn't have wanted a headstone out in some lonely field or even a plaque in a stuffy mausoleum, so in her honor they added some details to her favorite papier-mâché humpback. You couldn't see it from below, but once a year when Grandpa Gene brought out the extension ladder to check the smoke detectors, you could climb to the top of it and from above the whales you could see that one pectoral fin said *1980*. The other said *2007*. And the upturned tail fluke said *Amy Diedre Rousseau-Thomas*.

The second whale held the same pattern. It had been Amy's idea first. She painted it the summer after Gloria died. One fin said *1952*. The other said *2001*. The fluke read *Gloria Lahaina Phillips*. As a kid, May had always wondered whose name would get painted onto the third and final majestic humpback.

Maybe it was because somewhere inside her May knew the truth, but *early summer 2007* had always been a good enough answer. Her mom had died early in the summer of 2007. Early in the summer of 2007 she sat frozen in a lab while her mother died, a fact that was more than enough to try and wrap your mind around.

So of course no one had told May that her mom had died on June 21, 2007. Today. Solstice. When May was born just one day shy of a year later, no one could believe it. June 10 had been the due date. Given the very controlled nature of the pregnancy, there was no question as to what the due date was. But June 10 came and went, and May seemed to be in no hurry. Day by day as the anniversary approached and the baby still hadn't been born, Shep started to feel more anxious. This was a mistake. Why had he taken this step so quickly? He was selfish. Gene tried to reassure him that Amy wanted this too, that she would be so proud of him. If the child was born on the anniversary, well surely it meant Amy was there with them. But when May was born on June 20 and not June 21, Gene breathed a sigh of relief. It was Elise who realized that even though it was a day different, both days were the longest days of the year. Of course they were.

May walked up the beach, busted board in tow. She was tired of lugging it around. The new board Amy had gifted her last year was tucked in its spot in the secret cave. May pulled it out and onto the sand, leaving the busted board in its place. Apparently the cave wasn't actually too much of a secret though, because May could see some fresh dings and scratches. At least whoever had used her board had the decency to put it back.

There was enough light to get out in the water now. The thing May had dreaded for the first seventeen years of her life, had been the thing which saved her these past ten years. The waves were big. That was alright, a good thrashing would feel nice today. May loved being on a longboard, but getting such a big board out past big waves had never been her strong suit. She had always felt somewhat embarrassed that she couldn't get the hang of the duck dive. It felt like she was betraying her heritage. Eventually she had accepted that she was more of a turtle roller than duck diver. *Turtle Roll* would be a cute name for a restaurant, but some people might think it was a turtle sushi place. Probably best that Gene had gone with Duck's after all.

Duck diving was all about finesse and angles and maneuvering. *Turtle rolling* was just what it sounded like. Right before the wave came, you flipped on your back, held the board up and slightly out from your chest, and then just let the wave roll over you. It wasn't particularly impressive looking, but maybe turtles knew something about the ocean that ducks never could.

"M! M! Is that you out there?!"

May squinted to see Amy waving from the beach. With age they had developed even more of a likeness to each other. Perhaps, it was more the work of the sun and salt water than just time. May could see that Amy didn't have a board with her. What did that mean on today of all days? May waved back.

The universe might let her stay here. What if this year she didn't agree with being sent back, maybe if she didn't touch the board, maybe if she wanted it badly enough when the clock hit 11:06, maybe if she said some magic words, maybe then she could stay, here with Amy. She could stay by Amy's side. According to the death certificate May just needed two extra hours. Well, two hours and thirty-three minutes to be exact.

Death by drowning – Found Jun. 21, 2007 at 1339.

In some world, Amy had drowned. But here, right now, she hadn't drowned yet. Could today's outcome be different? If May stayed two hours and thirty-three minutes longer, two hours and thirty-three minutes past the solstice, maybe she could still stop it all from happening. But it wouldn't just be two hours would it? If May stayed, could she ever get back. Is that what the universe was asking of her? Is that what all of this came down to? Is that what her mom wanted from her? Is that what she wanted? If she stayed, she could live in this space for a while. Maybe that's how it worked? But she'd be absent from the future. She could save someone else, but lose herself? Was that it? Was that the only deal? Were these even her choices to make? May shook her head. It didn't make any sense. None of it ever had.

May watched as wave after wave crashed in the space between her and her mom. Wave after wave after wave. They never stopped. Sure they ebbed and flowed, but they never stopped. There had been moments in her life when the ebb and flow felt comforting. Right now, it felt exhausting. May had tried so hard to stop it all from coming. But it never stopped, did it?

Gloria still died. Amy was still hurting in her body and in her heart. Abee could only come so far with her. So here she was, not sure there was a point to any of it. There was no holding the waves back. If the waves were going to break her, they were going to break her. Isn't that what all of this had taught her? Everything happened just as it always had.

May didn't have any more expectations of today or herself. These past twelve years hadn't been a mission after all. They were a gift. Today she would just enjoy the gift one more time. She let the next wave take her all the way in and to her mom.

~~~~~~

May tried to soak up every part of her mom, without staring too long or intently at one spot. Amy's t-shirt hung loosely. Her pants were held up by a cinched drawstring, not the curves of her hips. Her cheekbones had appeared as prominent features.

"Hey, don't take this the wrong way, cause I'm being serious, I'm not teasing. I really dig that you turtle roll out there." Amy leaned back into the sand, staring up at the sky as she spoke. "Sometimes we make things more complicated than they have to be, don't we? And by *we*, I mean *me*." Amy paused. "You know I've always loved talking to you, right? It's like we're kindred spirits or something, so just be honest with me—are you an angel?" Amy tilted her head to look at May. Her smile had a hint of mischievousness to it, but her eyes were serious, pleading.

"I don't think so?" May's voice rose with *so*. It was her honest gut response. And it was her gut that pushed her on. "But I know that you've known for a while now that something—well, that something odd—is going on here, and—you're not wrong. And I'm not even worried at this point that'd you'd think I was crazy if I told you everything. I don't think you would think that, but I'm afraid it would mess with things. Things that would be too big to unravel. Or maybe so big that it would all unravel?" May's voice quivered. "I don't know what to do anymore. I hope I've been a good friend to you over the years. These days together have meant the world to me. I just really feel like I should have been able to do more to help you and Gloria. I'm so so sorry." And in an instant the kind of cry that feels like a yell escaped from May's mouth and her heart.

Amy grabbed May's hand, and with one squeeze their fingers were woven together. "None of this is yours to fix. Oh, Love. Not a single thing." Amy's face was wet too. "Everything is going to be alright. And if this helps, I don't want to know what happens next. I really don't. I think I'd rather just wake up every day and see what it brings." The lump in Amy's throat stopped her from saying more.

"What if I told someone else? Someone who could just help while I'm not here." May felt desperate.

"My sweet girl, you've been with me all along; you are with me. And whatever magic has made this possible, it's more than I deserve."

Clarity of thought possessed May, and her next sob stopped halfway out. What was the magic? *What was it?* After all these years of not allowing herself to just look straight at the thing—what was it that was actually strong enough to rip through space and time and reorder her world? She finally, suddenly saw it.

"I miss you so much."

"I miss you too."

"And I think I have to go now."

"That's okay; it's all okay. It's okay for you to go."

Amy meant it, but it didn't mean she was ready to let go of May's hand.

~~~~~~

Amy watched as May walked up the beach. May's skin was the same color as the sand, and the farther away she got, the harder it was to distinguish her shape from the shore. Amy felt herself shaking her head. In disbelief? In awe? Or was it just a learned reflex? Her whole life she had watched her mom shake her head and stare off into the distance. Who was Gloria watching walk away? Who was Gloria squinting to see on the shore?

Amy ran her hands over her flattened chest. She was so tired of being sad. Everything ached. She hadn't felt determined to be done with it all, but it was more like she felt resigned to it all being done. She had come down here this morning resigned to the fact that it was done, it was time to be done. She knew where she needed to swim, the place where the current would take her far away, and pull her down, and if she didn't fight it, it could all be done. She thought she was done.

But she had known the girl would be here, hadn't she? The girl was always here on these days, the solstice days. The days where the sun magically stood still for just a moment. Maybe Amy hadn't resigned all hope after all. Maybe there was still a bit more magic to be had.

Listen: "I'll Follow the Sun - Remastered 2009"
by The Beatles

TWO

~~~~~~~~~~

JUNE 2007 CE

Amy went to find Elise. Elise had been begging to help her, begging. But Amy kept pushing back. Elise had never officially said *no* to the unaskable thing, but Amy knew. Elise had her own family; she would probably keep having more of her own family. Amy's family wasn't Elise's responsibility. Amy didn't begrudge Elise, and she really never had. She didn't push Elise away, but she turned her angst on herself and ended up pushing herself away. Which was an imperceivable difference to the people in her life. Pushing herself away, or pushing them away, either way, it was distance that they were still failing to bridge.

But today—today Amy was ready to stop pushing and punishing everyone she loved. Amy called out as she came in through the back door. Surely Elise would be here. She was always just getting Andrew up from his nap or just getting ready to put him down for his nap.

"Els, Els. It's me. I don't want to scare you, but I don't want to yell and wake up the baby, either." Amy whisper-yelled for a few more sentences trying to make her presence known but not too known. No one responded.

"Amy?" Tal had come in behind her; she hadn't heard him over her own quiet racket. She jumped. "Abee was up all night with a cough, so she took him to the pediatrician. The appointment is at noon, I think, but you know, the doc's in Santa Monica, so it will be awhile before she's back."

Amy didn't know. She had made a point of not knowing too much about Elise's life lately. But she nodded like she did.

An idea came out of Amy's mouth before she even thought it, "How long has it been since we've surfed together? That used to be everything. It was all we had to care about. Come down with me for a bit? It's beautiful out today."

Tal smiled as if remembering, but his eyes gave him away. His eyes were full of pity. Amy felt the acid rise in her throat.

"You know, never mind, that was silly of me; you have work, and well—" Amy headed toward the door.

She hadn't been this vulnerable, this open with Tal in years. It wasn't unwelcome; it was just a surprise. "I do have some work right now, but I can come down later. That would be nice. Are you doing okay?"

"I will be." Amy gave one solid nod, as if that settled the matter.

Tal felt the urge, or was it a reflex, to say *I love you*. To make sure Amy still knew. But he held it back. Amy hadn't been okay. Tal knew that. Bones stuck out where they had never stuck out before. He wasn't sure what sinewy actually meant, but it's how she looked. What happens to muscle memory when the muscles are gone? Amy opened the door. She was walking out. *I love you* felt caught in his throat; he couldn't force it up or down. Tal's brain raced to find a workaround. "*Mon Amie*, I'll see you down there in a little while."

Amy nodded one more time and smiled. He still loved her.

~~~~~~

The restaurant was full. Amy knew they could use her help. She knew her absence had made their lives harder—at Duck's, but mostly just in general. Shep was working hard. Gene was drinking hard. She caught Shep's eye from across the kitchen. The steam coming off the dish in front of him blurred his expression, but she could still read the surprise. He had a right to look surprised. She was surprised with herself, too. It was like she was back from the dead.

Amy mouthed, hoping to communicate under the din of clanking pots, and pulsing fans, and chopping onions, *come down after lunch, I'll be at El Matador*. She mimed balancing on a surfboard. She could see his mouth open into a laugh.

I love you, Shep mouthed back.

~~~~~~

She was going to be okay. Amy tugged open the rusty door of the shed, but a rise in the ground stopped it from opening all the way. She kicked at the grass, making a divot. It swung open. Hot dust puffed out. Hot light poured in. Amy spotted a broom just inside the threshold, grabbed it and quickly started swiping webs out of the air. Even if she couldn't see them, a lifetime of hating this shed had taught her that *they were there*. Luckily Amy had no trouble seeing the thing she came for. You couldn't miss it—the board that still shimmered like the ocean. It was bigger than she remembered, or she was smaller than she realized. She hadn't used it in years. But today was a day for walking on water and flying at the same time. Amy heaved it out onto the grass. The sun was hot and bright; it wouldn't take long for the old wax to get softened up. Then she could scrape it off and start over.

Amy leaned forward and over the board and then slowly knelt to examine it for any new or old scratches, dings, cracks. She stared at the tail. Tal's fix was almost imperceptible. The new flowed into the old. As her gaze slowly moved up, she had to look hard for the patches that she knew were there. And then from the bottom of her vision she saw a black orb, floating down from her hair, hanging by an invisible strand, or maybe just free falling. Either way it felt like it was in slow motion. She meant to scream, but she couldn't. She froze. She just watched as the shiny black body with the perfect red hour glass fell onto the board. The spider landed on its back, hour glass up, legs contracted, motionless. Amy didn't move either. A mature female Black Widow. Was it dead?

Amy timidly ran her hand over the back of her neck and through her hair. She watched as the spider sank down into the softening layer of wax. She couldn't say why, but she moved to help it—to move it out of the baking sun and the melting wax. Amy grabbed a stick and began nudging the spider toward the side of the board. The first nudge was met with no reaction, but the second nudge pushed the spider from prone to supine and in an instant its legs were moving. Had it just been playing dead?

The spider dashed and then decided to resume its act. Belly up. This time she nudged it all the way off the board, into the grass. It righted itself and froze. It was covered in wax. It was definitely alive, but it was changed. It had taken on an unintended layer. Amy couldn't fix that. But the yellow sun and the black body might work together; the wax might roll right off its warm back. Or it might hide in the shadows and get heavy and still and stuck. Would it be alright? Or was it doomed? If it was doomed, should she fast-forward to the inevitable? Amy closed the door to the shed. She dragged the board up to the deck. She left the spider to work out its own fate.

~~~~~~

They told her eight weeks of no strenuous exercise. When Amy mentioned surfing, the doctor upped that to ten. But that had been over a year ago and Amy had barely even been outside. Amy had to stop and put the board down every 50 yards or so. It wasn't fair. Your strength could be cut out of you in an instant, and then you had to fight to get it back one long day at a time.

She shook her head as she looked up and down the beach again. Mel was really gone. What a strange world. What could Mel have told her though? Surely nothing Amy didn't already know—*at some point this ends*. Death and taxes and all that. It ends for everyone, that was more than enough to know. Amy smiled to herself, glad to have settled that, and glad to have settled that the end didn't need to come today. She could imagine tomorrow. A better one.

Amy got to the spot on the beach she had in mind, but for a different reason now. She needed to feel the pull and prove to herself that she could push back. She wasn't as strong as she used to be, but she was strong enough for today. Amy walked her board out into the waves. She looked toward the horizon and waited for the set to pass. She watched as the pink heart bobbed up and down in front of her. Then, she hopped on and started to paddle out. The board was the same as it had ever been, but she had changed. Tal made the board for a different person. A braver, stronger, softer person. Now Amy's knees and elbows knocked around it. Her hard angles twitched against the places she used to melt into.

The next set was coming more quickly than Amy had guessed and the waves were big. She didn't make up her mind in time, and so her body didn't get in position in time. A wave picked her up and threw her down in a heap. The water pulled her forward. Her leash pulled her back. Another wave crashed on her head before she had time to even realize she had broken through the surface. It was just water on top of water. She felt things spinning into chaos, but she also felt the strange comforting sensation that she had been here before.

Amy had to get control of the board, or she had to get rid of it. Up was down and down was up, or maybe it wasn't. And then the swirl threw her back and out and her body took a breath before her mind could even comprehend she had access to oxygen again. She opened her eyes long enough to clock that she had two seconds to make a move before it all started over. Her mind set up the neural chain of command that it had initiated thousands of times before. This is what you do feet, this is what you do legs, this is what you do shoulders, this is what you do breath. This is how we dive under this wave. This is how we get through it. This is what we've always done. DUCK. DIVE.

And she couldn't. While Amy's brain raced forward, her muscles had lost the memory. She was going to have to find a new way to work it out.

Amy meant to scream, but she couldn't. Instead, the seconds in front of her melted into minutes, and the sky and the water and the board in front of her melted into an unending landscape of blue fractals. She could see it all and she wasn't scared anymore. And she wasn't alone.

Amy could still feel her fingers woven in between her own. She had gotten to hold her hand. What magic was that? She could hear her laugh; she could sense her strong body moving through the water next to her. She could see her as she let the waves wash over her. And in an instant or an infinite moment Amy's body knew what to do.

Amy's leg moved, which moved the leash, which moved the board. Her shoulders curved forward, which brought her hands in reach of the rails, which gave her fingers something to hold. She rolled, twisting her torso and kicking her legs to get enough momentum to flip the board. Now, she was purposely under it. She pulled down on the board just enough to make sure the nose was submerged, but not so much that the whole thing was pulled below the surface. Her arms stayed bent to absorb the shock that was surely about to come. She held her breath. She felt the wave knocking, crashing, but she wasn't swirling this time. She was safe under the shelter of the board. She had turtle rolled her way out. But she couldn't stay; she had to keep going.

Amy used what strength she still had to pull the right rail down and into the water, and then she used the momentum of her own body to roll it and put it all right side up again. She shook her head to get her bearings, up-check, down-check, horizon-check, shore-check, breath-check. Amy immediately started paddling parallel to the beach. She had to get out of the riptide, but then where? The deep water was closer than the land at this point. Break free of the current, get to the calm of the deep water, and then she could rest.

Back, up, over, down, pull. Back, up, over, down, pull. Breathe. Back, up, over, down, pull. Back, up, over, down, pull. Breathe. And she was free.

The gentle crests and troughs rocked her, but they were in no hurry to crash out here. Amy let her head rest on the board. She closed her eyes. The sun was warm on her back. She lifted her arm and let her hand rest on the nose of the board, on the bright pink heart. Her finger traced the outline without even looking.

And just like her body had helped her know what to do in the chaos of the waves, now she felt certain of what she needed to do out here in the deep. She sat up to straddle her board. She was shaking from exhaustion, but it was more than that. Her neck felt stiff. She would never make it back in with the board; it was too big, too much. She lifted her right leg onto the deck. She pulled the strap off her ankle and let the end of the leash sink down into the water. She bent over, hugging this old piece of herself. She loved it, she was thankful for it, and it didn't fit anymore, and that was okay.

She slid off the back. Gave herself a minute to make sure she had her breath, and then pushed the board away. Pushed it back toward the current, the invisible river that would take it on. No one else was around, but someday, someone, somewhere would find some part of it, up the beach or down the beach or out at sea. They would wonder how it got there, and perhaps they'd even be concerned about what happened to its rider. They wouldn't know. But she'd know, and she'd know that everything was okay. Amy started to swim, free of the current, free of the board, just herself.

In the middle of a shaky up stroke, as she turned her head to the side to take a breath, she spotted her best friend waving on the shore. Tall, dark, and beautiful as always. She wanted to shout out, *I love you, I'm so sorry, I miss you*. And she would, she would say it all soon enough. But right now, she just had to get back.

Even from a distance Elise could see Amy was struggling. Amy was making the right motions, she was swimming, but something was not right. Elise clumsily splashed through the water until it was deep enough to dive into. Elise grabbed her hand at the first break. Amy let herself be pulled forward, and she let herself melt into Elise's arms.

Listen: "Baby"
by Oh Wonder

THREE

~~~~~~~~~

JUNE 1967 CE

The sun was warm on her face. The sand was warm against her back. She wanted to just sink into the warmth. And then she was coughing, choking, vomiting. It was all happening too quickly, and it was all too bright in her eyes, but an unseen hand rolled her to her side and started pounding on her back. Her lungs burned; her throat burned; her nose burned.

The hand had a nice voice though. It was calling, yelling for help. The voice sounded scared. Lola didn't feel scared; she just felt tired, so tired. The fire had finally stopped spewing out of her. She could breathe. She was breathing. The voice sounded less panicked. Other voices were there now, too. There were enough voices to lift her up. The sand underneath her was replaced by something stiff. A deep voice, not the voice attached to the hand, asked her what her name was. The answer was right on the tip of her tongue, on the edge of her brain, but she couldn't say it. Every time she was just about to grab it, it disappeared, and slipped through her fingers. She couldn't get a hold of it. The same thing happened when the deep voice asked her how old she was and where she was from. She knew these things, she knew she knew, but she didn't.

"Her sweatshirt says Malibu Sharks," one voice said. "What do you think that means?" The crowd seemed to have no idea. They agreed that it looked like a school shirt, but Spartans and Vikings were the only mascots around here.

Malibu. That sounded right. "I'm from Malibu," she said weakly. She didn't have her eyes open yet, but if she had, she would have seen a group of fellow teenagers exchanging incredulous looks. They were from Malibu, and they had never seen this girl before. The deep voice wanted to know who her parents were. Your mom's name, the voice clarified, hoping a more specific question might be easier to answer.

Mom. That felt right. "My mom's name is Diedre." The answer slipped through her lips without even having to think about it. She felt the nice hand on her arm now.

"Far out, that's my name too," the nice voice said.

Lola's eyes flew open. At her left arm was a very tanned, very handsome boy. A blur of tanned bodies stood behind him, and then to her right she saw a face that made her stop breathing again. She wasn't sure who she was, or where she was, but she knew without a doubt that the person touching her right arm at that exact moment was her mother.

~~~~~~

"My parents are musicians. They're in Monterey right now, or maybe they're back in San Francisco." Lola nodded as Diedre talked. And she watched as Diedre put a vinyl record on the player. Diedre's hair was perfectly styled, curled and bouncy, with a bright green paisley scarf tied around it. Her bikini was the same green. Lola was looking at her mother, but a version of her mother she had never known before.

"You can't buy this in the states yet," Diedre explained as she held up a yellow record jacket with purple writing for Lola to see. Lola could make out a big J and H. The other letters were too curvy for her to read from her spot on the sunken square-shaped couch. "They got it sent over from the UK." Diedre carefully dropped the needle and Jimi started to fill the room. "My mom called a few days ago. She said Hendrix lit his guitar on fire and then smashed it on the stage. Whatever happened, she sounded different. I don't think they're coming home any time soon."

Lola's grandparents were musicians. Lola knew that. Somehow she already knew that. But she also knew her mom didn't talk about them. They were never to be talked about. It made her too sad. Why was her mom talking about them now? Lola closed her eyes. The memories were there like faded impressions, not bright flashes.

"You must be so tired. Lie back. You should just rest. Wait, first, are you hungry? Thirsty? I have water and coffee. That's pretty much it actually. With just me here I don't shop much. I mostly eat at the diner. Do you remember anything yet?" Lola slowly opened her eyes and timidly shook her head—*no*. What she did remember made no sense. She could feel the tears coming.

"No worries; don't cry," Diedre offered quickly, her sweet face full of sympathy. "Honestly, it's no rush. You can stay as long as you want. I could use the company.

And I'm having a few people over later for a summer solstice party. It's the strawberry moon tonight, too, so you absolutely have to stay and celebrate with us."

"You would always wake me up to see the strawberry moon," Lola said quietly, but not too quietly. She remembered this. Her mom would get her out of bed; they would pluck the biggest strawberries from the garden, and they'd eat them under the full June moon.

"What?" Diedre heard just enough to be confused.

"I'm just starting to remember some things—maybe."

"With the solstice and the full moon happening on the same night, they say it's the perfect time to wish for your greatest desires. So maybe it'll all come back to you. Do you remember your name yet?"

Lola shook her head again, still *no*. She felt so silly. She didn't even know her own name, and yet she thought this nice girl was her mom. Maybe she did need a nap.

Diedre sat down next to her and grabbed her hand. "Hey, it's really okay. It's going to be okay. What if we just pick a temporary name for now. It can be anything, it can be like a nickname, just between friends." Lola nodded her assent, but couldn't think of anything to say.

Diedre took both of her hands now and closed her eyes for a few seconds, like she was thinking hard, or dreaming. "Okay, I've got it! To me, you feel like a Gloria." *Gloria Lahaina.*

That was her name. And she remembered now that her mom had always called her Lola.

"Alright I like that. But what if you call me Lola for short?"

Diedre squeezed her hands. It was settled.

~~~~~~

After Lola took a nap and showered, Diedre gave her some clean clothes to wear for the party. It was not just a few people. Lola recognized some of the tanned faces from down on the beach, but most, she didn't. At 7:20 Diedre ushered everyone out into the back yard. The sun hung just above the horizon, a perfect floating ball of light. Diedre informed everyone that the solstice was in three minutes and at that moment they should all make a wish. But the magic of tonight, she went on to explain, was that after the solstice, there would be exactly two hours and thirty-three minutes before the full strawberry moon rose. If you made the same wish on the full moon that you had made at the solstice, well then the sun and the moon and all the stars would be on your side and all your wildest dreams could come true. Most people giggled. Lola heard whispers of kissing under the moonlight. But this was no joke. This was her chance, her chance for another chance.

The first time she wished it, it was a simple—*I want to stay here.*

Two hours and thirty-three minutes later, the desire had grown—*I want to stay here. I can't go back. I need to be where she is.*

Lola could never explain it. She worried she was crazy. But the universe let her have a bite of its magic. She got more time with her best friend in the whole world— her mom. And she devoured every second like it was a ripe June strawberry.

~~~~~~

Diedre was right. Her parents didn't come home. So, it only made sense for Lola to stay with her. Malibu in the 60's was a literal acid trip. Whether it was hallucinations brought on by the sun or the chemicals, no one was sober enough to care where Lola had come from or where she was going. In people's minds she existed as Diedre's cousin. Or maybe they were sisters. Either way, she was there.

Lola enrolled herself in school. She used Diedre's last name, *Phillips*. There were less questions that way. And she couldn't remember her real last name anyway. She started her sophomore year right on schedule. They rode the bus into Santa Monica; that's where the closest high school was. The teachers wore suits and ties and dresses and panty hose. There was no gum chewing allowed, and every student was called by the name on the roll sheet, no nicknames. Lola was officially Gloria Phillips, and she had never been happier.

Gloria and Diedre became family to each other, they were family. They learned to cook for each other. They surfed together. They shared a love for poetry and sat on the sunken couch at night, reading together. They read Patchen and Plath, Baudelaire and Bukowski, Donne and Dickinson. They drank cup after cup after cup of coffee together.

Gloria's memories felt like the beach. Sometimes things would feel clear, but in a moment a wave could knock down the sandcastle of her certainty, and she'd have to start piling it up and smoothing it together all over again.

Diedre's parents came home for the girls' graduation in 1970. Some combination of touring Europe, and protesting Vietnam, and campaigning D.C.

had always kept them far away. They were in no position to ask questions of the girl who had appeared in their absence. So all they asked was where she planned to go to college and if she needed any money. They said they'd have their manager make sure her account was paid in full. Then as quickly as they dropped in, they were gone again.

Gloria sat with Diedre under another strawberry moon and wiped her tears. Diedre hated them—but she loved them—and she missed them. Gloria said she understood, and somehow she knew she did.

They were going to Berkeley, Diedre to study marine biology, Gloria for the fine arts program. Diedre loved the ocean, but she also loved doing whatever the opposite of music was. She couldn't risk being anything like her parents. Ironically, but maybe not surprisingly, studying the songs of the humpbacks became her obsession and her medicine.

Diedre met him the first day of Bio II, during their second year at Berkeley. He sat at the desk next to hers, and that's all he had to do. Gloria knew this day had been coming. Somehow she knew. She knew this person, and he scared her. But he was new to Diedre, and Diedre was in love. He was just mean enough to remind Diedre of her parents, but he was just nice enough to make her hope that he could be different.

When Diedre plopped down on the bed next to Gloria and said she was going to go to the Registrar to submit her withdrawal, Gloria just nodded. Diedre said she was going to Hawaii with him. She said Gloria could come too if she wanted. Gloria knew she couldn't. They had lived five perfect years together. It had been a gift, and now she had to let the gift go. The tighter you grab onto sand, the more you lose. You have to just enjoy the feeling of letting it flow through your hands. She couldn't keep her. Diedre deserved to go and live a life full of highs and lows, mistakes and stumbles, and love so big it can't help but break your heart. Diedre deserved to go and have it all, but she didn't deserve him. No one did.

So Gloria looked Diedre in the eyes and told her what she remembered about her own father, how mean he was, how much he drank, how he hurt her and her mother, and then she begged Diedre not to waste her time repeating that story. Diedre nodded. She knew Gloria was telling her the truth. A week later Gloria came back from her figure study class and found Diedre's side of the room cleared out. There was a note on Gloria's bed.

~~~~~~

NEW

January 11, 1972
My darling Lola,

I need to go, and so right now that means I need to go with him. But I promise I won't waste all my time on him. I'll love you forever and always. I wrote this for you...

A mouth painted red with stick and seeds.
Full and ripe between tiny chubby fingers.
Some waned bite by bite.
Others disappeared with a single chomp.

There and then gone.
There and then gone.
But not gone.
Just changed.

The sweet and the blush.
The sugar and the rush.
They linger, they spread.
They grow, they become you.

You are red and sticky and sweet now.
And you are mine now and I am yours.
Even as you grow and change.
Even as I am gone.

There and then gone.
There and then gone.
But not gone.
Just changed.

You are my sunshine. Go get your sunshine, Lola.

Diedre

DUCK DIVE

~~~~~~

Diedre's parents must have assumed that Gloria left Berkeley too, because no more accounts were being paid—in full or in part. It was 1972 now, and the only thing Gloria knew for sure was that she needed to get back to the sun. If she got back to Malibu, she felt certain the rest would work itself out.

But Diedre followed her own sunshine to the Big Island. He took her to a little hideaway cottage in Ocean View, a place borrowed from a friend. There weren't many other people around. At first it was romantic, and then it was lonely, and then it got scary. Mauna Ulu, on Kīlauea's East Rift Zone, had been erupting since 1969. The reports described the activity at the crater as alternating between high fountains and long periods of peaceful overflows. When they showed up in early 1972, it looked like the eruptions were coming to an end. For a few weeks the lava stilled itself, but on February 3, it became clear that Pele was far from done with her work. The crater erupted—again—this time with fountains higher than the Empire State Building. And so did he. They hadn't even been there a month.

As Diedre pressed a towel against the gash on her forehead—he had thrown a bottle—she knew she had already wasted too much of herself. Even if the fountains went back to peaceful overflows, she could see now that she'd always get burned. With Gloria's voice clear in her mind, she did the bravest thing she'd ever done. She decided for herself that she didn't deserve him after all, and she left. With each step she took—away from him—Diedre could feel a world crumbling. A world that could have been, or had been already. Either way, she knew it couldn't go on, and so she kept on walking.

Diedre couldn't afford to get back to California, but she also didn't want to get back. Instead, she found her way to Maui, Lāhainā to be exact. She sat under the great banyan tree for a week. She got a job on a tour boat. She met the humpbacks, the guardians who always came home. She met their babies in the Auau Channel. She went back to school, Maui Community College this time. She listened to the whales sing. Her professors said their deepest, lowest songs could travel to the other side of the world. There was no place their song couldn't reach.

Every June, when the full moon spoke to the strawberries, Diedre sat under the banyan tree, and she thought of Gloria. Her memories faded throughout the years; one day she couldn't say Gloria's name anymore. It was there, and it wasn't. But even as the memories escaped her, every time she touched the great tree, she felt a love that cut through the distance. Diedre became a professor herself, and a researcher. Her research team was working to understand the humpback's resistance to cancer. She drank coffee grown just up the mountain. Her body stayed strong until the end—full of sun and salty air and free of fear. The whales became her family too. And Diedre never left.

In the old church graveyard, the one with the Kings and Queens, there's a simple slab.

Diedre Phillips
1952-2023
forever in the sun

Listen: "Up From A Dream"
HAIM

FOUR

~~~~~~~~~~

JUNE 2023 CE

May could see the sun peeking in through the slats of her shutters. June could be notoriously gloomy, but not today. Today, June 10, was her birthday. Her fifteenth birthday. It *was possible* she had just slept through the morning fog, but whether it had never come, or come and gone, it was just sunshine now. May flipped over to look at her alarm clock—11:24. Still two hours til the party; maybe she could sleep a little longer. Once a year, just for her, they closed Duck's and brought everything down to have a birthday-bake-on-the-beach. When everyone you knew and loved worked at a restaurant, it was a big deal to close it for a day. May loved the food—crab, lobster, clams, scallops, potatoes, corn, and Grandpa Gene's seasoning—and she loved the party and all the attention, but the fact that they stopped everything, just for her, meant even more.

Sleeping longer sounded nice, but the waves were probably good today, and that sounded nice too. Before her brain even had time to decide, May's body was up and out of bed. She put on her new bubble-gum pink bikini. Well it was new to her, but she'd found it at the vintage store. She opened her shutters and hopped out her window; it was quicker that way. She started to grab her board from the side of the house, but it'd be easier to grab Abee first and then come back for the board. Abee was definitely still asleep. Elise always called him the sleeping giant.

The door of the Berenson house swung open, banging against a stack of boxes. Elise had a book signing and tasting event up in Ojai next week. Elise was a big deal, but she still had to schlep her own boxes around.

May took the stairs two at a time and was jumping on the end of Abee's bed before he even knew someone was in his room. He pretended to keep sleeping even after he was very aware May was there. She jumped all the harder. Bounce. Bounce. Bounce. Crack. Thwap. Shit.

Abee jumped up and May rolled off the bed so her eyes could be first on the damage. A slat—or three—had snapped under the mattress. That explained the crack. A thick book was spread open on the floor. That explained the thwap.

Why did Abee have a book under his mattress? At first glance May thought it looked like some sort of text book, that was strange, but as she stuck her head further under the bed to see how to get the busted slats out, rows of smiling faces stared up at her. She abandoned the boards and grabbed the book. She closed it. Her eyes scanned the black cover with teal lettering. It was the Malibu High School Yearbook from 94-95.

"Abee, why do you have an old yearbook under your mattress?"

After his initial jump scare, he had flopped back down and pulled the covers over his head. He didn't respond. May hopped back up on the bed, cupped her hand around her mouth, and leaned forward toward the round spot that looked like a head. "There–was–aaaa–yearrrrbookkkk–unnderrr–your–maaattressssss."

"I cannnn–hearrrr-youuuuu," the covers mumbled. "And–noooo–there's–nottttttt."

She grabbed the covers and yanked them back. "Yes, there is. Look." She held the book up in front of his face, too close in front of his face. He scooted back and blinked the sleep from his eyes.

"94-95, as in 1994-1995?" He took in the cover. "Why would I have an old yearbook, Mays? It must be my dad's."

May nodded absentmindedly as she flipped back into the book. She had stopped listening to him. She turned to the middle, thought better of it, and turned to the inside cover. Was this really Tal's?

Don't ever change! XOXOXOXO Molly
LYLAS! Ashly
BFFS4LYF4RL ~Your girl Brit

This was not a boy's yearbook. May flipped to the next page. In lieu of any sort of (mildly) clever or (barely) meaningful message, this person had opted to just tessellate the message recipient's name across a whole signature page for them.

> *AMY*
> *M*
> *AMY*
> *M*
> *AMY you'll go on forever in my heart.*

May rolled her eyes, the 90's were a strange time, but at least this note offered definitive information. This yearbook belonged to her mom. "Abee, why do you have my mom's yearbook?"

"Why do you keep saying ridiculous things while I'm trying to sleep?"

May turned the page. A scrap piece of paper was tucked into the seam. The first thing she noticed was the handwriting. It was not the bubbly loud scrawl of the other messages. It was tight and exact and meaningful. It was a poem. A few pages over there was another one. And another.

May flipped the whole book inside out and shook it to release all of its extra contents. Small scraps floated down onto Abee's bed like confetti. The handwriting was so familiar. They were all poems. She flipped it back over and two full size pieces of paper revealed themselves to still be wedged into the center of the book. The first paper started with—

June 20, 2001
My darling May...

A letter to her? She tried to keep reading it while simultaneously seeing what the second page said. They were crafted separately. The papers were different weights and shades of white, but they had been placed there together. The second one said—

January 11, 1972
My darling Lola...

May's body flushed from top to bottom. She scooped up all the loose pieces of paper, tucked them in the front pocket of her hoodie and tucked the yearbook under her arm. As she sprinted down the stairs she thought she could hear Abee yelling something like—*oh, that yearbook?* But it didn't matter, she just had to show her mom.

Listen: "Manifest"
by Andrew Bird

FIVE

~~~~~~~~~~

JUNE 2023 CE

Her mom was sitting on the back patio, intent on finishing her crossword. May threw the book down on the table without saying a word. "Well good-morning birthday girl. Is this how fifteen is going to be?" Amy was all smiles with only a slight roll of the eye toward the drama that had just interrupted her puzzle. May was too flustered to care if she was teasing her or being serious.

Everything after that came out as one enormous run-on sentence-paragraph-novel. The yearbook, Abee's room, poems, notes, Diedre, Lola. From Nonna Lola to May. But how? Amy set down her phone. Her fingers tingled as they touched the book. This was her yearbook.

"In Abee's room?"

May nodded *yes* emphatically.

Amy remembered it, sort of. It had been so long ago. 28 years ago. She barely remembered what she had for breakfast. Well that wasn't true. She knew today. Every Saturday she still had a donut—in honor of Isaac.

Amy flipped through the pages—believing but not believing. It was just like May had said. But how? Gloria had died what, six or seven years before May was even born? She waved for May to come closer. She pointed at her own picture. Her red-headed self, deep in the middle of puberty, not grown, but not a kid. She looked so much like May.

They were beyond words. It was all pointing and sounds. Amy pointed to the box next to her picture. *No Portrait Available.* May buzzed with energy as she watched her mother's finger slowly slide across the page. They read it together. Silently but together. Lola Rossi.

~~~~~~~~~~~~~~~~~~~~~~~~~~~~~~~~~~~~~~

It came to Amy in shallow murky waves. At fifteen she had been far too in love with Tal to think much about anything or anyone else. But she could almost see a poster in her mind. It was like seeing a memory of a memory though. The poster was on the bulletin board in the school hallway. A girl was missing. Amy remembered feeling sad, and mad, and not surprised as she stared at the board. It wouldn't be the first or the last time someone went missing here. Amy almost remembered her, but she must have gone to the other lower level school. Amy didn't remember knowing her. She could almost hear a teacher calling her name though—Lola, Lola Rossi. But there was never any *here* in response. Lola was always absent. Then Amy remembered a teacher saying something to the class about a death, a mother, a mother named Diedre. Lola and Diedre. Like the letters. Somehow like the letters in the yearbook.

That memory, and the letters, and that gray box that said *No Portrait Available* were all they had—at first.

~~~~~~

Amy was glad to be in the quiet clean lab come Monday morning. She was the mother of a fifteen-year-old now. She shook her head; time was so strange. Amy could still see May's tiny fingers, her red hair, her red body, like they were printed on her mind. May had come into the world like she was on fire, and she'd been keeping Amy warm ever since. The party, all the people, the weird thing with the yearbook; it had been a lot. Yes, she was glad for her quiet lab now.

Amy sipped her coffee. May had become obsessed with learning how to brew the perfect pour-over. Amy knew she should probably try to dissuade May from drinking too much caffeine as a teenager, but she was getting used to having this perfect cup made for her everyday. So Amy was actually doing the opposite of trying to discourage May; she was encouraging her habit. Amy even gave her some fancy beans for her birthday. Amy had a longtime colleague who could get green coffee beans from the mountains of western Maui—straight from the farm, and then May could roast them herself. Not that it was a competition, but if it was; her present had been the winner.

Amy clicked to the tab for her email. Spam. Ad. Spam. Meeting reminder. She stopped. The fifth message down was from a name she didn't recognize, but the name in the subject line she knew immediately; it was about her colleague, from Maui, the one who sent the coffee she was currently drinking.

Tyler, whoever Tyler was, was writing to let everyone know the very sad news that their beloved colleague Diedre Phillips had passed away on Saturday. Her team, and the community on Maui was heartbroken. The cancer had been swift. She hadn't suffered long. If anything, her own sudden diagnosis had seemed to infuse her with superhuman strength for their research. Diedre made great strides in the last few weeks of her life. Her team would continue her work. She had taken them far. Tyler assured everyone that they would see it to the end now. They expected to still publish within the year. He would send out more info about a service once arrangements had been made.

Amy swiveled around on her stool. She was still in her lab. That was good. But everything felt strange. There was that name again, Diedre, and Phillips. Phillips was Gloria's last name; she had kept her own name. But there were a million Phillips in the world, and their family didn't know anyone in Hawaii. But Diedre Phillips. Amy did know her; she was sure of it. And not just because they had worked together for the past twenty years.

It didn't take much convincing; they all wanted to come. A trip to Hawaii, yes please. Even Grandpa Gene was ready for a break. Shep decided they would close the restaurant. They had done it before and the world hadn't exploded. This trip felt similar, but the differences were striking. For one, Isaac wasn't with them and now they were flying first-class, which was out of the question twenty years ago. And of course now they had the kids. Amy knew the kids obviously hadn't been on that first trip with them, the one to Poland, but sometimes she had a hard time remembering that. It seemed like May and Abee had always been with them.

The time change had Amy up early. Same for May. Same for Abee. 4:00 a.m. early. They walked along the beach which was so beautifully different from their own. They squinted to see the misty spouts popping up from the horizon. They walked toward the center of Lāhainā. It wasn't even 5:00 a.m. yet, probably still too early to find coffee. And then May saw it. The great banyan tree. Without speaking they walked toward it, like it was calling them.

They wrapped their arms around it—or they tried—like they were hugging a long lost friend. The watch on Abee's outstretched arm dinged with a reminder. It was 4:57 a.m. *Solstice* the alert read. He swiped it away, and they all leaned in a little closer.

They brought Elise back later. Elise brought Tal. Tal brought everyone else. They all felt it. *A thin space,* Elise said. *A vortex,* Shep said. It looked like a forest. But it was all one. The tree started out as an eight foot tall sapling, and now 150 years later it was over sixty feet tall and stretched wide enough to cover a whole city block. As the branches spread from the original trunk; they sent aerial roots down from the canopy to the ground. The roots hanging in the air grew and strengthened, and eventually became the strong vertical support the sprawling tree needed. These roots turned trunks gave the appearance of separate trees, but they were all one.

Tal spoke, but only loud enough for Amy to hear.

"That first board I made—" he paused like she might not know what he was referencing. She did. "Well it was made with banyan heart wood. The stringer I mean. The stringer was banyan. My dad found it, and he somehow knew it was sacred. Seeing this here now though, I hate to think about any part of a tree like this being cut down or even just naturally broken off."

Amy ran her hand over one of the newest aerial roots, still soft and dangling. "Sometimes things have to be pruned though. Let's just assume it came from a branch that had to be pruned."

And then she could see it, for just a blur of a second. Her grandmother, her mother, her daughter, worlds that had done and undone themselves in a million ways. It all mattered, it all made sense, it all was part of the same story, but at the same time none of it mattered. These people, here in this moment, so full of love and life, that's all she needed to know right now.

Listen: "I Know The End"
by Phoebe Bridgers

SIX

~~~~~~~~~~

AUGUST 2023 CE

The restaurant had cleared out, but in just a little over twelve hours it would be full again, so they had to be quick. May wasn't sure if it had been her idea or her mom's; maybe they had both thought of it. Gene and Shep pieced together a makeshift scaffold for them. On the first one May held the paint steady as Amy carefully added her memory to the top of the dusty, beautiful, old whale.

They switched roles for the next one. They weren't sure if they understood it all exactly. They actually assumed that they probably didn't, but it felt important to try and honor what they did know.

From up above the first whale you could see that one pectoral fin said *Lola*. The other fin said *Gloria Lahaina*. The tail fluke said *Nonna Lola*. The second whale held the same pattern. One fin said *Diedre*. The other fin said *Dr. Phillips*. The tail fluke said *Grandma Di*. They decided not to put any dates. *When* was the least important thing about *who* these women were.

And there was still one majestic humpback left. May knew that someday she would add the memory of her own mother to that whale. *Amy Diedre Rousseau-Thomas. Daughter. Mother. Best Friend.* Someday, many days and years from now.

SEVEN

~~~~~~~~~~

JUNE 2035 CE

There were so many things about today that felt too good to be true. But having Elise next to her, for that Amy felt unbelievably lucky. This yard looked perfect now, the pool that had been made to look like a natural spring, the sprawling patio that was set with tables covered in white linens glowing with candles, the dance floor spread out over the perfectly green lawn, but it seemed like just yesterday when that rickety, nasty, hell hole of a shed had been all this yard had to offer.

28 years ago now, Amy had spent two days in the hospital, the neurotoxic venom had hit her—already fragile body—hard. Her heart had stopped. But Elise had been there, and it hadn't been the end. When Amy got home from the hospital, she didn't have to explain anything to Elise. Elise found Amy in the yard pulling apart the shed one board at a time. Elise joined her. Amy wanted to burn it. Burn it all down. It was a terrible and not to mention an illegal idea, but all Elise said was that she was there with her, whatever Amy needed. And as it turned out, that's all Amy really needed. So instead of burning it down, bit by bit Gene hauled the debris of the spider infested shed to the dump.

After that, Elise looked Amy in the eyes and told her she loved her. She wanted their families to be family, always. And she was ready to say *yes*. She wanted to help Amy and Shep. She would carry for them. Elise wasn't scared anymore.

Three months later, Elise was positively pregnant, again, with her best friends' baby. On June 10, 2008, not a day late, not a day early, May Vere Thomas was born.

And today, their babies were getting married.

~~~~~~~~~~~~~~~~~~~~~~~~~~~~~~~~~~

Abee held May's hand in his. His finger traced the scar on her palm as he looked into her eyes. They had written their own vows. The rush of emotion tried to blur his memory, but he could never forget her words to him.

Andrew Benee Berenson, like the sun needs the moon and the moon needs the sun, like Castor chooses Pollux and Pollux chooses Castor, like the ebb bleeds into the flow and the flow bleeds into the ebb, I, May Vere Thomas, promise to give you a love that will be long and a long time full of all my love.

He would always be her very best friend.

NEW

Listen: "One In the Same"
by My Morning Jacket

EIGHT

~~~~~~~~~~

The sun was coming through the window in hot, bright stripes. It was too early. She held still for a minute, mentally going through the list of everything she was thankful for. There was so much. Him, and her, and him, and oranges, and lemons, and avocados, and the waves, and the cat who had started coming by, and this house, and him again, and the sunshine—even if it was forcing her out of bed in this peaceful moment—and coffee. She could get up for coffee. She slowly slid out of the covers, doing her best not to jostle the bed.

She started the kettle, ground the beans, ran hot water over their mugs. She whisked together the muffins, and started cracking the eggs. She loved the certainty of breakfast. The day might bring a million different things, but at least this was a given. Dark coffee, fluffy eggs, muffins bursting with last summer's juiciest berries— frozen in perfection for just a moment like this.

The sun eventually did its work on the rest of the house. Someone started the record player, someone took the muffins out to the patio, someone spilled the orange juice, and someone added bananas to the shopping list. As they walked out the back door together, dressed and most teeth brushed, some headed to school, some across the yard, some down to the beach, they gave hugs and hand squeezes and reminders about meetings and lunches. And there were no clouds in the sky, and the sun was particularly bright and particularly hot, and they had no idea the end was just eight minutes away.

APPENDIX A – THE MUSIC

It's like a soundtrack for a book. Find it on Spotify by searching playlists → Duck Dive or use this list to make your own

NEW	ARTIST	SONG	ALBUM	SOURCE	DISTRIBUTORS/HOLDERS	RELEASED
1.1	Jim James, Teddy Abrams, Louisville Orchestra	"Back To The End Of The World"	Back To The End Of The World	UMC - Decca Gold	A Decca Gold release / ℗© 2019 UMG Recordings, Inc.	September 27, 2019
1.2	Tyler Childers	"Lady May"	Purgatory	Hickman Holler Records	℗© 2017 Hickman Holler Records marketed & distributed by Thirty Tigers	February 9, 2022
1.3	Shakey Graves and Sierra Ferrell	"Ready or Not"	Ready or Not (feat. Sierra Ferrell)	Dualtone Music Group, Inc.	℗© 2022 Dualtone Music Group, Inc.	February 9, 2022
1.4	Rayland Baxter and Dylan LeBlanc	"Mother, Mother"	Luck Mansion Sessions	Third Man Records	℗© 2017 Third Man Records, LLC	March 17, 2017
1.5	Willie Nelson	"Something You Get Through"	Last Man Standing	Legacy Recordings	℗ 2018 Sony Music Entertainment	April 27, 2018
1.6	Dr. Dog	"The Breeze"	Fate	We Buy Gold Records	℗© 2008 We Buy Gold Records	May 2, 2008
1.7	Stephen Sanchez	"Lady by the Sea"	Lady by the Sea	Republic Records	℗© Stephen Sanchez, under exclusive license to Mercury Records/ Republic Records, a division of UMG Recordings, Inc.	December 18, 2020
1.8	Jim James	"I Just Wasn't Made For These Times"	Tribute To 2	ATO Records	℗© 2017 ATO Records, LLC. All Rights Reserved.	December 8, 2017

APPENDIX A – THE MUSIC

It's like a soundtrack for a book. Find it on Spotify by searching playlists → Duck Dive or use this list to make your own

WAXING CRESCENT	ARTIST	SONG	ALBUM	SOURCE	DISTRIBUTORS/HOLDERS	RELEASED
2.1	Sleeping At Last	"One"	Atlas: Enneagram	Asteroid B-612	℗© 2019 Asteroid B-612	July 11, 2019
2.2	The Beatles	"Here Comes the Sun"	Abbey Road (Remastered)	EMI Catalogue, Concord Music Publishing	© 2015 Apple Corps Ltd / ℗ 2015 Calderstone Productions Limited (a division of Universal Music Group)	September 26, 1969
2.3	Free	"Oh I Wept"	Fire and Water	UMC (Universal Music Catalogue)	℗© 1970 Universal-Island Records Ltd.	June 26, 1970
2.4	Tyler Childers	"All Your'n"	Country Squire	Hickman Holler Records / RCA Records	℗ 2019 Hickman Holler Records, under exclusive license to RCA Records, a division of Sony Music Entertainment	August 2, 2019
2.5	The Beatles	"The Long and Winding Road"	Let It Be (Remastered)	EMI Catalogue	© 2015 Apple Corps Ltd / ℗ 2015 Calderstone Productions Limited (a division of Universal Music Group)	May 8, 1970
2.6	Noah Kahan	"Everywhere, Everything"	Stick Season	Mercury Records / Republic Records	℗© 2022 Mercury Records / Republic Records, a division of UMG Recordings, Inc.	October 14, 2022
2.7	Maya Manuela Featuring Pembroke	"multiverse"	multiverse	Maya Manuela	℗© 2022 Maya Manuela	November 11, 2022
2.8	The 1975	"When We Are Together"	Being Funny In A Foreign Language	Dirty Hit	℗© 2022 Dirty Hit	October 14, 2022

APPENDIX A – THE MUSIC

It's like a soundtrack for a book. Find it on Spotify by searching playlists → Duck Dive or use this list to make your own

FIRST QUARTER	ARTIST	SONG	ALBUM	SOURCE	DISTRIBUTORS/HOLDERS	RELEASED
3.1	Fruit Bats	"When U Love Somebody"	Mouthfuls	Sub Pop Records	℗ © 2003 Sub Pop Records	August 4, 2003
3.2	The Avett Brothers	"I Wish I Was"	True Sadness	RRE, LLC /Republic	℗ © 2016 Republic Records, a division of UMG Recordings, Inc.	June 24, 2016
3.3	Nathaniel Rateliff & the Night Sweats	"The Future"	The Future	Stax	℗ © 2021 Stax Records, Distributed by Concord	November 5, 2021
3.4	Jason Isbell and the 400 Unit	"If We Were Vampires"	The Nashville Sound	Southeastern Records	℗ © 2017 Southeastern Records	June 16, 2017
3.5	Nick Drake	"Pink Moon"	Pink Moon	UMC (Universal Music Catalogue)	℗ © 1972 Island Records, a division of Universal Music Operations Limited	February 25, 1972
3.6	John Prine	"I Remember Everything"	I Remember Everything	Oh Boy Records, Downtown Music Publishing	℗ © 2020 Oh Boy Records marketed and distributed by Thirty Tigers	June 11, 2020
3.7	Taylor Swift	"Midnight Rain"	Midnights (3am Edition)	Taylor Swift, Universal Music Publishing	℗ © 2022 Taylor Swift	October 22, 2022
3.8	M. Ward	"Chinese Translation"	Post-War	Merge Records	℗ © 2006 Merge Records	August 22, 2006

APPENDIX A – THE MUSIC

It's like a soundtrack for a book. Find it on Spotify by searching playlists → Duck Dive or use this list to make your own

WAXING GIBBOUS	ARTIST	SONG	ALBUM	SOURCE	DISTRIBUTORS/HOLDERS	RELEASED
4.1	Johnny Flynn	"Einstein's Idea"	Country Mile	Transgressive	℗© 2013 Transgressive Records	September 30, 2013
4.2	Shakey Graves	"Chinatown"	Role The Bones X	Dualtone Music Group	℗© 2021 Dualtone Music Group, a division of MNRK Records	April 2, 2021
4.3	Fleet Foxes	"If You Need To, Keep Time On Me -Solstice Version"	A Very Lonely Solstice	Anti / Epitaph	℗© 2021 Fleet Foxes, under exclusive license to Anti	December 10, 2021
4.4	The Mamas & The Papas	"Gemini Childe"	All The Leaves Are Brown (The Golden Era Collection)	Geffen	A Geffen Records Release © 2001 UMG Recordings, Inc. ℗ This Compilation ℗ 2001 UMG Recordings, Inc.	August 28, 2001
4.5	Bakar	"Hell N Back"	Hell N Back	Black Butter, Sony Music Publishing	℗ 2019 Bakar under exclusive license to Black Butter Limited	August 15, 2019
4.6	flipturn	"August (Acoustic)"	August (Acoustic)	flipturn	℗© 2019 flipturn	February 15, 2019
4.7	Mr. Joy	"Astrovan"	Mt. Joy	Dualtone Music Group, Inc.	℗© 2018 Dualtone Music Group, a division of MNRK Records	March 2, 2018
4.8	Father John Misty	"Goodbye Mr. Blue"	Chloë and the Next 20th Century	Sub Pop Records	℗© 2022 Joshua Tillman, under exclusive license to Sub Pop Records	April 8, 2022

APPENDIX A – THE MUSIC

It's like a soundtrack for a book. Find it on Spotify by searching playlists → Duck Dive or use this list to make your own

FULL	ARTIST	SONG	ALBUM	SOURCE	DISTRIBUTORS/HOLDERS	RELEASED
5.1	Jimi Hendrix	"The Wind Cries Mary"	Are You Experienced	Legacy Recordings	℗ 2009 Experience Hendrix L.L.C., under exclusive license to Sony Music Entertainment	May 12, 1967
5.2	Everclear	"Santa Monica"	Sparkle And Fade	Capitol Records	A Capitol Records Release ℗ © 1995 Capitol Records, LLC	May 11, 1995
5.3	Big Thief	"Change"	Dragon New Warm Mountain I Believe In You	4AD	℗ © 2022 Big Thief under exclusive license to 4AD Ltd	February 11, 2022
5.4	Corey Kilgannon	"God Is Just the Universe"	God Is Just the Universe	Corey Kilgannon, under exclusive license to Amuseio AB	℗ © 2020 Corey Kilgannon, under exclusive license to Amuseio AB	April 12, 2020
5.5	Fleet Foxes	"I'm Not My Season - Solstice Version"	A Very Lonely Solstice	Anti / Epitaph	℗ © 2021 Fleet Foxes, under exclusive license to Anti	December 10, 2021
5.6	Billie Marten	"La Lune"	Writing of Blues and Yellows (Deluxe Version)	Chess Club / RCA Victor	℗ 2016 Sony Music Entertainment UK Limited	September 23, 2016
5.7	HAIM	"Leaning On You"	Women in Music Pt. III	Columbia, Sony Music Publishing	℗ 2021 Haim Productions Inc. under exclusive license to Columbia Records, a division of Sony Music Entertainment	February 19, 2021
5.8	Bob Dylan	"I Contain Multitudes"	Rough and Rowdy Ways	Columbia	℗ 2020 Columbia Records, a Division of Sony Music Entertainment	June 19, 2020

APPENDIX A – THE MUSIC

It's like a soundtrack for a book. Find it on Spotify by searching playlists → Duck Dive or use this list to make your own

WANING GIBBOUS	ARTIST	SONG	ALBUM	SOURCE	DISTRIBUTORS/HOLDERS	RELEASED
6.1	Maria Kelly	"the sum of the in-between"	the sum of the in-between	Veta Records	℗© 2021 Veta Records	October 15, 2021
6.2	Love You Later	"Growing Season"	Growing Season	Love You Later	℗© 2018 Love You Later	November 23, 2018
6.3	John Mayer	"You're Gonna Live Forever In Me"	The Search for Everything	Columbia	℗2017 Columbia Records, a Division of Sony Music Entertainment	April 14, 2017
6.4	Fleet Foxes	"In the Morning - Solstice Version"	A Very Lonely Solstice	Anti / Epitaph	℗© 2021 Fleet Foxes, under exclusive license to Anti	December 10, 2021
6.5	boygenius, Julien Baker, Lucy Dacus, Phoebe Bridgers	"True Blue"	the record	boygenius under exclusive license to Interscope Records	℗© 2023 boygenius, under exclusive license to Interscope Records	March 1, 2023
6.6	Bonny Light Horseman, Eric D. Johnson, Josh Kaufman, Anaïs Mitchell	"Deep In Love"	Bonny Light Horseman	37d03d, Shelly Bay Music LLC	℗© 2020 37d03d	January 24, 2020
6.7	Oshima Brothers	"Love is Tall"	Dark Nights Golden Days	Oshima Brothers Music	℗© 2022 Oshima Brothers Music	April 1, 2022
6.8	Petey	"Microwave Dinner"	Lean Into Life	Terrible Records	℗© 2022 Terrible Records	September 29, 2022

APPENDIX A – THE MUSIC

It's like a soundtrack for a book. Find it on Spotify by searching playlists → Duck Dive or use this list to make your own

THIRD QUARTER	ARTIST	SONG	ALBUM	SOURCE	DISTRIBUTORS/HOLDERS	RELEASED
7.1	Father John Misty	"Nancy From Now On"	Fear Fun	Sub Pop Records	℗© 2012 Sub Pop Records	May 1, 2012
7.2	Bermuda Triangle	"Till the End of Days"	Till the End of Days	Blackfoorwhitefoot Records	℗© 2018 Blackfoorwhitefoot Records	June 21, 2018
7.3	Ye Vagabonds	"Blue is the Eye"	Nine Waves	River Lea Records	℗© 2022 River Lea Recordings	May 13, 2022
7.4	Quiet Houses	"Cold Water Swimming"	Cold Water Swimming	Lab Records	℗© 2021 LAB Records, Ltd	October 8, 2021
7.5	Lorde	"Secrets from a Girl (Who's Seen it All)"	Solar Power	Universal Music New Zealand Limited	℗© 2021 Universal Music New Zealand Limited	August 20, 2021
7.6	John Mayer	"Emoji of a Wave"	The Search for Everything	Columbia	℗2017 Columbia Records, a Division of Sony Music Entertainment	April 14, 2017
7.7	The Wild Reeds	"Fall With Me"	New Ways to Die	Dualtone Music Group, Inc.	℗© 2018 Dualtone Music Group, Inc.	September 28, 2018
7.8	Palace	"Where Sky Becomes Sea"	Where Sky Becomes Sea	Fiction	A Fiction Records Release ℗© 2021 Universal Music Operations Limited	November 12, 2021

APPENDIX A – THE MUSIC

It's like a soundtrack for a book. Find it on Spotify by searching playlists → Duck Dive or use this list to make your own

WANING CRESCENT	ARTIST	SONG	ALBUM	SOURCE	DISTRIBUTORS/HOLDERS	RELEASED
8.1	The 1975	"All I Need To Hear"	Being Funny In A Foreign Language	Dirty Hit	℗© 2022 Dirty Hit	October 14, 2022
8.2	The Beatles	"Across the Universe"	Let It Be (Remastered)	EMI Catalogue	© 2015 Apple Corps Ltd / ℗ 2015 Calderstone Productions Limited (a division of Universal Music Group)	May 8, 1970
8.3	May Erlewine, Woody Goss	"Palm of My Hand"	Anyway	sapsucker productions	℗© 2020 sapsucker productions	August 14, 2020
8.4	The Brook & The Bluff	"Don't Worry Baby"	Don't Worry Baby	The Brook & The Bluff	℗© 2020 The Brook & The Bluff	October 9, 2020
8.5	Lizzy McAlpine	"Ceilings"	five seconds flat	Harbour Artists & Music	℗© 2022 Harbour Artists & Music under exclusive license to AWAL Recordings America, Inc.	April 8, 2022
8.6	Lizzy McAlpine	"When The World Stopped Moving"	When The World Stopped Moving: The Live EP	Harbour Artists & Music	℗© 2021 Harbour Artists & Music	April 21, 2021
8.7	My Morning Jacket	"Wordless Chorus"	Z	ATO Records	℗© 2005 ATO Records, LLC	October 4, 2005
8.8	Fruit Bats	"Ocean"	Gold Past Life	Merge Records	℗© 2019 Merge Records	June 21, 2019

APPENDIX A – THE MUSIC

It's like a soundtrack for a book. Find it on Spotify by searching playlists → Duck Dive or use this list to make your own

NEW	ARTIST	SONG	ALBUM	SOURCE	DISTRIBUTORS/HOLDERS	RELEASED
9.1	Adam Melchor	"Last Time"	Last Time	R&R Digital / Warner Records, Sony Music Publishing	℗© R&R Digital with Warner Records, ℗© 2021 Coquito Records LLC, under exclusive license to Warner Records	January 8, 2021
9.2	The Beatles	"I'll Follow the Sun - Remastered 2009"	Beatles for Sale (Remastered)	EMI Catalogue	© 2015 Apple Corps Ltd / ℗ 2015 Calderstone Productions Limited (a division of Universal Music Group)	December 4, 1964
9.3	Oh Wonder	"Baby"	22 Break	Universal-Island Records Ltd.	An Island Records Release ℗© 2021 Universal Music Operations Limited	October 8, 2021
9.4	HAIM	"Up From A Dream"	Women in Music Pt. III	Columbia, Kobalt Music Publishing, Sony Music Publishing	℗© 2021 Haim Productions Inc. under exclusive license to Columbia Records, a division of Sony Music Entertainment	February 19, 2021
9.5	Andrew Bird	"Manifest"	My Finest Work Yet	Loma Vista Recordings	℗© 2019 Wegawam Music Co., under exclusive license to Loma Vista Recordings, distributed by Concord Music Group, Inc.	March 22, 2019
9.6	Phoebe Bridgers	"I Know the End"	Punisher	Dead Oceans	℗© 2020 Dead Oceans	June 18, 2020
9.7	Trampled by Turtles	"Walt Whitman"	Stars and Satellites	Banjodad Records	℗© 2012 Banjodad Records	April 10, 2012
9.8	My Morning Jacket	"One In the Same"	It Still Moves	ATO Records	℗© 2003 ATO Records, LLC	September 9, 2003

ACKNOWLEDGEMENTS

The idea that people can just think up stories, put those stories into words, and then print those words on pages for other people to read has always seemed like magic to me. Wonderful magic. The first book I ever got to "publish" was as Co-Editor of my high school yearbook—*Las Memorias*, Tascosa High School, 2001-2002. I poured my heart and soul into 296 pages. Every word, every picture, the paper weight, the fonts, the bleeds, the timelines. I. Ate. It. Up. And as a Senior in high school, a seed was planted in my heart and mind. *You can make books.* So my first thank-you has to go to Mrs. Amy Stahl, who as I write this, 21 years later, is still helping kids make books. Every day she would tell the yearbook staff, "Thank you for your help!" And now I say to her and all the beautiful teachers and librarians at Wolflin Elementary, Austin Middle School, and Tascosa High School in Amarillo, Texas—thank you for *your* help. Thank you. Because of you, I get to make books. And Amy, I'll see you at book club.

AND TO SYLVIA MCTAGUE. My amazing neighbor, brilliant editor, and treasured friend, I deeply apologize for my complete ineptitude when it comes to semicolons. I'd like to promise you that by the next book I will have gotten better, but don't hold me to that. Your expertise, administered with a kind and gentle hand, gave me the confidence to see this story through. Thank you for your knowledge, your care, and your support. I am so grateful.

MOM AND DAD. I love stories because of you two. My childhood was rich with books, movies, and music, and maybe even more importantly our home was always full of real people (real characters) talking and sharing, and you two were always listening and caring. Stories matter because people matter. Thank you for living that out.

ALICIA, REAGAN, JORDI, LINDSEY, SARAH, DEB. You helped me birth this book with your incredible talents and your incredible friendship, and whatever you need help birthing, I got you. Thank you for believing in me and helping me believe in myself. I love you all.

STALEY AND GUNNAR. Thank you for always encouraging me to be my weird self. I'll do my best to never be a normal mom. You two are my sunshine, forever and always.

ANDREW. Because of you, I have the courage to go for my dreams. I've always said this and I always will—you are my hero. PTL and YTB. Thanks for being my very best friend.

www.ingramcontent.com/pod-product-compliance
Lightning Source LLC
Chambersburg PA
CBHW030806020726
47499CB00006B/1787